The Latest F
is

M000189025

"This riveting saga will engross any interested in police procedural mysteries, adding a powerful sense of purpose and angst between two protagonists who must not only face the demands of their jobs; but their own relationship.

"As the detective and P.I. struggle to regain their lives and find new purpose in them, readers are swept along in a mounting story of intrigue and strange associations in a satisfyingly complex, engrossing mystery from start to finish." – *D. Donovan, Senior Reviewer, Midwest Book Reviews*

"Ms. Carline has outdone herself in *A More Deadly Union*. The writing is solid, the suspense gripping, and the heart of the story, touching. As with all the Peri books, I finish one and can't wait for the next." – *Claudia Whitsitt, Award-winning Author of the Samantha Series and the Kids Like You Series*

"Gayle Carline and her P.I. Peri Minneopa have done it again. *A More Deadly Union* is a great read filled with suspense, twists and a little romance that keep you turning the page to find out what happens next. I consider this a must read." – *Dot Caffrey, Author of the Trilogy of Power Series*

A MORE DEADLY UNION

A Novel

by
Gayle Carline

This is a work of fiction. All characters, organizations, places, and events portrayed in this novel are either products of the author's imagination or are used fictitiously.

Cover art by Joe Felipe of Market Me (www.marketme.us).

ISBN: 1-943654-06-9
ISBN-13: 978-1-943654-06-2

 Published in the USA by Dancing Corgi Press

This book is dedicated to love.

CHAPTER 1

His partner's words were nearly swallowed by the morning fog.

"I got a bad twitch about this."

Minutes later, he was in a dim warehouse, high on a catwalk, looking down at the chaos below. Bullets flew in and around travel trailers, men screamed. The air reeked of gunpowder and death.

He recognized a figure in a police stance. In front of the officer, someone turned, one arm outstretched and pointed. Training had become instinct—the detective stood, aimed, and shot within a millisecond. The pointing figure crumpled to the ground.

Something bumped into his thigh. It was hot and pushed him off balance. He grabbed for the rail of the catwalk, feeling too top-heavy to stay upright. His hands hit the railing, palms slapping, nails slipping. His rifle clattered to the concrete below, awaiting his arrival.

CHAPTER 2

"Miss Peri, come see what Willem found." Benny Needles gestured at the door, as if his manic flailing could whisk the blond private investigator into the house.

"Chill, Ben, I'm coming." Peri unfolded her tall frame from her Honda sedan. "I can't teleport."

She scrutinized the front of the house as she strode through the gate and up the walkway. Even before the fire, Benny's house had suffered from neglect. The upside of having an arsonist destroy much of her part-time client, part-time assistant's living room was it meant a new roof and a fresh coat of paint. Of course, insurance wouldn't pay to weed the garden.

The gnomes' hats were barely visible above the crabgrass.

Benny's friends, the Nickels, were overseeing the house repairs, but everyone left it to Peri to keep Benny from going on a buying spree to replace his precious Dean Martin collectibles. They didn't know how hard it was to convince a man with OCD and Asperger's that he didn't need twelve packages of matchbooks with Martin's likeness on the covers.

Call me Peri Minneopa, Dino Police.

She spotted a black and white lump staring at her from the porch. An American Pit Bull Terrier sat askew, its back legs jutting at awkward angles, and a goofy grin splitting its broad face. One eye had a black half-moon underneath and the other had the matching half over, giving it the look of someone who'd been in a fight but was still too dazed to remember who won.

"Hey, Moonie." Peri rubbed the dog's head as she passed. Moonie's tongue rolled sideways, the grin widening.

Benny still stood in the doorway, eyeing the dog as if it had two heads. As soon as Peri crossed the threshold, he shoved a round object into her stomach.

"Oof! Benny—" She pushed the item back toward him.

"It's a spittoon." Benny sounded thrilled. "Willem found it for me."

"Uh-huh. Why do you need a spittoon?"

Benny's eyes lit even brighter. "It's from *Rio Bravo*, the movie Dean Martin did with that cowboy."

"You mean John Wayne?"

"Yeah, whatever. This was the spittoon in the first scene, where the villain offers to buy Dean a drink. Only he's not Dean in the movie, his name is Dude." He looked over at a figure standing in the living room. "Isn't that a great name, Willem? Dude?"

Willem Chen stood in the middle of the room, staring at a blank wall. The lanky man's shock of white-blond hair was at odds with his Korean features, and his over-sized red-framed glasses gave him an avant-garde appearance, but no one in the small town of Placentia cared. He had a winning way with colors, textiles, and clients, and was one of the most sought-after interior decorators in southern California.

Peri strolled into the house. "You've got a real fierce protector on the front porch."

"Everything needs Miss Moonie's seal of approval." Willem extended his long arms for a hug, and Peri obliged.

She gestured around the room. "I didn't think you'd be in here decorating until Jared was finished with the construction. Looks like there's still some work to be done."

"True, but, ah, Benny was anxious to re-Dino-fy the space." Willem's expression took on a quality of forbearance. "Jared thought perhaps it might speed the work along if I helped our client envision the next step."

Peri smiled and nodded. Benny was driving them crazy.

Heavy footsteps interrupted them and a tall, muscular workman entered, dust and paint covering his jeans and t-shirt. Willem's face brightened.

"Nice to see you, Jared." Peri offered her hand. "I stopped by to make sure my friend wasn't spending all his insurance money on eBay."

"You'll have to talk to Willem about that," he told her. "I'm spending money on lumber and drywall, and so far, Mr. Needles is signing all the checks."

"Jared, dear." Willem touched his partner's arm. "I finally got hold of Garrett Miller. He said he can sing at the wedding and the reception."

"The wedding?"

Willem turned to Peri. "We're so excited. After ten years together, we're finally going to be married."

"Oh, how lovely. Congratulations. I'm not into marriage myself, but I'm thrilled you're able to tie the knot."

"Thank you. It's going to be such a fabulous day. I'm working with the planner, Craftsman is catering—oh, of course you'll be invited, and Moonie's going to be our flower girl." He paused and beamed. "As you can imagine, we've prayed for this for such a long time, I'm afraid we're going a bit overboard."

"We?" Jared asked.

"Okay, me. Jared's not much for the frills. I'm just happy he's not complaining about anything. He's such a good sport."

"Just one of the reasons you love him," Peri said. "Like I love Skip for not pressing me about marriage."

"He wants to?" Willem asked.

"Brings it up every now and then, usually after I've had a dangerous case and he'd rather I retire and let him support me."

"It's not like he's in a safe job."

"Exactly." She was interrupted by the buzzing of her cell phone in her pants pocket. The ID said *Chief Fletcher*. Pressing the button, she moved away from the men.

His words were blunt and loud, as if he pushed them out of his mouth. "Peri, there's been a shooting…Skip."

Her response was half-whispered, half-gasped. "What?"

"They just took him into surgery at Placentia-Linda. I'm on my way to the hospital. Thought you'd want to meet me there."

Peri heard herself mumble something affirmative as she lowered the phone, leaning against the door frame.

5

Someone was erasing her legs from the ankles up. There was a clatter in the distance. Hands were on her arms. She turned her head and saw Jared, propping her upright.

"What's wrong?"

The words were simple, but when she opened her mouth to say them, her lips trembled uncontrollably. She sucked the tears back into her eyes while she whispered, "Skip. He's been shot."

The look on Jared's face slapped her into reality, and the tears spurted out. He embraced her, his arms strong and supportive, enfolding her in comfort.

"He's at Placentia-Linda," she stammered. "I have to go."

Willem appeared at her side, holding her phone. "Jared and I will drive you. You're in no shape to drive yourself."

Benny was holding the spittoon again, rubbing it, moaning, "No."

Peri moved to him. "Benny, listen to my words."

He raised his head, his vision skittering across her face.

"Skip will be fine." Her voice tried not to wobble. "It will all be fine."

There was the chance she was wrong, and Benny would hold her responsible for lying. But she had to say Skip would live. An attempt at honesty would leave her weeping, possibly on the floor in the fetal position.

Skip wouldn't want to see me like that. She stumbled into the sunshine, toward the car.

CHAPTER 3

The Placentia-Linda emergency room was not usually a hotbed of activity, but Peri and her entourage walked into the small admitting foyer to find a bustling crowd of people, including what looked like the town's entire police force. She searched for familiar faces. Officer Chou was not there, nor was Skip's partner, Craig. She wove through the masses, trying not to breathe the disinfectant-laden air.

"Peri." A hand stopped her and she turned to see Chief Fletcher.

Grabbing his arm, she spurted the obvious question. "What happened?"

"There was a gun battle. Couple of our guys were investigating suspicious activity in a warehouse down on Crowther, and were ambushed. Skip and Craig went to help, plus a couple more squad cars. We got one of the bastards."

"And Skip?"

"All I know is that he was shot and he's in surgery."

A woman in scrubs appeared and signaled to the chief. He squeezed Peri's arm. "Be right back."

Peri found Willem and Jared and filled them in. Benny had refused to move any closer to the crowd than

7

the door. She ran through the facts in her head as she joined him.

"Skip got hurt, Ben. The doctors are doing everything they can to make him better."

He frowned. "I am not a baby. You sound like I'm too young to understand."

"Sorry. He's been shot. I don't know how badly, but he's in surgery now."

Benny bobbed his head, looking at the ground. "We will be here when he wakes up."

Peri fought to keep her eyes from filling. She needed that little ray of optimism.

"Can I have everyone's attention?" Chief Fletcher's voice commanded the room. "I'd like all my officers and staff to go with Dr. Marx to be debriefed."

A tall, dark woman holding a clipboard waved her hand and motioned for them to follow her as the chief continued.

"If you are related to Officer Chou, or Detective Carlton, you need to go with Carla. If you are related to Detective Daniels or Officer Gomez, go with Vivian."

Peri turned to the smaller blonde in scrubs who was waving. "Carla?"

"Yes, who are you related to?"

"I'm Skip Carlton's girlfriend."

Carla appeared unsure. "Um, I'm sorry. This group is for relatives and spouses only."

"But I've been dating him for ten years." Peri reasoned with her. "We lived together."

"I'm sorry, Ma'am." The nurse sounded contrite. "We have rules. Confidentiality, you know."

"I know, but—"

Chief Fletcher stepped between them. "Peri, why don't you come with us? We'll sort it out."

Her stomach fluttered, sick and worried, but Peri allowed herself to be led into what appeared to be a classroom. All the seats were taken. She stood in the back and watched the chief walk to the front with the woman holding the clipboard.

"This is Dr. Jackie Marx. She's been working on our guys and overseeing everything." The chief took a large breath. As he exhaled, his face grew ten years older. "She'll bring you all up to speed."

Dr. Marx stepped forward. "First of all, ladies and gentlemen, I want to let you know we have done—and are continuing to do—our best to save the lives of our faithful officers."

Her words lifted the hair on Peri's neck.

"Five people were brought into our ER today. Of the five, one person, the suspect, was DOA. Officer Kenneth Chou sustained multiple gunshots to his legs. He lost a lot of blood, but we stabilized him. He is in serious condition.

"Detective Charles Carlton had a single gunshot wound in his thigh, which was minor. Unfortunately, he fell from a significant height and has sustained a concussion. He arrived unconscious, and is currently in a medically-induced coma until the swelling in his brain subsides. Again, we have hope for a complete recovery, but the next few hours are critical."

The doctor looked down at her clipboard for a moment before continuing.

"We worked diligently on Officer Thomas Gomez and Detective Craig Daniels. They each received multiple shots to the limbs and the neck area, hitting many blood vessels. Despite our efforts, we could not save them." She kept her face expressionless, but her eyes were glassy.

Peri gasped. Tom Gomez was her own personal bodyguard when she was being stalked by a sociopathic socialite. And Craig? Dead? She remembered all the times Skip's partner had flirted with her, worked with her on cases. Her vision blurred. She turned to a female officer near her, who was also crying. They huddled together, sharing their grief.

"Take all the time you need here," Dr. Marx told them. "My condolences for your losses."

Chief Fletcher wiped his eyes as the doctor left the room. "I'd like us to be able to take all the time we need, but we've got a job to do. Let's find out who did this. I don't need to tell you, these guys are extremely dangerous.

"The suspect is on his way to the coroner's. He had no ID, so we're running prints. I know everyone will want to pitch in and catch these bastards, but I'm asking you all to do what is needed, even if what's needed is to work another case while someone else is chasing a lead."

Peri pressed herself away from the officer.

"I gotta get to work," the young woman told her.

"Yes." Peri's voice cracked and she tried not to burst into tears again. Instead, she wound her way through the exiting crowd, toward the chief. He was giving a few specific orders to his two other detectives, Steve Logan and Pat Spencer. Peri waited for them to leave before she approached. "Can I see him now?"

"Come with me." He escorted her past admissions, down corridors to the intensive care unit.

The nurse at the desk gave her a questioning glance, before leading them to a large room with beds concealed by curtains. She turned to one alcove and picked up the chart. "This is Charles Carlton."

"Skip," Peri said. "His name is Skip."

The young woman didn't look up. "We go by the name on the chart."

"But he's in a coma." Peri knew she should let it go, but she couldn't stop herself. "He needs to hear his name to wake up."

The nurse looked at her and smiled, with an expression of compassion and understanding. She scratched a few lines on his chart. "Skip. We'll make sure to call him that."

Calmed, Peri moved to Skip's bedside. A blanket covered him, tucked under his chin. Good, they were keeping him warm. His left leg was out of the blanket, elevated. His thigh was wrapped where he was shot. It didn't look too bad, nor did the bandage holding a tube in place on his left hand. Not what she liked to look at, but at least all the tape hid the needle. A bag hung on a frame and dripped clear liquid through the tube.

Her eyes drifted up to his face. She feared that Skip would not look like Skip, that it might look as though he didn't live here anymore. He had been intubated, the tubing held into place by tape across his cheeks. Machines monitored anything that could be measured, prepared to sound an alarm if the measurements went astray.

His eyes were not quite closed, giving him the appearance of a man in limbo, neither awake nor asleep, dead nor alive.

Schrodinger's cat.

For a moment, her heart broke and she felt like surrendering, admitting how badly he was hurt and imagining the worst. It took effort to make the glass half-full again, but she leaned in and kissed his forehead, lingering to absorb the familiar feel of his skin.

"I love you," she whispered. "Come back to me."

Chief Fletcher put his arm on her shoulder, to signal the end of their visit. "He needs lots of rest now."

She shuffled from the room, her heart and mind trying to process what had happened. There had to be a plan, to catch the guys who did this, to take care of Skip, to set everything back the way it was. The chief was saying something. She turned to hear him, trying to focus on the meaning of his words.

"...the guys can come see him as long as they're on duty and can say it's for the investigation. We'll let you know when we're visiting so you can go with us. That way you'll be able to see him."

"Why couldn't I see him anyway during visiting hours?"

"At the moment they're limiting visitors to the immediate family and of course, law enforcement." He shook his head. "It's got to be strange, Peri. We all think of you as Skip's wife. But without either the paper or at least a common address..."

His voice trailed off as they made their way to the foyer, where Willem and Jared waited to take her back to Benny's house. Benny still hung by the door, so they all moved to join him. She told the trio about the loss of the two officers and Skip's condition, trying to keep the news about Skip and Officer Chou upbeat. Jared took it well, and Benny stood looking down and bobbing his head.

Willem seemed unconvinced. "What aren't you saying, Peri?"

"Oh, it's nothing. It's just—they're only allowing immediate family to visit him. Seems I'm not on that list."

Willem rubbed Jared's arm. "That's why it's so important for Jared and me to be legal. We thought we had our bases covered until Jared was injured at work. His family wasn't accepting of our relationship. They flew in from Montana and basically kicked me out of the hospital until he was able to communicate. He let them know I was to be included, no matter what."

"But I thought you had it all worked out legally. Power of attorney and all that."

Jared shook his head. "That's no good in an emergency situation, especially with a family you'd like to reconcile with eventually. Unfortunately, I hadn't come out to my folks when the accident happened. They had a lot of shock to overcome. And the last thing Willem wanted was to make their relationship worse by dragging in a policeman with a court order."

Outside, Jared strolled with Peri while Willem and Benny forged ahead toward the car. Willem was trying to talk Benny into donating blood. Benny was trying to convince Willem this was not something Benny did.

She became aware of Jared's arm on hers, slowing her movement. Turning to him, she raised her eyebrows in query.

"I know the timing is horrible." His voice was almost a whisper. "But would you be available for a meeting? In your office...confidentially?"

"I'd love a distraction. Let's shoot for tomorrow at 2 p.m. If something changes, you know, with Skip—"

He squeezed her arm. "We'll pray it's only for the better."

Peri took his hand. Her parents had not made religion a big part of her life, although they practiced plenty of faith, and spoke of God often. Still, pangs of guilt hit her as she realized she never called for God's help unless she was in a jam.

God, I don't stop by often, but please let Skip be okay. Amen.

As a postscript, a small voice in the back of her head added, *and please help them hunt down the bastards who did this.*

CHAPTER 4

Oh no oh no oh no. Benny's mind raced about like a cyclone, a whirl of thoughts and ideas, swirling too fast for him to capture one and focus on it. The bright sun outside the hospital had reflected too harshly on everything. The people milling around inside the emergency room had been too loud and too colorful and too busy. It was all too much.

Thankfully, he was home. Home, where he could see all his things and relax. Now that structure was restored to the front of the house, he had been able to move back in. He went into his kitchen and poured himself a glass of milk. Milk was soothing. It was white, a blank slate to calm his brain.

Skip was shot. Skip. Shot. The words kept rolling around. Skip could be scary. Actually, all policemen were scary. He didn't see Skip, or any of the police, often. Still, there was a leaden feeling to his insides, all the way to his toes. Skip was hurt, and some of the policemen were dead.

Dead, like my mom. I miss her so much. I miss watching TV with her and the smell of her cooking. I wish she was here to tell me what to do.

Willem had told him to give blood, but that was out of the question. Doctors and needles made him want to pass out. Of course, so did talking to police most of the time. Benny waddled from one room to the next, his dress loafers making soft clicks on the wood floor.

I should give blood but I can't give blood. His brain buzzed in agitation again, and he started talking to himself as a way to focus.

"Skip needs help. How can I help him?"

Benny ambled up the stairs to his room, and looked at the Matt Helm posters on the walls surrounding his round bed, an original from the movie set. Every night, he went to sleep dreaming he could be like the man on the poster. Matt was sure of himself, just like Dean Martin. He knew how to do practically everything. He could drink and gamble and play golf. Sometimes he even played golf for charities.

Benny stared up at Martin, smiling, surrounded by beautiful women. What would Dino do?

An idea sprouted, a tiny idea. Benny wanted to grow it bigger, but he didn't know how. He knew who could grow it, though.

Picking up the phone, he dialed his friends, the Nickels.

CHAPTER 5

In the office, Peri divided her time between pacing around the small space and reorganizing it. Every two minutes, she checked her phone to see if somehow she had missed the call telling her Skip was awake and fine. It wasn't quite 2 p.m. but she wished Jared would get there, already.

I need something to do.

A soft rap at the door preceded its opening.

"Come in, please." Peri shook Jared's hand. "I'm not sure when I've ever been as glad to see someone."

She motioned to a chair as she walked around the desk and they both sat.

"I'd like to hire you, Peri. I think I'm being stalked."

The handsome young man looked down, avoiding Peri's eyes. "I need you to understand. Coming out to my family was hard, but coming out to myself was worse. I mean, I always knew, but I didn't want to know. I wanted to be like my dad, who found the woman he loved, or even my buddies who played around. Growing up in a small town in Montana wasn't the best place to be gay. It was a lonely life—I couldn't let anyone really know me. I hated myself."

She nodded, so he continued.

"In high school, I met Rick. He was a transfer from a big city, St. Paul. He'd been in some trouble, so his parents shipped him out to live with his grandma and go to school in a 'safer' environment." He laughed as he formed the air quotes. "We both played football—varsity squad. I thought football would make me straight. He knew I was gay the moment we met. When I told him I wasn't, he laughed."

Peri could see the struggle on his features. It must be awful for such a shy, private man to be so exposed, to broadcast to the world what he did with whom behind closed doors. Whose business was it to anyone but him?

"He was my first." A heavy sigh. "I believed he would be my last, or at least my only. I'd been told it was wrong for such a long time. The first time, it felt good and it felt awful. I promised myself I'd never do it again. Then I promised I'd only ever do it with this person, because he was The One. Only he wasn't. He was nothing but bad."

"And now, he's back?"

"I don't know. I haven't seen or heard from him in years. He spent our entire relationship abusing me in different ways, including threatening to tell everyone what I was. I was so happy to get away from him and come out here to college. Of course, I was still scared he'd tell the whole world. I managed to forget about him until a couple of weeks ago. Turns out, he not only lives in the area, he's running for some office over in Walnut Ridge. Got a wife, kids, playing the conservative card."

Peri laughed. "Sorry, couldn't stop myself. Boy, has he changed."

"Tell me about it." He gave a dry chuckle. "His campaign manager called me, out of nowhere, and told me to swear to never tell anyone that we—well, that we did what we did. As a matter of fact, he asked me to pack my business up and take it away, far away, so no one would find out that one of his high school classmates lived in the area. He suggested San Francisco."

"And you told him no. Nicely."

"Of course. But he didn't like it. Now I've been noticing things. I think I'm being followed—I keep seeing the same red sports car everywhere I go. And last night, someone broke into my truck."

"It didn't look like a normal burglary?"

"Nothing was stolen, first of all. Everything was completely unlocked, all the tool cases were opened, the stuff from the glove compartment was all over the seat. I mean, it looked searched."

"And naturally, you assume Rick is the one responsible. Did you report this to the police?"

"I don't want to worry Willem, but I don't want either of us hurt. And if the Rick I used to know hasn't changed, well...I've been on the receiving end of his cruelty." He cradled his forehead in his hands and propped his elbows on the desk.

Peri leaned back, running her hand across her neck. "Ah, politicians. When they deny their past actions, they take the chance no one will find out. Typically that doesn't end well."

"I know."

"What makes you think Rick couldn't lie and say it never happened?"

Jared's face took on a slow burn as his jaw tightened. He pulled a photo from his back pocket and, after a moment's hesitation, handed it to her. Two male bodies were entwined, both young and lean. Their faces were clear—it was a young Jared and a dark-haired boy. Jared had that dreamy-eyed look of someone lost in passion. The other boy's expression disturbed Peri. He was smiling, but he didn't look happy. He looked smug.

"How did you get this?"

"I was so naive. Rick had a camera hidden in his room. He taped us doing, you know, and made still photos from the videos. This is part of what he used to torture me. I stole this one and hid it away. I didn't know why I stole it at the time, but now I realize it was my insurance."

"And he knows you have it?"

"The day I left town, we spoke. He said, 'I'm missing my favorite photo of us. Do you know where it could be?' The way he looked at me, I knew he knew, but I told him, 'I don't know, which one is your favorite?'"

"Think they were looking for this photo when they broke into your truck?"

"It's possible. But seriously, why would I keep it there?"

"True." Peri twirled her pencil as she considered. "You know, Jared, if you took this picture to the newspaper, you'd have no reason to look over your shoulder. Or hire me."

"I know, but it's so sordid. I don't want to flash my indiscretions around. I'd rather pay for my privacy."

"Understood. Let me investigate, see if I can find out if Rick could have done this, or who he'd pay to harass you."

Jared reached toward the photo. As his fingers touched the edge, she pulled it back. "It might not be a bad idea for me to keep this, or a copy of it."

He looked horrified.

"If Rick is hunting for the picture, his hunt might escalate to breaking into your house. If you want to spare Willem any drama, we need this to stay safe."

He released the photo. "If I lose that, I think I might lose my mind. I mean, while I have it, I know it all really happened and I survived."

Peri put the picture in an envelope, and opened her safe. She taped it to the underside of the middle shelf before closing the door. "When this is all over, I'll give it back."

"I appreciate that." He stood. "I didn't want to bring you into this, especially under the circumstances."

"No, this is good. Gives me something to do besides worry."

"Skip will be fine. He's in great shape, and he's strong-willed. You'll see."

She came around the desk and took his hand. "Thank you for your support."

A merry ring tone interrupted them.

"That's Blanche," Peri said. "I gotta get this. Let me do a little digging, and I'll get back to you."

Jared let himself out as she answered her phone.

"Oh. My. God." Each word exploded in a husky, staccato rhythm. "Peri, I'm sorry I didn't get your message. I was at a conference in Sacramento and didn't realize my phone was still on mute. Got home this morning. What the hell is going on?"

Peri explained, shakily, trying not to weep. Blanche was quiet until she had completed her story, then said four of Peri's favorite words:

"I'm coming right over."

On her way out the door, Peri stopped and returned to her safe. She removed Jared's picture, took a photo of it with her phone, and put it back.

A little extra insurance couldn't hurt.

CHAPTER 6

Blanche arrived at Peri's Spanish-style bungalow with chips, salsa, and beer. Peri opened her mouth to say how glad she was to see her, but nothing came out, except more tears running down her cheeks. Blanche enveloped her in a loving embrace, stretching her small frame up to Peri's height.

"I'm sorry, I keep turning on the waterworks." They parked themselves on the sofa, placing the bag, the jar, and the bottles on the coffee table. "I'm trying not to worry about Skip, and I still can't believe Craig and Tom are gone."

"Oh, for Pete's sake, I think you're allowed. I've been crying and I'm not as close to any of them as you are."

"The doctors say they're hopeful. Or maybe they're saying that to keep everyone calm."

"No, from what you described, Skip's chances are better than good." Blanche grabbed a chip and dug a scoop of homemade salsa. "The gunshot wound is nothing, as long as there's no infection, which there shouldn't be. As for the head injury, well, I know it can be worrisome, but I've seen people come back from much worse."

Blanche's job as Assistant Coroner kept her busy with corpses, but she had a wealth of medical knowledge. Her career as a heart surgeon had been cancelled by an accident to her hand. Now she helped the living give closure to the dead.

Peri took a long swallow of beer. "The worst part is I can't be there with him right now. They won't let me visit, because I'm not family."

"That's bull. You two have been together for years."

"Apparently, that's not enough."

"Well, did they at least contact his *real* family?"

"Chief Fletcher said they'd gotten in touch with his oldest daughter. I guess both girls took the first plane out of Chicago."

"Think they can put in a good word for you at the hospital?"

Peri shrugged. "Dunno. I've met them both, I speak to them on the phone sometimes when I'm at Skip's— went to the youngest's graduation from college. Neither of them act like I'm some wicked stepmother. Matter of fact, even the ex-wife seems to get along with me. She's been remarried for about five years."

Blanche raised her beer to Peri. "Well, here's hoping they let you in."

Peri brought her bottle up to touch Blanche's. "I wish I could do something to help Skip."

"I hope you're not considering what I think you're considering."

"What?"

"Don't play coy with me, Girlfriend. It would be just like you to try to hunt down Skip's shooter."

Peri scoffed. "Please. I think the police can do their job. Besides, I have a new case to work on."

"Good. Because I will rat you out to Fletcher. If you want to help, what about his daughters? Maybe they'll need something."

"That sounds like a good idea. Maybe I should go over to Skip's and get it ready for them."

"Perfect. Want help?"

Peri smiled. "Race you to the car."

CHAPTER 7

"Hey, Peri." Blanche called out from Skip's kitchen, where she was wiping the counters. "What if I went out and did a little grocery shopping?"

Peri emerged from the hallway, dust rag in hand. "What do we have now?" She opened the refrigerator. "Two containers of leftover stew, a carton of orange juice and a six-pack of Sam Adams."

Blanche picked up one of the tubs of stew. "I don't picture two young women surviving on this."

"Well, I know they're both in pretty good shape. I'm going to assume they eat on the healthy side. Maybe...fruit, salad? Cheese?"

"I can work with that. We can always take them out for a meal."

"What would I do without you?"

"Your own shopping, for one thing." Blanche laughed and grabbed her purse. "Be back in a jiff."

Peri returned to her cleaning, running a dust rag over the furniture before doing a quick scrub-and-wipe of both bathrooms. She was vacuuming the family room, worrying about Skip, working on Jared's problem, and still trying to focus on the gray Berber carpet, when a woman's voice startled her.

"Excuse me? Are you the cleaning woman?"

Peri jumped and whirled, yanking the plug from the wall. There stood two young women, both tall and dark-haired, with familiar brown eyes. Skip's daughters.

"Sorry, you caught me by surprise. Amanda, Daria, I'm glad you're here."

The older girl, dressed in a navy suit with a cream-colored blouse, looked at Peri with a quizzical expression. The younger one, in leggings and a sweater, grinned and reached out for a hug.

"Peri, it's good to see you." Daria's embrace was full and comforting. "Sorry, I didn't recognize you at first. How's Dad? We heard he was critical."

"I was at the hospital yesterday," Peri told them. "They said the next few days will tell how much—" She couldn't bring herself to finish the sentence. *How much damage was done.*

"We haven't seen him yet." Daria glanced at her sister. "Amanda thought it would be best if we dropped off our luggage and freshened up."

"Sure," Peri said. "I've got everything ready for you. I'm afraid your dad's fridge is either feast or famine. This week it's on the lean side. My friend Blanche went to the store to stock the kitchen with a little food."

"That won't be necessary." Amanda spoke at last. Her face showed no emotion. "Daria and I can manage."

"Really, it's no trouble. I'd like to be of some help. Would you like me to take you to the hospital? Chief Fletcher might be there as well. He'll probably want to speak to you. And I can introduce you to the nurses."

"No." The eldest daughter sounded more emphatic. "Daria and I will handle this."

Peri was shocked at her attitude, but tried to understand. Perhaps she was afraid of what had happened to her father. "Like I said, I'd like to do what I can to help. I know your dad would want you to be taken care of."

"I'm sure." The young woman's voice was cold. "But *our family* can take it from here."

Her emphasis on "their" family hit Peri in the heart. Peri looked into Amanda's eyes, trying to find the girl who used to like her. "You know I love your father."

"Then you should have married him." The message was clear. Her opinion had nothing to do with Skip's injury and everything to do with his lifestyle.

"Amanda." Daria pulled on her sister's sleeve. "Why don't we get the bags from the car?"

A door slammed and Blanche's voice could be heard coming down the hall. "They didn't have berries in season, but I got some apples—" She stopped as she came into view.

"Blanche, these are Skip's daughters, Amanda and Daria."

"Let me help you with those." Daria stepped forward to take one of the bags from Blanche's arms and set it on the counter. "It's nice to meet you. I can't thank you enough for getting us something to have around the house."

Amanda took the other bag. "Nice to meet you."

Looking at her sister, Daria's face reddened. "Maybe we should help put the food away, Sis, so we'll know what's here and where it is."

Amanda stared at Peri. "No, I think it's best if we get our bags from the car. These ladies can put away the groceries."

She strode from the room. Daria gave Peri an eye roll and a shrug before joining her sister.

"*These ladies?*" Blanche asked. "Did I miss something?"

Peri rubbed her forehead. "The Amanda I knew has been replaced by some kind of bitchy nun. She's giving me a big dose of 'family values' because Skip and I aren't married."

"Seriously?"

"Here." Peri handed her a box of granola. "*These ladies* need to get their work done."

She and Blanche were still unpacking when Daria returned.

"Peri." Her voice was barely a whisper. "I'm sorry about Sis. She used to be fun, but ever since she got engaged to Mr. Ivy League Corporate Lawyer, she's changed. Basically, he's an ass and his ass-nocity has rubbed off on her. Together, they're asses-squared."

Peri chuckled. "I remember Skip talking about dear Drew and his rather pointed opinions. It's okay. I can deal with it. It'd just be easier for me to see your dad if you guys would put me on the approved visitor list. Amanda is right about one thing—marriage does grease a lot of wheels."

Amanda entered the room, silencing them.

Peri finished putting the yogurt in the fridge. "Blanche and I will be leaving, but if you need anything at all, my phone number is on the corkboard."

Amanda dismissed them with a wave. "I'm sure we won't be needing you."

Her sister reached out and hugged Peri, then Blanche. Peri turned her back on Amanda and strolled to the door, leaving because she decided to and not because she was being thrown out. Blanche followed her, staying silent until they had climbed into her white SUV.

"What a little brat," Blanche said. "I mean, the nerve."

Peri waved her hand. "Letting it roll off my back. This isn't even the real her. It's some skewed version of her, through someone else's filters."

Blanche started the car.

"Besides," Peri said. "When Skip wakes up, I'm tattling."

CHAPTER 8

Once home, Peri dug out a bottle of cabernet. It was the one she and Skip bought when they went wine tasting in Temecula. There was nothing particularly special about the trip. It was an unplanned jaunt, a pleasant, comfortable weekend.

Now every memory felt sacred. Was that their last trip to Temecula?

"No," she told the bottle as she returned it to the wine rack and chose another. "I'm going to open you when Skip is better."

Her glass full, she wandered into the living room and sank onto the couch. She took a long drink and let her head rest back on the leather, eyes closed, savoring the earthy tone of the wine, and feeling the warmth of the alcohol soothe her body.

I hate waiting. I want to be with Skip. She put down the wineglass and picked up her laptop. In the meantime, Jared needed her to work his case.

Rick Mayfield wasn't hard to find on the internet. He was aggressively pursuing the vote, trying to be Walnut Ridge's next mayor. His platform was all about families, and homeowners, but there were references to attending church that could be interpreted to mean he planned to favor Christians with money. It was his right, and the right of the voters to elect him, but was it his right to pose as having no past that contradicted his present?

She dug further into his background. No arrests. Perhaps he had juvenile records, and those would be sealed. She looked up court information for Glendive, Jared's hometown in Montana. She hoped it would only take a phone call, not a visit.

This was not a good time to leave town.

She looked further, digging for another angle, making notes of the people quoted in the various articles. One person, Sean Jackson, was quoted often. Sean was a chatty guy. One article described him as Rick's campaign manager, another referred to him as a "friend of the family." Either way, he did a lot of talking about Rick.

Unlike the candidate, Jackson had been in a few scrapes with the law. Nothing big, no felonies. Now he was a realtor with a degree in law.

According to a two-year-old news article, his 87-year-old neighbor had sued him for installing a fence several feet over his property line. The simple property dispute could have been settled in one court appearance, but Jackson kept filing delays, trying to wear down the elderly man with legal baloney.

Nice way to treat your neighbor, you blowhole.

If Rick's right hand man played ethical roulette in his personal life, he'd probably play it for his candidate/friend as well. Peri guessed he'd do anything he could to paint over that black mark in Rick's past.

Her phone buzzed. She grabbed for it, hoping it was news of Skip.

"Peri, please come over." Jared's voice was breathy, and she could hear Willem shouting in the background. "Our house has been broken into."

Good thing she'd only gotten one sip of her wine.

CHAPTER 9

Peri entered an expansive ranch-style home in the Fullerton hills, beautiful on the outside and desecrated within. Jared stood next to an empty couch, its cushions all over the floor, ripped open, spilling their stuffing. He was talking to a short, wiry man in slacks and a dark windbreaker, an "FPD" ball cap on his head. Moonie sat at Jared's feet, ears down, staring at her master with a pensive wrinkle in her brow.

Willem could be heard in a back room, bemoaning a broken cookie jar.

"Peri." Jared motioned to her. "This is Detective Berkwits."

She offered her ID, with her P.I. license, to him.

"Placentia?" His voice was unexpected, soft and southern. He studied her for a moment. "Ah, yes, I think I've seen you—y'all date one of the detectives that got hurt. How's he doin'?"

She managed to croak, "Okay so far."

"Tell them we're all prayin' for them at Fullerton PD." The detective handed her ID back. "Mr. Reese was telling me you been working with him on a harassment case."

"Yes, I've just started gathering information." She looked around at the disarray. Furniture had been gutted, ceramics broken, paintings and photos torn off the walls. "I may be wrong, but this doesn't look like a search. It looks malicious."

"Search for what?" Berkwits asked.

Peri exchanged glances with Jared, who nodded, his face ashen. "Mr. Reese is, or was, in possession of a photograph he believes someone may be trying to retrieve. Did he tell you about his truck being broken into?"

"Your truck was broken into?" Willem came from the kitchen. "When did this happen?"

"I didn't want to worry you." Jared hung his head. "They didn't take anything. I thought someone was pranking me."

"Pranking you? And that's why you hired Peri? For a prank?" Willem's voice rose an octave higher.

"Wait a minute, Willem." Peri interrupted before his voice reached a register only Moonie could hear. "Jared wasn't trying to hide anything from you, I swear. He was trying to keep you from being alarmed if it turned out to be nothing."

Willem swept his arm around the room. "Does this look like nothing?"

He was close to a breakdown that would be embarrassing, so Peri intervened again. "Detective, perhaps I could fill you in while these gentlemen take a moment."

Berkwits nodded and Peri followed him to the kitchen. She brought him up to speed on what she'd learned thus far, giving as vague and tactful a description of the photo as she could.

"I have to admit," he said at last. "When I arrived on the scene, my first thought was 'hate crime.' But in light of what you've told me, I think we'll look at this Rick Mayfield character first. Our CSU is on his way. Maybe we'll get lucky with some prints."

"I hope so. This is too nice a couple to have this happen, and I'm frankly worried about the escalation in the vandalism."

"I agree. Our department usually doesn't work with PIs, but if Mr. Reese hired you, I'd like to know anything you know."

"You're very gracious." Peri regarded him. "Thank you."

He shrugged. "We all take it hard when there's a cop shot. And I figure you deserve a break. We're all praying for Skip and that other officer to pull through."

The detective took out his phone to make the calls. Peri could still hear Jared and Willem in a quiet argument. Not wanting to interrupt them, she walked out the back door, to be out of everyone's way.

Their backyard was an oasis of beauty. Even on a February evening, with the furniture covered, the natural rock pool and the gardens were spectacular and inviting. She strolled on the stone path, gazing up at the sky. The moon revealed gray clouds, drifting from the ocean. More rain was approaching.

She scanned the yard, noting the small, twinkling lights on the path, along with backlights at the block wall. The back of their property butted against a steep slope of undeveloped land that ended on Bastanchury Avenue.

On a hunch, Peri selected the flashlight on her cell phone and peered around at the edge of the wall. In the corner, she found a small accent table where it didn't belong, and shoe prints around it. Something pale fluttered under the table. She reached underneath, taking care not to leave any prints of her own.

It was a piece of paper, a receipt for sliders and beers at Brian's, a local bar. She aimed her phone at the paper and took a picture. It hadn't been there long, as the ink was still dark and the edges were intact. Once she was satisfied with the quality of her photo, she called for the detective.

When he appeared, she pointed to what she'd found. "I'm guessing they used the table to jump down to the slope. You might get some useful information, if you can beat the next storm."

There was a hustle of activity to grab plastic and cover the table, the ground, and the wall, until CSU arrived. While the police hurried about, Peri took several shots with her phone, mumbling, "sorry" with every flash. When a man with a large case marked "CSU" walked up, she went back inside, pausing at the living room to see if the coast was clear.

Willem sat in the only chair that had been untouched, a simple maple rocker with no upholstery to destroy. He rocked in a measured rhythm, while Jared sat on the floor beside him, holding his hand. Moonie lay at Jared's side, her head on his leg, watching their every move.

Peri opened her mouth, then shut it. What to say? She couldn't ask if everything was better, or even okay. Nothing was okay. Someone had broken into her house once. They didn't do this kind of damage, yet it made her feel ill, physically assaulted.

She knelt in front of the pair. "I know how bad this is. But the police are taking it very seriously. We're going to find the person who did this. If they can't, I will."

Willem gazed at her, his eyes red. "How can you promise that?"

"Because I can cross lines the police can't."

"Peri, I don't want you in danger because of me," Jared said.

Moonie pushed her nose under Peri's hand. She stroked the massive head, massaging her ears. "Oh, don't worry, my sleuthing is completely in the background. They'll never see who's digging into their private lives."

"At least she wasn't home alone when it happened." Willem reached down to rub Moonie. "Everyone looks at her and sees a vicious dog, but she's not. Who knows what they would have done if they thought she might attack them?"

"Thank God she was with you." Peri stood up and stretched her long legs. "Now then, do you have a place to go tonight?"

"Well, I didn't think—" Jared stammered.

Willem stopped him. "Oh, no. We are not staying here tonight. We are not even coming back until this is all better and we have a security system in place."

"The security system is probably a good idea," Peri said. "I have one."

Jared squeezed Willem's hand. "Okay. We can get a hotel room for tonight. We'll figure out what to do for the long term tomorrow."

Peri gazed at the two men. "Listen, you two, be careful. This went from breaking into your truck to destroying your home pretty quickly. Stay in touch with each other when you're not together—don't even run a quick errand without letting the other one know where you're going. It wouldn't be a bad idea to have a code word in case one of you is in trouble."

"We'll be careful." Jared looked around. "In fact, I think we should pack our bags while the police are here."

Peri hugged the men and left, images of the vandalism running through her mind. If this was Rick Mayfield, or his henchman Sean Jackson, how far would they go to get what they wanted? If they couldn't find the photo, would they try to get rid of the young man in it? She returned to her car, determined to do more investigating.

Driving home, she fought her desire to go to Placentia-Linda Hospital. She yearned to sit at Skip's bedside and hold his hand, squeeze it, pray for him to squeeze hers in return. In addition to loving him, she knew he was her solid rock when she was on a case, offering words of encouragement and warning. Without his voice, who would tell her to be careful?

Who else loves me enough to save me from my own stubbornness?

CHAPTER 10

The hospital lobby was quiet on Wednesday morning as Peri sat waiting for Chief Fletcher. He had told her to meet him at nine. She was thirty minutes early, and pretended to read a book on her phone, while she constantly checked the time instead. In the background, soft footsteps walked in and out, and low voices murmured.

The police chief arrived a little after nine, striding over to Peri, who rose to greet him.

"Sorry I'm late." He took her hand.

"Oh, I just got here," she said.

At the desk, Chief Fletcher gave his name, along with Skip's. An older woman looked up the information.

"He's been moved to Room 241." She gestured toward the double doors.

Peri tried not to bolt ahead of the Chief as he pushed the doors open and followed the signs.

"Thank you for doing this."

"It's the least I can do, Peri. If I could get your name on the list, I would. Maybe soon they'll take the restriction off."

"Maybe soon he'll wake up and tell them to." The memory of the initial chaos flew across her mind. "How's Chou?"

Fletcher shrugged. "Alive. They nearly lost him a couple of times, but he's a strong guy."

"He's got family?"

"Oh, yes, both parents, his wife and two sons have been at his side the whole time. Real praying folk. Every time I go see him, they're holding hands with their heads bowed."

"I'm glad. Everybody should have someone to fuss and worry and pray over them."

There was a uniformed officer sitting outside the door to Skip's room when they arrived. Peri looked at the chief for an explanation.

"This might have been a deliberate ambush. Even if it wasn't, we're assuming Skip and Kenneth can give us information when they're able to speak. We don't want any of those bastards coming in to finish what they started."

She entered the room slowly, afraid of what she'd see, hoping he'd look better. A still figure lay covered in blankets and surrounded by machines.

"Take all the time you want," the chief said. "I'm going to get some coffee."

She approached the bed. Skip's face still lacked color, and his eyes hovered between open and closed. She ran her hand across his brow, then carefully traced his cheek with her fingers. Taking in the entire scene, she willed herself to believe he was improving.

She pulled a chair close, sat down and held his hand. Afraid to squeeze it, in case he didn't squeeze back, Peri caressed his fingers, running her own down each one and savoring the feel of his skin.

"I know you had a bad fall, Skipper, but it's time to wake up." She adjusted his blanket, smoothing it across his chest. "That's all I want. No matter what happens after that. Maybe you wake up thinking it's twenty years ago and we've never met. Maybe you'll wonder who the hell you are. I don't care. Wake up and I'll introduce myself. I'll introduce you, if you need it."

She leaned forward and kissed his forehead. Her voice became a ragged whisper as a tear spilled from her eye. "Just wake up."

"I'm certain you aren't on the guest list." Amanda's acidic voice shot across the room.

Peri remained in her chair. There wasn't going to be a snap to attention because this child demanded it. She lifted Skip's hand once more and kissed it. The clock in the room clicked a few more seconds before she rose in slow deliberation, and turned to face Amanda.

"Good morning, Amanda. I hope you slept well."

Daria dashed in, still stuffing keys and sunglasses in her purse. "Wow, finally found parking, and—oh, Peri, how nice to see you."

Peri moved forward to hug her, then stepped aside so she could see her dad.

"He's looking a little better, I think, don't you?" Daria asked.

"Sure," Peri said, even if it wasn't true.

"Daria, really, the doctor is the best judge of whether he's better," Amanda said. "And I don't believe you answered—"

"Consider me Chief Fletcher's plus-one." Peri said. *Have a heart, you little brat.* "I'm here in an official capacity."

She was getting used to lying, especially to defend her territory.

"Do you often show such affection, officially?"

"Not usually, but this one's kind of cute." As soon as the words came out of her mouth, a lump hit Peri's stomach. "I'm sorry. That was rude. Please, Amanda, let's not get into a pissing match. I understand your disapproval of my relationship with your father. Well, maybe I don't understand it, but I respect your right to have it. But surely you know your dad and I are together, even if we don't have the papers to prove it. I love him. He loves me."

Peri looked at Skip. He was so still. "I confess, I'm frightened. I'm betting you are, too."

Amanda sighed. Maybe she could be reasoned with. A glimpse at the young woman showed lowered shoulders and softened eyes. Peri held her breath, and her tongue. One wrong move would push Amanda back into her steely frame of mind.

"I brought you some coffee." Chief Fletcher's voice barked into the silence.

Amanda straightened up, crossing her arms over her chest.

Damn. So close.

"Thank you, Chief." Peri took the cup. "I'm assuming you've met Skip's daughters, Amanda and Daria."

43

"A long time ago." He extended his hand to each. "Nice meeting you, although I wish the circumstances were different."

"We do, too," Daria told him, then tugged on her sister's sleeve. "Amanda, why don't we go get some coffee and let the Chief finish his business?"

"I don't want coffee."

"Tea, then." Daria increased her tug to a pull. Amanda turned, at last, and followed her sister out the door.

Chief Fletcher moved to Skip's bedside. "I hunted down the doctor while I was getting coffee. She thinks his prognosis is good. The swelling has already started to subside. Maybe a few more days and his brain will be back to normal."

Peri smiled. "Sounds good. Of course, brains and comas are weird. I did a little research on the internet. He may wake right up, or he may sleep a little longer."

The chief gave her a funny look, so she added, "I know, it's not my normal glass-half-full self. Today I feel like being realistic."

He put his arm around her shoulder and squeezed. "He'll wake up. In the meantime, they're going to open the visitor's list to friends."

"Let's hope Amanda doesn't put my name on the No Admittance list."

"If she does, I'll cross it off."

Peri laughed, and followed the chief out. As they walked down the hall, she decided to press her luck. "Any leads on who did this?"

Chief Fletcher patted her arm. "This is something I'm not going to discuss with you, Peri. Guys who'd shoot cops are doubly dangerous."

"What? I'm curious. I don't want to get involved, but I'd like to follow along."

"And I know you can't follow along without getting involved." They reached the front door. The winter sun bounced off the puddles from last night's shower. "I promise I'll let you know when the arrest is made."

"I guess that will have to do." Skip's face appeared in her mind, frowning. He wouldn't want her to get involved. *The chief is right. As much as I want to keep digging until I find the bastard who did this, I need the police to follow their procedures. If the shooter got off due to a technicality I was responsible for, I'd never forgive myself.*

CHAPTER 11

Brian's Bar and Billiards didn't open until eleven-thirty, so Peri had some time to kill. She could drive to the bar early and do a little work on her cell phone while she waited. Or she could pick up a few things at the grocery store in the same shopping complex as the bar.

But the warehouse where Skip and his co-workers were attacked was calling to her. She had no business there, and it was in the opposite direction from Brian's. Still, her car turned right out of the hospital instead of left, as she gave herself a dozen excuses for why she needed to see the scene of the crime.

Not to investigate. To see where it was. To feel like a part of what happened, to help Skip process it when he wakes up. Yes, when he wakes up.

The parking lot was empty, giving the place a silent, sinister feel. She eased from her car and shut the door. It echoed in the quiet. The crunch of her shoes was too loud. Even the odors were over-enhanced by the rain. She studied the building, committing it all to memory, from the block lines to the tiny windows at the top.

There were two doors, a large roll-up door for loading and a small door for people to enter. They were probably locked, but she strolled over to make certain.

The small door to the right held fast. She moved to the roll-up door and gave a half-hearted pull on the handle. To her surprise, it yielded a bit. She pulled harder. The door rose, allowing sunlight onto the travel trailers Skip and the others had fought around.

She took a step inside and stopped. The place had the feeling of a graveyard. Her will faltered for a moment, then she straightened her shoulders and entered. It was cold in the building, yet she could hardly breathe, and opened her jacket to keep from sweating.

About eight small RVs were scattered throughout the space. She moved between them like a visitor to an old cemetery, reading tombstones. This trailer had bullet holes in it... this one had a dent... this one wore a dark brown stain...blood.

Peri's stomach knotted as she considered whose blood it was. Placentia's CSU officer, Jason Bonham, had processed everything already. He would know where each man stood, where everyone went down.

She glanced at her watch. Time to go to Brian's. As she turned to leave, her foot caught on something, pitching her into the side of one of the trailers. The trailer rocked, and she heard a clinking noise.

Peri knelt and looked underneath the trailer. A gold chain, with a charm, was caught on a piece of metal molding, dislodged when she bumped into the trailer. Reaching into her pocket, she withdrew a tissue. After snapping a few pictures on her cell phone, she plucked the jewelry from the frame, using the tissue to keep her fingerprints off.

The chain was thick, like a man would wear, and the charm was more of a medallion, large and heavy. A dragon curled around the front of it, fierce and breathing fire. In its talons, it held the word "Drachen." On the back was a phrase that appeared to be German. *Reinheit oder Tod.* She took out her cell phone and selected the translation app.

"Purity or death."

That sounds distinctly Hitler-esque. Jason needs to have this. Wrapping the tissue around the charm, she pocketed it, closed the warehouse and drove to the bar.

Brian's had been a fixture on the Fullerton-Placentia border for over thirty years. Beer was featured on the menu, although wine was served if patrons didn't mind asking for it by color. Next door was Big B's Barbeque, a rib joint with a pass-through to the bar. It was a hangout for locals, including students from the nearby Cal State Fullerton campus.

The servers always remembered Skip and Peri, what they drank and what they ate. She had a feeling someone would recall two guys who each ordered one beer and shared a plate of pulled pork sliders.

Peri stood for a moment to let her eyes acclimate to the low lighting. A busy young man with a beefy face and spiked hair looked up from his task of stocking glasses.

"Hey, Peri, you're here early. Red wine today, or a Bass?"

"Cup of coffee today, Garth. I'm working a case." She sat down at the bar, and showed him the receipt on her cell phone. "I know how busy it gets here, but who might have served a couple of guys on Monday night?"

"Okay, sure, Table 8." He slid a white mug toward her. "Yeah, I was working that night. I didn't have that table, Shawna did. Can I see your phone?"

He went to the register, where he alternately looked at the photo and pressed his index finger against a touchscreen. "Ah. They used a credit card."

"Garth, you're a genius. Any name on that card?"

"Brandon Mayfield."

Peri inhaled the coffee's aroma. "Mayfield. Well, that's a coincidence. Thanks."

She drank her coffee. *Was Rick Mayfield bold enough, or stupid enough, to use a family member for his dirty work?* In Jared's story, he was a cruel young man. His expression in Jared's photo did nothing to contradict that. But using a relative to retrieve that photo seemed reckless.

A pretty young blonde darted in the back door, fumbling to get car keys in her black leather hobo. "Sorry, the babysitter was late."

"No prob," Garth told her. "You can take over setup. Peri's got a question for you, while you get settled."

Peri showed her the receipt.

"Brandon and Jessica? Sure, they're regulars. Twenty-somethings, okay but not big tippers, not that I expect them to be."

"Could you describe them?"

"Sure. He's average height, about like Garth, but thinner, with light brown hair, and brown eyes. Kind of looks like a model. Jessica is maybe five-four, long dark hair. Curvy, but I wouldn't call her fat."

Peri pushed her cup aside and rose to leave. "Thanks, guys. You've been a big help."

Peri considered calling Detective Berkwits and telling the Fullerton police what she'd found. It was always a fine line for a private investigator. Maybe they'd want her to check in with what she'd discovered. Of course, they have the receipt, too, and maybe they'd rather do their own investigating. She dug a five-dollar bill from her tote.

Garth waved her off. "On the house."

She put it under the empty mug. "Consider it a tip then."

The noontime temperature had warmed enough for Peri to slip off her jacket before getting into the car. Getting older was easier with her medication, but the least bit of warmth could still trigger a hot flash.

She raced the car toward the police station, drumming her fingers at each red light. Every piece of evidence could help them find Skip's shooter. She made a weak promise to herself, not to try to extract any information from her favorite CSU officer. What good would it do, anyway? Finding the killer wouldn't wake her boyfriend.

Boyfriend. What a juvenile term. Lover, soul mate, significant other, they were all words that were either too much information or too little. And none of them gave her access to him in a health crisis.

"If I'd married him the last time he asked, I could be visiting him right now. I could say 'I'm his wife' and it would be like the password."

She looked in the rearview mirror, smoothing the wrinkles on her brow. Last week, marriage didn't mean anything to her. Suddenly, it was her entire world.

CHAPTER 12

Benny paced in front of the Alta Vista Country Club, waiting for Phil and Nancy Nickels. He checked his watch. It was 11:29.

They told me eleven-thirty. They only have one minute, and I don't see them. I didn't want to come. They should not be late.

When he told them about his idea, the Nickels said it was a good plan, but they insisted he help out.

"Benny, this is a wonderful thing to do," Nancy had told him. "You really need to see it through with us. We'll be a team."

I've never been on a team. He remembered his school years. *No one ever chose me. I don't know how.*

He was ready to get back in his Cadillac and go home, when he heard the familiar rumble of the Nickels' diesel Mercedes, rolling up the drive. Nancy waved at him from the passenger seat as they turned into the parking lot.

Benny looked at his watch again.

"You are one minute late," he said as the couple walked up.

"Sorry, Benny," Phil told him. "Matt Helm got out of the house and I had to coax him back with a can of tuna."

Benny frowned. If it was a choice between losing the cat and being late, well, he'd rather not choose at all. "You should be more careful."

Nancy smiled. "Let's go find Jo-Anne."

A tall, elegant woman greeted them at the front desk. In addition to her job as event coordinator for the country club, Jo-Anne Martin served on many volunteer committees with Nancy, and knew Phil from his weekly golf schedule.

She smiled and extended her hand to Benny.

He hesitated. Handshaking wasn't his thing, but he reminded himself of what Dino would do. He took her hand firmly and pumped it once as he introduced himself.

There, that's done. He checked it off his social to-do list.

"Let's go in the office and talk about what we need." Jo-Anne gestured toward a small room with a desk and chairs for two clients. "Let me grab another chair."

Benny stood in the doorway. The walls were too close, and the shelves were too full of books and trophies and photos. He squeezed his eyes shut, to keep out the swirl of color and shape. "This is too small. Can we have another room?"

"Yes, actually, I think we've got a conference room available." She ushered them across the entryway, down a hall, to a larger room with a table and chairs.

Benny found a chair that swiveled. *This is good.* His skin was prickly and his feet fidgeted back and forth. Swaying in the chair would help him calm down.

Jo-Anne sat with a folder and notepad. "I know we spoke briefly on the phone. You are interested in a fundraiser?"

"A special fundraiser," Phil said. "I'm sure you've heard about the recent shootings of our police officers. It was our friend Benny's idea to have a golf tournament and dinner to raise money for these officers and their families. A show of community support, right, Benny?"

Benny's head bobbled. "We need to help them."

"That's such a great idea." Jo-Anne pulled out her calendar. Her voice was low and calm, although her words spilled quickly. "I was sick when I heard the news. Normally, we're pretty booked, but we happen to have a free Saturday in two weeks. Is that enough time for advertising?"

"Ordinarily, we'd take months to plan something like this," Nancy said. "But we need to do this quickly. Strike while the iron is hot, so to speak."

"I'll check with management, but under the circumstances, I think we can discount a lot of our services. Nancy, were you planning on any kind of additional fundraising, like silent auction or something?" Jo-Anne asked. "I'd be happy to help."

"Yes, between the Women's Club, Phil's involvement with Rotary, and even the library Friends Foundation, we should be able to put together a table of items. Thanks for offering."

"Am I done helping?" Benny swiveled faster.

"Well, it depends," Jo-Anne said. "Do you want to help with the tournament?

Benny shrank into the chair, his eyes wide. "I don't know how to play golf."

"Don't worry about the golf," Phil said. "Nancy and I will handle the planning for that."

"All right." Jo-Anne scribbled in her notebook. "Would you like to select the menu? Or maybe come up with a name for the event?"

Benny flinched from her gaze, and stared at the floor. *Decisions. Menu or name? Which would be better?* He wrung his hands, smashing his fingers against his palms.

"You can help with both if you'd like," Nancy said.

Her words calmed him. He could do both. He wouldn't have to choose. "We should call it Help Our Police Tournament. Wait—Tournament and Dinner. And we should have Italian food."

"Why Italian food?" Jo-Anne asked.

"Because I like Italian food."

Phil and Nancy laughed.

"'Help Our Police.' It's simple, which is good." Jo-Anne wrote on her pad. "'HOP on down to the Help Our Police Golf Tournament and Dinner.' What do you think?"

"It sounds great," Nancy said. "I'll make phone calls this afternoon and get everything moving forward. It would be wonderful to hand a big check to Chief Fletcher. I'm sure these families could use the money."

They all stood, except Benny, who took one more twirl in his chair before rising. Jo-Anne extended her hand for a departing shake. He frowned, then acquiesced.

Two handshakes. Check.

"I want to thank you again, Benny, for this idea. It's an excellent way to rally the community around our police. I'll call you this week to set up an appointment to taste possible menu choices, okay?"

More decisions. He looked around. "Can you come, too?"

"Of course," Nancy said.

They left together. Phil gave Benny's shoulder a firm pat. "You're a good guy. I hope you're proud of yourself, because I'm sure proud of you."

Benny returned to his car wearing a big smile. Phil told him he was good. He was proud of him. It was almost as nice as hearing his dad say he was proud. Phil wanted him to be proud of himself. *Am I proud of myself?*

He shook his head. *Not yet. But when we raise the money, I promise I will be.*

CHAPTER 13

The receptionist buzzed Peri into the station, and she headed for Jason's lab. She saw him through the window, at his desk, writing. She knocked and waved when he looked up. It was hard to tell if he was grinning or grimacing as he stood and gestured for her to enter.

"Peri, good to see you, but you really shouldn't be here. Hate to tell you, but the chief specifically told me not to talk to you about the case. Have you seen Skip? How is he?" Jason flitted from his desk to a microscope while he spoke.

"I got to visit today. He's about the same, still on the ventilator, still...the same." Fear prevented any other words. "Anyway, I know I'm not allowed to get involved, but I come bearing gifts. I stopped by the warehouse and—"

Jason held up his hand, and picked up the phone. "No, no, no. At least let me get Steve or Pat in here."

Within moments, Steve Logan entered the lab. He was a tall man, broad and commanding, with a thick coppery mustache to match his auburn curls.

"Peri, how can I help you?"

"First of all, I'm not trying to get involved with the case. I went by the warehouse today, just to see it. I'm hoping you can understand."

He frowned. "Maybe, but I can control my impulses. Police training requires more discipline."

She narrowed her eyes. "Well, you're a better man than I am, Gunga Din."

"I'm sorry. That came out a little rough. I've never been in your position, so I don't know what I'd do. Must be tough to be shut out of everything. Too bad you never married Skip. I heard he asked often enough."

"Yes, yes, he asked often enough." Her insides grew warmer, the blood coloring her chest and moving upward. Kind of like a hot flash, except she wanted to hit something. "Yes, we could have married. No, we didn't. Yes, it's my fault. I don't know what the hell that has to do with anything, especially hospital visitations. Seems to me someone in a coma needs anyone who loves him, whether they're related or not. It's not like I'm asking to pull the freakin' plug."

She'd reached into her pocket for the medallion, but relaxed her hand and kept it there instead. Steve was an ass who didn't deserve what she'd found. It's even possible he wouldn't accept it, not being wrapped in police protocol and all. Skip would have used it. He might have yelled at her about how she got it, but he wasn't stupid.

"Is Detective Spencer any nicer than you?"

"Not really. He thinks you should never have given up the house-frau business."

She took her hand from her pocket, empty. "Then I've wasted your time, Detective."

"Jason said you had something to give me."

She glanced at Jason, who was staring into a microscope, obviously attempting to stay under their radar. "Jason misunderstood."

"Well, then, I guess you'll be on your way." The detective's jaw clenched. "Shall I escort you to the front?"

Jason leapt from his chair and handed him a stack of papers. "Here's the report on the bullet casings I collected from the scene, Steve. Don't worry, I'll see Peri out."

His hand was at her elbow, pushing her toward the door. She was surprised by his strength. He gave her no chance to resist. They strode down the corridor, past the receptionist and out to the civic center courtyard.

The sun was high, sparkling on the tall fountain in the middle of the court, the water rippling down the blue mosaic tiles. She turned to him, wrenching her arm from his hand.

"You're hurting me."

"Sorry. I'm also sorry Steve was such a jerk, but if you've got something, we need it."

"No evidence of your own?"

He shook his head. "Too much. I spent hours at that warehouse. Fingerprints everywhere—so many different ones. I'm still running them through the system, hoping for at least one hit. Bullet casings with nothing to compare them to. We're processing the blood DNA, but that takes time. I need something that pulls us in a direction."

"What about all the other officers? Didn't they see anything?"

"The warehouse was dark, and once they burst in, all hell broke loose. Shooting, shouting, bodies running and falling." He frowned. "And you're not supposed to be asking these questions."

"You're right. I promised I wouldn't. Guess it's a hard habit to break." She reached into her pocket, producing her find. "Here. I don't suppose you can say this is anonymous, but at least wait until I leave before you tell Logan who it's from. I swear I didn't break in. And the only reason I found this is because I tripped and fell against one of the trailers. It was stuck underneath."

"Peri, we all just want you to be safe."

"I know. I tried to stay away, but I had to walk through there. It was awful and eerie and I simply had to do it." She held out the tissue to him. "I took pictures before I retrieved it. I'll send them to you."

He pulled out the chain, wrapping the tissue around to keep his fingers from touching the metal. Holding it up to the light, he examined both sides. "This is great. Thanks, Peri."

"I hope it's useful. I don't know why it has a dragon on one side and German on the other. Aren't dragons symbols of Asian culture?"

Jason shook his head. "Not always, although often enough. But if you look at this dragon, it has more of a lion look to it. Asian dragons remind me of catfish, with all the long whiskers. This one looks like it would belong on a knight's banner or shield."

"Well, please let Detective Snobby know I don't want to get involved with the case, mostly because I'm afraid if I caught the shooter, I'd kill him myself. I'd hate to have to clean up the mess."

She marched back to her car, cursing Detective Steve Logan under her breath in language that made her brain cells blush. *The nerve of some men, thinking I should have kept my safe job. And what business is it of his if Skip and I aren't married? We tried living together and it was a disaster. Are we supposed to be miserably married in case one of us gets hurt?*

Sliding into her car, she whispered another prayer. "I'll do anything if he'll be okay, God. Even marry him."

CHAPTER 14

Peri checked her watch as she crawled along the freeway with the commuters. Like most inland towns, Walnut Ridge was lived in, not worked in. The residents left in the early morning, and drove south to Orange County, or west to Los Angeles. Their journey home began around three in the afternoon and lasted past six.

Four o'clock meant she was in the middle of traffic sludge.

Finally off the freeway, she wound through the wide, curving streets. As she rolled down the main boulevard, she noted a banner hanging overhead. A town meeting was scheduled for the next evening to discuss some issue plaguing the residents.

I'll bet Rick attends, and I'll bet he's got something to say.

By six, she had reached her destination, a tony little mini-mansion behind huge iron gates. Rick Mayfield had done well for himself. Of course, she'd already read up on his family. His wife came from wealth. She wedged her Honda along the curb between two Mercedes, hoping no one noticed her humble ride. It was already dark, which worked to her advantage.

For a long time, there was no activity around the house, at least that she could see through the gates. Around seven, the porch light came on, as well as accent lights around the yard, low enough to be attractive yet bright enough to reveal intruders.

She noticed an easement with a walking path along the west side fence. Stepping from her car, she adjusted her ball cap and checked the laces on her running shoes. She jogged down the street, away from the house, to get an idea of the neighborhood. The houses were all large and well-spaced. Most were two stories, with balconies over the front door.

At last, she turned and ran toward Rick's house. As she got to his gate, it opened. She stepped forward, only to pull back when a dark Jaguar blasted down the drive. The car stopped at the street, blocking her way. She couldn't see through the tinted windows, but she had the distinct feeling of being stared at by the driver.

Perhaps he's waiting for me to jog around him.

She gestured for him to drive on, but the car sat, idling. Peri shrugged and stepped in front. The engine growled, and the car rolled forward, threatening, so she stepped back.

She waited for a moment. The car stayed put, still idling. Stepping forward again, she stared at the tinted window. Again, the car jumped forward, engine roaring.

Screw this.

Swinging out to the left, she sprinted across. She could feel the warm air from the engine as the car pulled out, barely letting her get around it. The Jaguar turned down the street toward her, ruining her plan to run along the easement. It crept alongside, keeping pace.

Stopping, she turned and faced her stalker. She pulled her cell phone from her pocket and glared at the car while she pointed her phone at it, and pressed a button. A flash from the camera lit the night, and the Jaguar sped off, with a slight screech of tires.

After watching until she lost sight of the car, Peri doubled back. The encounter left her with a vague sourness in her stomach and prickles along her spine. There was no way Rick could recognize her, could know her business, could know that Jared hired her, unless he'd passed the stalking stage and was into surveillance, complete with listening devices.

She trotted down the path along the easement, glancing sideways at the house. Most of the home was obscured by trees and shrubbery. The path sloped down as the property rose, allowing the owners to have a magnificent view of the canyon below, while ensuring people on the path were too low to see the house.

Well played, topography.

The path continued to wind downward in the dark, lit from above by a fragment of moon and from below by the city lights. She realized she was moving too far away from the house, and would have to trek up a steep incline to return to the street. The night smelled of wet dirt, and chimney smoke. Turning, she saw something she hadn't seen as she jogged past.

Steps.

They were wooden and appeared ancient, swept over by loose dirt, reminding her of the steps down to the coves in Laguna Beach. The handrail was also wood, and quite weathered. She laid her hand gently on the rail as she climbed, noting the roughness and taking care not to pick up any splinters. Five tall, narrow steps and she was at a small wrought-iron gate that led into the yard. The gate was decorated with swirls and a large circle with an "M" inside.

The "M" could stand for "Mayfield," but the wealthy Mrs. Mayfield's maiden name had been Morrison. *Wonder who really holds the deed to this place?*

She listened for dogs, but none had appeared as she climbed, so she pressed against the iron bars and peered inside. The grounds were a gentle slope of lush grass. An extensive patio with an outdoor living area spilled from the back of the house, ending in a natural-rock pool and spa.

Lights were on in a room downstairs, and she could see straight-backed chairs through the window. The dining area. Figures moved back and forth, entering with objects in their hands and leaving without. Dinner was being served.

A woman's shape became recognizable. She moved as if made of steel rods. Every step she took looked angry.

A man joined her in the shadows. The woman raised her arms, a little fistball at the end of each. The man brought one arm up and leaned forward. She backed, turned, and strode away. He followed.

Nice family moment.

Soon the man's shadow re-appeared. It was probably Rick. She watched him come to the window and stare out at the blackness. Something was in his hand; he brought it to his lips. He seemed to focus on the gate, standing still, staring. Peri feared he had detected her. She ducked, but something stopped her.

Her sweatshirt was caught in one of the curls of wrought iron. She pulled at the shirt, trying to get it unwound. It came undone as she yanked harder, stepping backward. Now something was under her foot, causing her to lose her balance. Not wanting to throw herself at the gate and attract attention, she kept backpedaling, beyond the edge of the step. Shuffling and scrambling, she tried to get her feet under her and stop her momentum.

It was no use.

She stifled a scream as she fell to the bottom, giving a series of huffs and groans. Her back and hips hit the corners of the steps with each bounce. Grasping at the handrail on her way did nothing but drive splinters into her palm. With one final thud, she landed in the dirt.

Wheezing, she attempted to rise. Her lungs did not agree and forced her to wait until they worked again. Finally, she pushed herself into a sitting position, and looked up. An object rolled about on the middle step.

She stood on rubbery legs and brushed dirt from her clothes. Reaching to the step, she grabbed the object, an empty pill bottle. She resisted the urge to stop and read the label. Getting back to the car was a better idea. Pocketing the bottle, she staggered forward, attempting to look normal.

As she reached the top of the rise, she heard a familiar hiss and sputter. Little black heads popped up from the grass and sprayed water. *Sprinklers. Perfect.* She would have jogged out of the way, but her body was complaining about the walk. There was no way she'd coax it to run.

She got into her car, soggy, muddy, grass-stained and already feeling her muscles stiffen. Before driving away, she pulled a bottle of ibuprofen from her tote. Two was the recommended dose. She swallowed down six. Next, she reached into her pocket for the empty bottle and looked at the label. It was a prescription for hydrocodone for Leona Mayfield.

Vicodin. She rubbed her sore shoulder. *Too bad it's empty.*

Tomorrow morning she had to be outside Brandon's apartment in Fullerton. Hopefully, she could catch him leaving and follow him.

This case was not going to be fun.

CHAPTER 15

At five a.m. Peri lowered her battered frame into her Honda, wincing with every muscle spasm. *I should have just slept in the car last night. Too bad I was busy digging splinters from my palm. And icing my right hip, left ankle, and—oh, hell, it all hurts.*

There was a job to be done, however. Soon, she was sitting in front of Brandon Mayfield's apartment, waiting for him to appear, and popping her non-prescription, under-performing pain relievers. She had found a picture of Brandon on the internet, a Mayfield family photo used for Rick's political aims. Shawna was right. He was a good-looking kid.

An hour later, she had nearly given up on catching him at home. He was probably on social media—surely, she could dig a little deeper to find his place of employment. As she turned the key in the ignition, the front door of the apartments opened and the familiar face emerged. He stared at his phone, shuffling down the stairs, then stepped over to a bright red Audi coupe and into the driver's seat. Peri let him get almost to the corner before she pulled out.

Less than fifteen minutes later, the Audi rolled into a parking lot, and Brandon bounced to the front of the local Bank of America branch and knocked. Another employee met him and opened the door.

Peri checked the time. The bank wouldn't open for another hour. Seeing a takeout place across the street, she got a quick to-go order and coffee. As she returned, a short, curvy brunette was knocking at the bank's door.

Hmm, is that Jessica? Peri settled into her driver's seat and pulled a breakfast sandwich from the bag.

She had taken a bite, when a flash in her rearview mirror made her look up. It was a Placentia Police Car, parked behind her. A shadow passed to her driver's side. She looked over to see a gun barrel staring back at her, and stopped moving, stopped breathing, even tried to stop her heart from beating.

"Ma'am, roll the window down and put both hands out of the car." There was a dark blue torso behind the gun barrel, with a female voice.

Peri looked at her sandwich, her mind stuck on what to do with it. When she turned toward the bag on the passenger seat, she saw another gun barrel, at the other window.

"Ma'am."

"Yes. Um, I have to turn the key over to lower the window." Peri sat, afraid to reach for anything in the car and be misunderstood.

The torso to her left leaned forward and yanked the door open. "Step out, Ma'am."

Peri did her best to unwind her aching body from under the steering wheel, keeping her breakfast in her right hand.

"Drop the sandwich," the female officer said.

Peri couldn't stop herself. "But I just bought this."

"Turn around, please, hands on the hood. And put the sandwich down."

Sighing, she placed her breakfast on the top of the car, and felt a small, strong hand patting her down.

Several times, the officer hit her bruises. She winced but tried not to budge, focusing on the tall, slender African-American officer on the passenger side, who was going through her tote and glove compartment.

The patting stopped.

"Ma'am, could you step away from the car?" the patrolwoman asked, indicating with her gun.

Peri kept moving until the gun stopped waving. The male officer completed the search by checking out the driver's side, the back seat, and the trunk. Peri blushed as she watched him dig through unopened junk mail and unfiled papers. After a few moments in conference, the officers holstered their weapons.

The male uniform held up her wallet. "Miss Minneepah, can I ask why you're in this parking lot?"

"I'm waiting for the bank to open. I misjudged the time." Easy question. Maybe too easy.

"Are you a customer?"

"No, but I was hoping to get some information about opening an account here."

"I see you're a private investigator. Work anything interesting lately?"

Peri looked at him. The officer's face showed no emotion, but there was something there, in his eyes. The police didn't often ask questions they didn't know the answers to.

"What am I suspected of doing, officers?"

They exchanged glances again.

"We got a call," the woman said. "Someone claimed you followed them here. They said they thought they saw a gun."

A laugh burst from Peri. "Sorry. Didn't mean to do that. I don't own a gun."

"Really? An unarmed PI?"

She shrugged. "What can I say? Not anti-gun, just don't personally want one."

"But, you are working something, aren't you?" the patrolman asked.

"Yes." A flash of red caught her attention. Brandon's car zipped out of the parking lot. As he drove away, she saw a brunette in the passenger seat. "But I'm done for the moment."

The patrolwoman looked at the disappearing car. "Sorry about that."

They handed Peri her things and returned to their vehicle. She picked up her breakfast from the hood and examined it, brushing at the bottom of the English muffin and considering how badly the five-second rule had been violated.

Sliding back into her front seat, she waited for the police to unblock her car. It was hard to attach her seatbelt, her hands were trembling so badly. Looking down the barrel of one gun was bad enough. Two barrels reduced her limbs to noodles.

She'd lost Brandon and Jessica, probably for the day. How did Brandon know she was tailing him? She tossed her partially-eaten sandwich in its bag and pulled out of the parking lot.

CHAPTER 16

Driving down Yorba Linda Boulevard, she paid cursory attention to the road, while her mind reviewed the morning. Brandon could not have spotted her, so who tipped him off?

Before she realized where she was headed, she had driven to the hospital. Chief Fletcher had said she'd get visitation privileges soon. She parked and went in, hoping it had happened.

"Peri Minn..." the receptionist's voice trailed off as she looked for Peri's name. "Yes, here it is. You can go on in. Room 241."

She stifled her urge to dash down the hall, keeping herself to a quick stride. As she turned the corner, it occurred to her Amanda and Daria would be there. Maybe Amanda would at least respect her relationship with Skip, even if she didn't like it.

Maybe unicorns were real and Skip's coma was a dream.

The officer at the door stood as she approached, looking at her with eyes as black as his hair. She announced herself.

He grinned. "Yes, I know. I've seen you with Skip around the station. I'm Ara Markel."

Happy to know the friendly face at the door, she entered Skip's room. The nurse was the only one with him, taking vitals.

The nurse tapped her chart on her way out. "He's all yours."

Peri pulled a chair over and sat, taking his hand. She stared at him. Was there more color in his face today? Leaning forward, she kissed his forehead and let her cheek rest against his temple.

"Hey, Skipper. How's your day been? Getting a lot of rest? Jason's working hard to process all the evidence. Sure would help if you were there. You're so good at putting clues together, solving puzzles. I'm busy helping Jared, the contractor working on Benny's house. Someone's stalking him." She rubbed his hand.

"Geez, Honey, I wish you could talk to me. I was trying to tail this guy and he made me somehow and got away. I've been over and over my actions all morning, and I can't figure out how he knew I was following him."

She leaned back. Pain shot through her hip. "Ow. I fell down a bunch of steps, into a flower bed last night. Stupid. Really hurts."

The memory of visiting the Mayfield home flitted across her mind, especially the Jaguar looking so menacing. She told him what had happened, from the Jaguar to the fall, to this morning's fiasco tailing Brandon.

"I couldn't see who was in the car, but what if it was Brandon? Or maybe…what if whoever was following Jared followed him to the meeting at my office?"

A sudden idea froze her blood.

"What if Rick knows I'm working for Jared? What if he's already ahead of me?" She kissed him again. "I'll be back—I need to check on something."

She scurried to her car and sped the mile to her building. Everything took too much time. As she put the car in park, her hands fumbled with the car keys.

Damn it. She sprinted to her office, and her heart fell. The door was ajar. She could hear noises inside. Not good noises, either, but the sounds of objects being thrown.

Double damn it.

Peri pulled out her phone to call 9-1-1. She had raised it to her ear when two figures came out of her office, dressed in black and wearing ski masks. One was short, one was tall, and both were lumpy. The trio looked at each other, three pairs of wide eyes.

"Son of a—what are you doing in my office?" Peri tossed her phone in her tote and reached forward to grab the short one's mask.

Before she could pull, the tall one had pushed her against the wall. She pushed back, then felt something sharp at her throat, and retreated.

"What do we do now?" the short one whispered. It was a woman's voice.

"Shut up." The tall one, a man, kept the blade tight at Peri's throat while he dragged her along the wall, into the office.

The short one followed, and shut the door.

"Now—" Short Gal began.

"Shh!" Tall Man cut her off, and stuck his leg out, tripping Peri, and tossing her to the floor. Landing on her bruised hip, she yelped. Tall Man's eyes wrinkled in a smile. He put his thick hiking boot on her leg and stood, putting all his weight on her. She gritted her teeth and glared at him, suppressing any more sounds of pain. Still, it hurt like hell.

Bastard.

He stepped off and stood by Short Gal, whispering. Peri studied the pair. Tall Man was running his fingers over his knife, a slim switchblade. Short Gal was unarmed, and stood flatfooted, as if she relied on everyone else to give her the next move.

Peri looked around for something to strike back with. Her desk was upended, and there were papers and books strewn around the floor. Apart from a letter opener and a stapler, she didn't keep a lot of sharp objects in the office. There was a pair of scissors in one of the drawers, but nothing within her reach, at least nothing that trumped the knife Tall Man had.

She looked for the safe in the corner. It had been dragged away and had obvious scratch marks and dents. But they hadn't been able to open it, thank God. She looked over to see Tall Man watching her. Without the rest of his face visible, his eyes were more expressive. They stared at her, then shifted to the safe.

Damn it.

It took two steps for him to reach her. She felt him grab a fistful of her hair and pull. Her hands went up to try to take the pressure off her head—they were met by his blade. A sharp prick on her left pinkie made her yank her hands down, using them to crawl in the direction he was jerking her.

He gave her head one more vicious tug toward the safe, then pointed the tip of the knife at the keypad. No words were needed.

Peri glanced at her left hand. Blood was dribbling down the side. She wanted to wipe it off, but Tall Man seemed insistent that she open the safe first. Her pulse rose as she reached out and tapped the code. The back of Tall Man's hand caught her cheek and slapped her aside. She flew backward and landed flat.

That's when she noticed his hands. He had taken off one of his gloves.

Rolling over, she struggled to a sitting position, then felt another boot, this one on her shoulder, pushing her back. Short Gal had moved behind her and kept her on the floor. Peri stopped resisting and watched Tall Man open the safe door, her heart beating against her ribcage.

He tore out the few items from the shelves. Peri waited for him to find the picture she'd taped to the underside, but instead, he rifled through the papers and books. It took all her cunning to keep her expression neutral as she watched him slam the safe door shut, then stomp around the space.

"Where else would it be?" Short Gal asked.

"Shut. Up." Tall Man sounded angry.

"Relax. She'll never ID us."

Peri looked up at the shorter intruder, who was now going through her pink snakeskin tote. "Hey, get out of my stuff."

A sharp pain in her ribs made her curl in the fetal position, wheezing. She felt her hands being yanked behind her back, and her wrists being wound with something sticky. *Great, they found my duct tape.* Soon, both wrists were bound together, followed by both ankles. The coup de grace was the strip of shiny gray across her mouth.

At least they didn't tape her ankles to her wrists. She laid very still, so they wouldn't get ideas. Both of her assailants moved to the door, then gave her a final look before leaving.

Not even noon and this day has gone to hell in a hand basket.

She waited a few minutes, until she didn't hear footsteps. Certain they were gone, she began the long crawl toward the door. She wished her office was not carpeted. It would have been easier to slide her body along tile, instead of scooting her shoulders over, then her hips, then her feet, then shoulders again. Not to mention cleaning up the blood she imagined was everywhere.

Everything hurt, from the bruises on her back to her hands. Her palms had been taped facing each other, making their abrasions rub together. Meanwhile, the knife wound on her finger dragged across the carpeting with each motion.

Fifteen minutes later, her feet were at the door, she was drenched in sweat, and her entire body was aflame.

Now what?

She could see the door wasn't quite shut. The problem was, it opened to the inside. She scooted down and right, then backed her heels against the sliver of door available. Bending her knees and pulling up with her calves, she tried to open the door. It budged a little, but dropped back to its sliver when she took her heels off.

For several minutes, she worked at it, trying to open the door wide enough to put her feet through. Each time, she was able to catch it before it swung back to its original place. It was a slow process, giving her ample time to kick herself for all the mistakes she had made, beginning with getting out of bed that morning.

There was a knock at the door, and Peri squealed through the tape. The door pushed open. In walked one of Placentia's finest, who rushed to her side. The female officer peeled the tape from Peri's mouth.

"Ma'am, I'm Officer Gwen Driver. Are you okay?"

"Yes, just embarrassed and aching." The officer helped her sit, then removed the rest of her bonds.

"Dispatch got a call from your phone, no voice, so they sent Officer Powell and me to check it out."

"I'm so glad you did." Peri stood up, shaky, and brushed herself off.

"Can you tell us what happened?"

Officer Powell came to the door. He started to enter, then looked at the mess. "Shouldn't we stay out of the area so CSU can process?"

"Call them in, George, but we still need to take care of—" She looked at Peri, who identified herself.

"Thanks." Peri allowed the officer to help her to her feet, and limped out the door. "There were two of them."

Driver pulled a chair out to the hall so Peri could sit. She motioned to Peri's hand. "Let's get you bandaged up."

Powell handed her a first aid kit. She turned Peri's hand over, cleaning it with an antibacterial wipe. Peri flinched from the sting. "Sorry. Looks like it's a small cut. Just bled a lot. Now then, want to tell me what happened?"

Peri described her assailants in as much detail as possible, which wasn't much. "The man took off one of his gloves. You should be able to get prints."

"Good." Driver turned to her partner. "When will Jason get here?"

"Sounds like it'll be at least half an hour."

"Peri, would you like to stay?"

Peri shook her head. "No, I think I want to go home. But could I get my tote, and something from my safe?"

Driver nodded, so she limped in and got her things, including the picture, still taped to her shelf. The picture. It wasn't safe in her office. Neither was she. In the meantime, how was she going to find a spare moment to clean up this mess? Too bad she couldn't hire someone. Or could she?

Peri retrieved her phone from her tote and pressed numbers. "Hello, Benny—would you like a job? Can you meet me at my office, say 2 o'clock?"

CHAPTER 17

"Miss Peri, this is a mess." Benny stood in the doorway, looking in at the tangle of papers and books in the office, while the locksmith tried to maneuver around him to change out the lock on the door.

"Excuse me," the man said. "I really need to work here."

"Benny, in or out." Peri stood in the midst of the chaos. Her desk was still toppled, the safe in the middle of the room, and papers covered everything. She had at least picked up all the papers with blood on them. There was a limit to what Benny would clean.

"It's messy in there."

She looked up to see him still in the doorway, looking for a place to put his feet. *Ah, Benny.*

"Yes, it's messy, but I need your help. See if you can step over there." She motioned to a place where the floor could still be seen. "I know it's hard to know where to start or what to do."

The little man rocked his body as though preparing to leap. Taking a big breath, he launched himself, tiptoeing to the bare spot. He landed and stood, his eyes wide.

Peri kicked the papers from the center of the room, making a path to the desk. "Here, come help me turn the desk upright."

She grabbed one side and waited while he took the other. They lifted, not quite together, and not with the same strength, but managed to somehow get the desk back onto all four legs. Peri pushed the safe back into the corner.

"It's still messy."

"Yes, Benny, that's why I need you. I can't spend the time putting this place back together, so I'm willing to pay you to straighten it."

He appeared stricken. "Miss Peri, I don't know where anything goes."

"Don't worry, I don't want it organized. All I need is for the books to be put on the shelves—not in any particular order—and the papers put into stacks. I can file them later." She reached down and picked up a small box, placing it on the desk. "Here. My business cards."

"No particular order?"

"Any way you want to get the books on the shelves, I will be happy with. The papers can be stacked on the floor, or the desk, or wherever you want."

His head bobbled. "Okay."

"Thank you, Benny. I have to run some errands." She focused on the locksmith. "When you finish, give the keys to my associate."

First thing she needed was a new cover to follow Rick Mayfield and his loving family around. Her little blue sedan wasn't as inconspicuous as she believed. And the blond hair definitely needed a makeover. She pulled out her cell phone and touched a familiar number.

"Beebs? I need a favor. Can we switch cars for a few days?"

Her best friend did not disappoint. "Sure."

"Thanks for not asking me why. I could use some ideas on disguises, too."

Blanche laughed. "It's not Halloween."

"Shut up and help me."

"Come on over and I'll set you up."

The Debussy house sat on a large, rolling lot in an upscale Yorba Linda neighborhood. It was two stories of beautifully bricked, immaculately maintained luxury. Peri ran up the porch and rang the bell, then opened the unlocked door before calling out.

"Upstairs." The voice beckoned her to the second story guest bedroom, where there were several colorful scarves on the bed, along with what appeared to be animal pelts.

"What is all this?"

Blanche appeared from the closet. "You said you need a disguise. I've got some wigs, scarves, glasses..."

"What are you, part of the Witness Protection Program?"

Her friend laughed. "They're my sister's. A few years ago, she had breast cancer. She used all these to cover the effects of the chemo."

"Kathleen? I had no idea."

"She kept it as private as possible. I was barely given permission to tell Paul. But two years, cancer-free."

"Oh, I'm so glad." Peri picked up one of the animals. It was a brunette wig, cut in a bob style. "Maybe this."

She slipped it on, tucking her golden curls inside. The image in the mirror startled her. "Wow, I don't even look like the same person."

Blanche took Peri's wrists and turned her palms up. "Dear God, girl, what happened?"

"Mostly I was stupid." Peri pulled her hands away and explained her latest injuries.

"You worry me." Blanche shook her head, and handed her a pair of Oakley sunglasses, large and dark. "What do you think of these?"

"I think I might blend in with the benevolent crowd. By the way, has anyone ID'd the dead guy from the warehouse yet?"

"Peri, you know I can't talk to you about it."

"Oh, please." She took off the wig and glasses. "I promise I'm not trying to get involved in the case, but can you blame me for being curious?"

"No. But can you blame me for not wanting to press your detective button?"

"I guess not."

Blanche patted Peri's arm. "How's Skip doing?"

"Well, at least he's in a regular room but he's still on the ventilator. I don't know, maybe I see more color in his cheeks. The bottom line is he's not...awake."

"Aw, Peri."

"I miss him so much, I can't stand it. The way he cautions me about staying safe, the stern looks and the nagging. I miss holding him, miss arguing with him."

Blanche ran her fingers through her short, dark hair. "Okay, I'm sure I'm going to regret this, but yes, I heard they got an ID on the shooter. Lawrence Kelly, 31, member of the Drachen Bruderschaft, a white supremacist group out of Victorville."

"Drachen Bruder-what?"

"Dragon Brothers. They're not really German, they're hate-mongers who latched onto a German moniker." She grabbed Peri's shoulders. "Listen to me. These are hard-core criminals. In the past two years, I've probably had six thugs on my slab that were killed as a result of either being a Drachen, or crossing one. Do not get involved in Skip's case. Promise me."

"Pinky swear I'll be good." Peri held up the wig and glasses. "My own case seems to be getting interesting enough."

"So, what do you hope to do with the getup?"

"Go unnoticed, for one thing. There's a town meeting tonight in Walnut Ridge. I'm hoping to be a concerned citizen and look around for some suspects."

"Good God, don't do anything dangerous with those people, either. You know what, call me once a day, okay? As a check-in."

"Yes, Mom. I guess someone has to keep tabs on me."

"I know Skip can't advise you, so let me give you some police-style advice: grow some healthy paranoia. Assume the bad guys are always around the corner."

"Sounds exactly like something Skip would tell me." The rich rumble of a car engine outside caught her attention. Peri peered through the side of the bamboo shades, down the street. "As a matter of fact, I'll take your advice right now."

The car that had just pulled up looked like the Jaguar that confronted her the night before. She couldn't see who was inside, due to the tinted windows.

"Looks like I accidentally brought company."

Blanche looked out. "Damn, now what?"

"Now I ask you for a couple more favors." She dug the envelope from her tote and handed it to Blanche. "Can you store this?"

"Depends. Am I storing it or hiding it?"

"Yes. It's what I think the people in that Jaguar are looking for."

"We have a safe in the floor of our closet. What next?"

"I need to get away from these guys. It's kind of a long shot, but I got an idea." Peri held up a blond wig from the bed. "Care to switch places?"

"Won't they notice I'm shorter than you?"

"Maybe, but I'm hoping without anything to compare you to, they won't be able to tell, at least not right away."

"Well, hell, I'm game." Blanche took the wig and tried it on. "I look good as a blonde."

Five minutes later, Peri watched her friend leave by the front door. Her short, dark hair was covered by the blond wig and Peri's red baseball cap, and her dark eyes were shaded by Peri's sunglasses. She was too short to trade clothes, but she had put on a pair of khakis and a long-sleeved tee-shirt that looked similar to her friend's. Peri's pink tote swung on her arm.

Blanche slipped into the blue Honda and drove away. Just as they hoped, the Jaguar took the bait and pulled from the curb. The plan was for her to drive to the police department. Peri prayed they would follow her friend without harming her.

Peri put the dark wig and glasses back on, then went to the garage and got into Blanche's white SUV. She turned the car in the opposite direction, and hoped she could go unnoticed for a change.

CHAPTER 18

This is too messy.

Benny stared at the papers and books on the floor. Miss Peri had at least helped him turn the desk right side up, but everything else was a whirl of white. It was hard to figure out how to make it better. He picked up one piece of paper and put it on the desk. There was another piece of paper under it.

"That didn't make anything better."

He could see the center courtyard from the floor-to-ceiling window in Peri's office. The sky clouded over, making the plants in the atrium look dark green. Little brown birds flitted up and down from the bushes to the ground, pecking at something. He strained to watch them.

"What are you eating?"

It was fun, watching the birds. He almost forgot about his chore for a few minutes, but a little voice nagged in his head.

Benny, you need to do your work.

He frowned and studied the room. So messy. One piece of paper on the desk. Many papers on the floor. Miss Peri expected him to pick them up.

What would Dino do?

"Maybe he'd sing." Benny reached into his pocket and got out his iPod. Soon, his brain was flooded with the smooth baritone of Dean Martin, crooning about amore.

As Dean sang, Benny decided to start in the corner near the window. He picked up a piece of paper, then another, until he could see the beige carpet underneath. Happy, he went to the next group of papers and picked them one by one, placing them in the next pile.

An hour later, Benny regarded the ten piles of paper on Miss Peri's desk. It was good, but it was still messy. Some of the file cabinet drawers were open. He peered inside one of them. It was empty, so he was able to stack four piles of paper inside. The next drawer had room for three piles. By the third drawer, he'd hidden all the loose papers.

Wow, Dean Martin is really good at helping a guy clean.

He turned and looked around, expecting everything to be nice again, but there were still books on the floor. What did Miss Peri say about the books? He closed his eyes. She'd said, "All I need is for the books to be put on the shelves—not in any particular order—and the papers put into stacks."

Okay, she did tell me to put away the books. He turned the volume up and worked for another hour, picking each book up and placing it on the shelf, in order of height and color. He was almost finished when the office door opened.

A large man came in, wearing a white t-shirt and beige camouflage pants. Tattoos crawled all over his neck and down his arms. They seemed to slither and move. Benny looked around searching for an escape, but the doorway was blocked. He backed until he was against the atrium window.

The man's t-shirt was too white, and his pants pattern didn't match his wiggly tattoos. Benny closed his eyes, then, worried the man would do something mean, he opened them. Then he couldn't stand the visual and closed his eyes again. He tried opening and closing his eyes in a staggered rhythm.

The man stood, studying him. "You, uh, you can't be the private detective."

Benny squinted, trying to hear what the big man was saying. Dean was singing too loud, so he took out his earbuds. A small strain of *Mambo Italiano* could still be heard. He was frightened, but Dean's voice kept crooning.

This man would not scare Dino.

"What do you want?"

"I'm looking for the detective."

This man looks bad. I need to protect Miss Peri.
"Miss Peri is not here."

"When will she be in?"

"She is not here."

"You just said that. Does she keep office hours?"

"No, you have to call her." Benny looked around and spotted her box of business cards on the desk. He selected one and held it out to the man, his fingers on the farthest edge.

"Thank you." The man took the card and looked at it. "Tell her John Smith will be contacting her."

Benny looked at the floor. "You need to leave now."

The big man did as he was told, and Benny exhaled, realizing he hadn't breathed in several minutes.

I need to see Miss Peri.
He locked the door and scurried to his car.

CHAPTER 19

Still paranoid about being followed, Peri parked down the street from her house and sat for a few minutes, observing the traffic. No suspicious cars were parked or cruising, so she dashed to her front door, keyed in the security code, and bolted the door behind her.

Relaxing, she wandered to the kitchen and dug a bottle of cranberry juice from the back of the refrigerator.

Footsteps on her porch startled her. She stood, waiting for a knock, but none came. Opening a nearby drawer, she removed a large carving knife. Her heart rate jumped into Mach 5 territory.

This is when I wish I had a gun.

She slid around the corner into the living room and made her way to the window next to the front door. There was a small space between the curtain and the glass. As she peered through, a pair of eyes stared back at her, surrounded by a face smashed against the pane. She leapt back, her hand over her chest.

"Benny!" She threw the door open to his round little form, standing on the porch. "Why didn't you knock?"

"Your car isn't in the driveway. What did you do to your hair?"

"Come in."

He waddled in, glaring at her. "I don't like your hair. Why is your hair different?"

"It's a wig, Ben. It's not my hair. I'm working undercover."

"Well, I still don't like it. You're home now so you can take it off."

Peri put the knife on the coffee table. "I'm not off work yet. What do you need?"

The words burst from him in a tangle. "I-I-I brought your keys and then a man came to the office and he was big and white and had wiggling snakes all over his body and he wants to talk to you."

"Whoa, slow down, Turbo. A man came to see me?"

Benny took a deep breath. "Yes, he came to see me, I mean, you. He was very big and I didn't like him."

"Did he leave a name or anything? What did you tell him?"

"I gave him your card and told him to leave." He stared at the ceiling. "He said, 'Tell her John Smith will be contacting her.'"

"John Smith? I'm guessing the wiggling snakes were tattoos. Did any of the tattoos look like dragons?"

"I don't know, they were all squiggly and moving around and his shirt was bright and his pants didn't match the marks on his neck." His words sped up again and he sounded breathless.

"Okay, okay, calm down. Thank you for taking care of that, and for cleaning up my office. I appreciate it." She got her wallet and counted out several bills. "I'll pay you for today."

"Miss Peri, I'm worried. Jared and Willem weren't at work today. When will my house be done?"

Peri considered how to tell him about Jared's problem. "Someone's being mean to Jared, and they broke into his house."

"Oh, no. No one should be mean to Jared. He needs our help. Aren't you going to help him?"

"I'm actually working on the case. Don't worry, Jared and Willem are staying in a hotel until I catch the person who is responsible."

"Oh." The worried crinkles left Benny's face. "Then why weren't they at work today?"

"They probably had to meet with the insurance company, like you had to when your house was burned."

"Oh. Well, are you helping the police find the man who shot Mr. Skip?"

"No, they don't need my help. I've really got to get changed and go to a meeting."

"What do you want me to do next?"

"Next? Oh, I don't need you to do anything else."

His expression was so downcast, Peri worried he might spring tears. "I mean, I don't need anything done tonight. When I get home from my meeting, I'll know more, and be able to come up with a plan."

She shooed him from the door, then ran back to the bedroom to slip into a simple black dress with black tights and a herringbone jacket. Checking the mirror, she adjusted her wig and regarded her reflection.

I still look too much like me. She darkened her makeup, giving her eyes a more almond shape and her lips a fuller appearance, then reached into a drawer for a pair of eyeglasses with a mild prescription. It was slightly disconcerting to her that she could see better. At least the black frames made her eyes look darker, more greyish blue.

After resetting the security alarm, she got in Blanche's SUV and drove toward Walnut Ridge. The entire way, she checked her rearview mirror for any car that hung back yet stayed with her. No one seemed to be on her tail.

Her first trip had taken hours, but this time it took less than sixty minutes. She barely had time to invent a cover story before pulling up at the civic center. There were clumps of people wandering toward a door that said Community Room. She watched the women, noting their clothes and hairstyles, happy with her choices.

I'll fit right in.

The room was set up like any lecture hall. Rows of chairs faced a long table with microphones. Most people in the room were helping themselves to coffee, greeting others they knew, and pointing toward seats. She strolled to the coffee urn, smiling at strangers, and poured herself a cup.

"Hi." A slender blond woman approached her. "I'm Holly Duchamps, event organizer."

Peri held out her hand and repeated what she had rehearsed in the car. "Kate Spears. I'm not exactly a resident. My husband and I are looking to buy a house here, and when I heard about this meeting, I thought it would be a good way to check out the neighborhood."

Holly smiled as if impressed. "We hope you'll join our community."

"I'm assuming the city's leaders and council members will be here."

"Oh, yes. As a matter of fact, our current mayor is right there. Let me introduce you."

She led the way to two men who looked as if they were discussing something serious. Peri slowed her steps as she recognized one of them—Rick Mayfield.

"Mayor Sutton, I'd like to introduce you to a potential new voter." Holly slid out of the way to allow Peri to grab the mayor's outstretched hand.

"Greg Sutton." He was a tall, lean man, very angular. His handshake was pleasant, firm without crushing bone. "Where do you live now?"

"Rancho Palos Verdes." She watched the mayor's face. "The last of our kids left for college, and it's time to downsize and possibly relocate."

At the mention of Rancho Palos Verdes, the mayor's eyes gleamed. Palos Verdes was a peninsula known for its extreme wealth. Even Wikipedia defined it as "affluent."

"Well, I hope we can convince you to choose our little town," he said with a big smile. Peri knew what he was thinking: *Ka-ching.*

He turned toward Rick. "Mrs. Spears, may I introduce you to one of our city leaders, Rick Mayfield. Rick is running for mayor this year." The mayor grinned even wider. "Since I'm retiring, I've endorsed him."

Peri extended her hand to Rick, and received a quick, friendly shake.

"Glad to meet you. Did Mayor Sutton say you don't live in Walnut Ridge?"

"Not yet. I read about the meeting tonight and it seemed like I could get a good flavor by listening to your political discussion."

Rick gestured. "Then perhaps we should all take our seats."

CHAPTER 20

For the next hour and a half, she listened to a lively discussion about updating the downtown area. Some people wanted trendy restaurants and boutique stores, to increase the city's revenues. Rick belonged to this group, and often referred to other locales that had revitalized their city centers.

Others just wanted to give their downtown a coat of paint and new signage. This group was led by one of the council members, Peter Marshall, an attorney in a gray suit. He was large and square, like a chunk of granite.

She was intrigued by watching Rick and Marshall try to present themselves as the voice to be heard. Neither had a higher position on the council, yet their views appeared to carry more weight than the other members sitting on the dais. Rick, in particular, seemed to have an edge with the audience. Whether he was a shoo-in for mayor or not, his backers were more vocal than Marshall's.

She tried not to be cynical about Rick's political aspirations, but it was difficult to overlook his slick style, a combination of perfect grooming and excessive charm. She could picture him as a teenager, manipulating the insecure young Jared into doing, well, anything.

When it was over, nothing had been settled, but everyone had voiced their opinion and could now rehash it with their friends. She drifted around the crowd, getting snippets of their reactions. Everyone agreed about two things: no one wanted to pay more taxes, and Rick Mayfield was at least earnest, if not correct.

She turned to find Rick talking to a young man she recognized. Brandon Mayfield, dressed casually in jeans, was listening to his father intently. For a moment, she froze, fearing he would recognize her, then told herself she was Kate Spears, PTA mom, and stepped forward.

"Mr. Mayfield, I had to tell you how impressed I was by you tonight. I hope you do win the election, you'd make a wonderful mayor."

His smile was as big as his ego. "Thank you, Mrs. Spears. May I introduce my son, Brandon? He's helping us with the event."

Peri held her hand out. As Brandon took hers to shake, she looked down at the ink scribbling on his arm. It was a dragon, curled in the same pose as the medallion she found in the warehouse. She grinned and made eye contact, noticing he was looking at his tattoos, as well.

"I apologize for staring, but my son also has tattoos. I think they call it a sleeve? Anyway, at first I admit, I hated them, but now I'm trying to learn about their meaning. So many young people have them, they've become the new normal." She hoped she had babbled enough to sound like a slightly ditzy mom.

Rick chuckled. "It has been Brandon's constant argument with my wife."

"Could I get a picture for the newspaper?" Holly joined the group, dragging a young man with a camera.

Peri scooted away from them, but Holly insisted. "No, I want you there, too, Kate. Now, get a little closer."

The group shuffled together. Standing between Brandon and Holly, Peri had an idea. She moved to Brandon's right side. "It would look better boy-girl."

"Good idea," Holly said. "Closer, everyone."

Peri moved in closer to Brandon, causing them both to stand at a slight angle. He was taller than her by maybe an inch or two, which made him too short to have been the man who attacked her in her office. His dad was about the same.

After several rounds of "cheese" and "one more," the photographer had several shots.

"Thanks, we'll be putting these on our Facebook page," Holly said.

Peri turned to Rick. "It was nice meeting you, Mr. Mayfield. This visit tonight has been very informative."

He smiled, holding eye contact. "I hope we didn't scare you off."

She felt an additional warmth from his almost-flirtatious gaze. Adjusting her glasses, she put on her toothiest beam in return. "Not in the least."

From the corner of her eye, Peri saw a flash of color. A woman invaded the party, giving Holly a firm push to move her out of the way. Tall and wraithlike, the woman's porcelain skin and long dark hair reminded Peri of characters in Charles Addams' eerie drawings. Her dress, though, was silky and bright, in shades of red and orange. It was also short.

Wow, Morticia, you look better in black.

To Peri's surprise, the pale woman put her arms around Rick and gave him a kiss, sensual and long to the point of embarrassment. Rick reddened and unwound himself from her grasp before addressing Peri.

"Mrs. Spears, I'd like you to meet my wife, Leona."

"Nice to meet you." Peri held her hand out, receiving a tepid shake in response. Leona's hand was so bony, she was afraid she might break it. The beads of sweat on her upper lip told the story, even if last night's pill bottle hadn't. Leona needed a fix.

A hefty, broad-shouldered man walked over to them. Peri had noticed him earlier, standing in the back of the room. His only interesting quality was his intense stare, two large blue eyes in a round face, almost owlish. She kept waiting for him to turn his head 180 degrees, which he might have been able to do, since he had no neck to speak of.

"Ready to go?" He pulled on Rick's arm. "We have a reception at your house."

Leona's eyes widened. "Shouldn't I know when there are people tromping through my kitchen?"

"If you'll excuse us." Rick smiled at Peri, then turned to his wife, whispering. "We did discuss this, dear. Last month, when we went over our schedules."

"Don't worry about a thing, Leona." The owl-faced man gathered her shoulders in one of his enormous arms and nudged her toward the door. "The caterers are already there, getting everything set up. You don't have to do a thing except stand by the tapas and look sexy."

He caught Rick with the other arm, and Peri watched the trio bustle from the room, each one trying to steer the other and all mumbling arguments through their wide grins. She studied Holly, who was looking down with an irritated expression.

"Who was that man?" Peri asked her.

"Sean Jackson, Rick's campaign manager."

"He seems very—assertive."

Holly sent the photographer to another group, her focus on the door where the three had exited. "He's an ass. But he's an ass who'll get Rick elected."

"Darn, I wanted to get his phone number. Do you happen to have it?"

"Certainly." If Holly had been rattled by Leona's shoving, she'd made a quick recovery. She pulled a stack of business cards from her purse and rummaged through them. "I know I've got one somewhere…"

"Can I help? I have Rick's information." Peter Marshall held a card out to Peri. "I don't believe we've met."

She told her lie one more time, scrutinizing Marshall as she spoke. He leaned into her space, causing her to move back. There was something unsettling about him.

Peri glanced at Holly, whose face was a complete blank. For the coordinator of an event like this, she was either surprisingly disengaged, or hiding something.

"Palos Verdes?" Marshall asked. "That explains why you'd favor new development, instead of cleaning up what we already have."

Peri forced a small laugh. "Please, Peter. I don't even live here yet, and I'd have to see specific plans before I'd vote on anything."

His mouth smiled, but his eyes narrowed. "When we start voting, everyone will have *all the plans*." His emphasis on the last part of the sentence made the hair on her neck stand up and dance.

"Thanks." She turned away to find Holly, who had disappeared to clean up the coffee area. "Holly, this was such an informative meeting. I'm glad I came. Would you mind sending one of those pictures to me? I'd love to have a memento."

"Certainly, what's your email address?"

The email she wrote down was a non-gender specific address she used to keep people from getting too personal.

"mydirtymartini?" Holly asked.

"Yes, it's...a family joke." Each lie she told was making the next one easier. *I'm going to be a sociopath by the time I get off this case.*

On the way to her car, she saw Rick and Sean in a corner of the parking lot, face to face. Sean's cheeks and neck burned scarlet as he spoke. She couldn't see Rick's face, but his posture looked rigid, as if he was holding his ground.

Leona stood to the side, watching them, smirking.

Peri felt drops on her face and shoulders. Sean and Rick hadn't noticed, but Leona held her hand out, yelled something about getting wet, and turned away, no doubt toward her car.

Rushing to the SUV, Peri jumped in and turned the vehicle toward home. At least she had more suspects to add to her list.

CHAPTER 21

Peri turned the corner onto her street, looking for a place on the curb to pull over. She was distracted by flashing lights a block down. Two police cars blocked her driveway, and the rays of several flashlights swept around her house.

She jumped from the car and sprinted down the street. "What's going on?"

An officer met her at the yellow tape in front of the house. "Ma'am, I need you to stay back. Do you know the owner of this residence?"

"I *am* the owner of this residence." Peri rummaged through her handbag, searching for her wallet. "Here, here's my license."

The policeman read it and stared at her.

"Oh, I forgot." She took off the glasses, then peeled the wig from her scalp, working her fingers through her hair.

He looked at her ID again, then called to a man in a dark suit. "Detective?"

Steve Logan joined them. "Hello, Peri. We got a call from your security company. Your alarm went off. There's no evidence of a break-in, so maybe it scared them away."

"What time did the alarm go off?"

The detective checked his notes. "Seven twenty-five."

"Damn." She was at the community center, meeting Brandon Mayfield at that time. He might have broken into Jared and Willem's, but there was no way he could have done this.

"You sound disappointed."

"A little." *How much should I tell him? He's definitely not going to help me. Unless...*

"I'm working on a stalking case that seems to be escalating. Whoever tried to break in was probably looking for a piece of evidence in my possession."

"If it's escalating, you should get the police involved."

"They are involved. The client lives in Fullerton." She tried to keep the neener-neener quality from her voice.

Logan had a comeback. "Yes, but they seem to be leaking into Placentia."

"You'll be happy to know I don't have a suspect. The person I've been focusing on couldn't have been here tonight."

"No, Peri, I'm not happy. Working your little break-in means I'm not working on catching the cop killer."

The creaking of Peri's backyard fence caught their attention. Jason Bonham was coming from the gate to join them. "No sign of entry. Hey, Peri. Dead bolts are intact on both doors, windows all locked."

"Why don't you go in and see if anything is missing?" Logan asked her. He gestured to a familiar female officer. "Driver, accompany Ms. Minneoper around her house."

Peri opened her mouth to correct her name, then decided to leave it alone. Instead she stepped forward. "Good evening, Officer Driver."

"First your office, now your home." Driver put her arm out to stop Peri at the door. "Let us go in first, Ma'am."

Peri handed her the key. "There's a light switch by the door, on the left."

She watched her enter, along with Officer Powell, guns drawn, sweeping the space as the light in the room popped on. They disappeared, and Peri saw the shadows change with each light in the house. It took a while for the officers to return, enough to make Peri worry someone had gotten in and overpowered them.

Her place was not that big.

At last, Officer Powell returned, holding the door for her. "All clear."

Everything looked normal. Dishes were still in the sink, her clothes were still strewn across the bed. No drawers were pulled out, no papers on the floor.

She returned to the detective. "It all looks fine. The break-in at my client's house was destructive. Fabric slashed, pictures torn off the walls. Even when they broke into my office, they weren't gentle about it."

"When did they break into your office?"

"Earlier today." She pointed to the uniforms walking toward their car. "Those officers took my statement."

"Great. Now we have to add that to the report." Logan took out his pad and wrote.

"Why are detectives even responding to my house alarm?"

"Because Chief Fletcher heard the address come in over dispatch and worried about you. He assumes you're looking for the cop killer, even though he told you not to."

Peri didn't bother to protest, remembering Brandon's tattoo and the Drachen Bruderschaft. She had intended to pass this information to the police. Disclosing it now would confirm the chief's suspicions.

"Tell him to stop worrying. The case I've got is keeping me busy."

"Not too busy to visit the warehouse. Jason gave me the evidence you found." The detective's face did not look grateful. "Stay away from that warehouse. Stay away from Jason. And stay away from the Drachen Bruderschaft."

"Glad to be of help."

"I can't say this any clearer, but let me say it one more time. I. Don't. Want. Your. Help."

"Gotcha." She leaned against the CSU van and stared at the crew, now packing.

Skip, I need you so much. Why the hell did you have to get shot? She pictured herself chattering at him while they sat on the couch, drinking beers and watching a movie. A memory of Craig Daniels popped in, asking her when she was going to "dump that old guy" and go out with him. Laughter. All that laughter, all gone now.

Now she was unwanted, unnecessary, unflirted with.

Tears threatened, and she covered her mouth with her hand, trying to stop herself from breaking down. Jason appeared, wrapping his arm around her shoulder, and giving her a gentle squeeze.

"It'll be okay, Peri."

"I miss Skip's judgment right now. And I miss Craig."

"I know, I miss them, too. We're gonna get those pricks who did this. And when Skip wakes up, he's gonna kick some ass."

"Thanks. I needed that." She patted his arm. "I'm sorry I got you in trouble with Logan."

"No worries. He yelled about it, but he was still glad to have that evidence, no matter who found it. That medallion pointed us toward the Dragon Brothers."

The yellow tape came down and everyone left. Peri retreated to her house. Whoever was after the photo was relentless. They didn't get into her place this time, but maybe next time they'd disable the alarm and tear her place apart. It was time to have a chat with Rick Mayfield.

She looked at the clock. It was past visiting hours, but she needed to talk to Skip. *If I can't get permission, I'll go for forgiveness.*

CHAPTER 22

The staff at Placentia-Linda Hospital had rules about visiting patients. They also had hearts full of understanding, so when Peri pleaded to sit for a few minutes with the man she loved, they understood. Officer Markel was again on duty. He nodded and let her pass.

She was both relieved and disappointed to see Skip in the same position, on his back, arms at his sides, eyelids at half-mast. The dim light filled the room with shadows. She could hear the faint sound of bells ringing, and the shuffle of feet as staff attended to patients.

Sitting down beside Skip, Peri stroked his arm. "I need you so much, Skipper. I miss our talks. Not because you could always tell me what to do—I mean, you usually told me to stop doing stuff—but talking things through with you helped me find answers. My case is…a mess. I feel like I'm floundering, knowing who is bothering Jared but not being able to prove it."

She studied his face.

"I won't lie, I'd like to help catch your shooter. But I'm afraid. These guys are hard core. Now it appears my suspect's son has a tattoo of the same dragon I found at the warehouse. What the hell do I do with that? Logan probably doesn't want to hear it. I'm not sure I care whether Brandon's connected to the gang or not, unless I can prove he's the one who vandalized Jared's house and my office."

She bent down and kissed his hand, then laid her cheek next to it.

"I love you." Her eyes closed as she focused on the feel of his palm against her face. She stayed that way for a while, eyes burning from exhaustion and tears.

A gentle shake woke her. The night nurse had her hand on Peri's shoulder.

"Oh, I'm sorry. I must have dozed off."

"It's no problem. We could move a cot in here, if you'd like to stay with him."

"Thanks, but that's okay. I need to get home, and not all his family would be happy if I moved in."

"Oldest daughter giving you a hard time?"

"Skip and I have been together for ten years, but we're not married. Amanda finds that unacceptable."

"You'd think you weren't adults making your own choices." The nurse took Skip's temperature, then checked the numbers on one of the machines.

"I'd like to be angry about it, but I'm too busy wishing Skip showed some sign of life."

"Well, his vitals have stayed consistently good. It wouldn't surprise me if the doctor took him off the ventilator and allowed him to wake up soon."

"That'd be great." Peri managed a grin. "I don't do patience very well."

After one more kiss, she was back on the road. Back at home, she made a thorough sweep of the house again, kitchen knife in hand, to ensure no stranger lurked in any dark corner or closet. Satisfied, she poured a glass of wine and opened her laptop. Holly had sent the photo to her, so she opened the message and downloaded the file.

Holly's photographer was good. There were three pictures, all clear with great resolution. Brandon's tattoo was easily seen. Peri zoomed in on the ink, and pulled up the photo gallery on her phone. The dragon looked almost identical to the one on the medallion, including the word "Drachen" etched under the dragon's talons.

Brandon's affiliation might be important to their case, but giving Detectives Logan and Spencer any intel would probably result in an argument about her investigation, her non-marriage to Skip, and possibly women's right to vote.

Another large sip of her wine relaxed her brain. Jason would understand. She pulled up his email address, composed a straightforward note, and attached the picture.

As she re-read the message, checking for errors, she reconsidered. Yes, Jason would understand, but she'd already given him the medallion. That put him on the detectives' bad side.

I can't do that to him again. How can I get it to him anonymously?

She dug a flash drive, still in its packaging, from the desk drawer. After slipping on a pair of gloves, she copied Holly's photos onto the drive. Hopefully, Jason could accept this, and the detectives wouldn't press him to find out who sent it.

Hopefully.

As she stuck the drive in her jacket pocket, planning to slip it by Jason's tomorrow, her phone rang.

"Ms. Menopeeze?" It was a young man's voice.

"Close enough. Who is this?"

"This is…Ernie…Valdez from Mr. Mayfield's office. He'd like to set up an appointment with you."

"All right." She was surprised, but decided to save her questions for the interview. "I'm available tomorrow."

They agreed on a time and she hung up. This was not what she expected, but it could be a good thing. She was tired of spinning her wheels. Speaking directly with Rick might give her some traction.

CHAPTER 23

Interviewing a subject can be tricky. Peri mulled over her approach as she drove north on the 57 freeway, through the rain, to Walnut Ridge. *If you're scheduled to talk, the person has time to create a story of lies to tell you. If you catch them by surprise, they may not talk at all.*

Rick's assistant had arranged a noontime meeting at the Mayfield home. What could he have to say?

The gate was open when she arrived. Peri drove in, pulling Blanche's SUV up the circular driveway and parking to the side. Hers was the only vehicle in sight. Perhaps Rick had pulled into the garage, to avoid getting wet.

The rain had slowed to a drizzle. She got out and studied the house in front of her. It looked even more impressive in the daylight—two stories, with soft corners, and a turret to her left. Columns supported a balcony over the front of the house.

She chuckled. *Does Rick plan to give speeches to the masses from up there, or just raise both arms and sing, "Don't Cry for Me, Argentina"?* The image was still on her mind when she noticed the front door. It was large and red, with an ornate brass knocker. It was also open.

Peri stood on the doormat, stymied. Finding a door ajar was usually a bad thing. Her gut said call the police. Her brain said that was stupid. Leona probably didn't pull the door completely shut on her way out. A breeze whipped across the porch, causing her to wrap her jacket tighter.

She rang the bell. Getting no answer, she rang again, and pounded on the brass knocker, waiting each time for the sound of footsteps. No one appeared. She pushed at the door, leaned in, and called, "Hello?"

The house was silent, so she stepped over the threshold, and into the foyer, repeating her call. To the right was a staircase. To the left, a curving wall led further into the first floor. She inched her way along the wall, calling and listening for signs of life.

The interior décor was basic English country—deep colors, ornamental furniture and overstuffed everything. She followed the dark wood floor into the dining area, her voice echoing as she continued to ask if anyone was home. The dining room flowed into a cavernous kitchen, easily able to feed an army of guests.

She turned to leave and wait in her car for Rick, when she noticed a shoe, next to the island. Curious, she moved around to investigate, and found its owner.

Holly Duchamps was staring at her from the floor, her body twisted and her eyes cloudy. A dark pool haloed her head, and a smudge marked the hole between her brows.

CHAPTER 24

"Dear God." Peri pulled out her cell phone and pressed the Emergency number.

In her shock, she couldn't remember the address. "It's Rick Mayfield's house," was all she could manage. She heard sirens almost immediately.

As she ran from the kitchen, her foot kicked something small. Glancing down, she saw her flash drive had fallen from her jacket. Scooping it up, she threw it back in her pocket as she hurried to the front of the house, only to be met by six officers with guns trained on her.

"Whoa, whoa." She held her hands up. "I'm the one who called. She's in the kitchen."

The cacophony of what sounded like a thousand voices answered her.

"Put up your hands."

"Turn around."

"On your knees."

"On the ground."

She wasn't certain which one to obey, but she knew disobedience made cops mad.

Okay, my hands are already up. I'll kneel. Okay. Turn around. She looked at the stone porch, not sure how to lay down without lowering her hands. Finally, she compromised and leaned forward, putting her palms out at the last minute to catch herself.

The abrasions on them still stung when she landed.

Gruff hands yanked her arms down and back. It hurt, but she wasn't going to complain, or talk back to them. That would make them even madder. Large boots stomped by her head, into the house. She stayed quiet, waiting. This couldn't be good, having the police see her coming out of a house with a dead body inside.

The same hands lifted her to her feet, then patted her body, down her sides, and up her inner thighs. The metal cuffs were hard and cold as they pushed around her wrist bones. It was difficult to keep from squirming, to keep the pain at bay. She waited for them to find her flash drive, cursing at herself for not dropping it off with Jason earlier. If they felt it, they didn't confiscate it, which was odd.

Oh. They're searching for a weapon.

Her first impulse was to reason with them, to explain she'd found the body. She had called them.

Or had she?

After a few minutes, a man in a suit emerged from the house, looked past Peri and nodded. Within seconds, the cuffs were gone and her hands were free. She rubbed her arms and rolled her shoulders. It had been mere minutes, but everything ached.

The suited man approached her. "I'm Detective Wolfe. Care to tell me your name, and explain why you were here?"

His voice was a Barry White song, so deep and velvety, she nearly giggled like a schoolgirl. Circumstances squelched her natural impulse.

"I'm Peri Minneopa. If you look in my tote, you'll find my ID. It's in the kitchen, the pink snakeskin—no, wait, Blanche has mine. It's a black leather bag. You'll also find my private investigator's license."

The detective held up his hand and mumbled an order to one of the officers, who went in the house and returned moments later with Peri's bag. The officer reached inside with his gloved hand and pulled out her wallet.

Identity confirmed, Detective Wolfe resumed his enquiry. "Continue."

"I had an appointment to meet Rick Mayfield here." She considered how to discuss the case without revealing it. "He might have information on a stalking case I'm working on."

"Stalking?"

"The client would like to know they're not imagining things before they go to the police." That was true enough. "When I arrived at the house, I was surprised to find the gate open. I drove in and parked, then went to the door and found it ajar."

"And you went in?"

"Not immediately. I knocked and rang the doorbell. Yes, it seemed suspicious, but sometimes I've been in a hurry and not quite closed my own door. I thought there might be an explanation."

"When did you decide to go in?"

"I didn't exactly make a decision. I rang and called, then knocked and called. Then, one foot kind of went in front of the other, kind of inching in and calling. I thought maybe I'd gone too far and should leave, then I found Holly."

"You know the deceased?"

"Met her once. Holly Duchamps. Seemed very nice. She had organized a town meeting to discuss some issues."

"Do you know why she'd be in the Mayfield home?" Detective Wolfe wrote as he spoke.

"No idea."

"You called 911 as soon as you found her?"

"Yes. I have to say, I was shocked to hear sirens so quickly."

The detective gazed at her, pen paused.

"As a matter of fact, it was as if someone else had called earlier." She stared at him, trying to discern what he knew. He continued to watch her with no expression. *I wouldn't want to play poker with this guy.* "Maybe someone who said the shooter was still in the house? Or that I was the shooter?"

"I have a gun." An officer stood by her open car door, holding something black in his gloved hands.

"Was your car locked?" the detective asked.

She shook her head. "Holy hell."

Wolfe did not seem excited. "What can you tell me about the gun in your car?"

"Only that it's not mine. It's also not my car—I'm borrowing my friend's car, but she doesn't own a gun either. I don't even have a permit."

"And you're a P.I.?"

"Yes, but I work nonviolent cases. Background checks. Surveillance on cheating spouses. I've never needed a gun...Except for when a cheating spouse tried to shoot me. And the time a psychopath kidnapped me and tried to murder me and left me in the desert. And when—"

He stopped her. "Are you sure you shouldn't have a gun?"

"Sometimes I think I should, but Skip always talks me out of it. Skip Carlton, he's my boyfriend."

"The detective who got shot?"

She nodded.

"We're all pulling for him and the other officer. Goddamned gangs."

"How did you know it was a gang?"

"You'll find the police departments have their own version of social media. When there's a crime against one of our own, we're all anxious to help out."

Peri looked him over. Young and African-American, of an imposing height and width, he wore khakis and a polo shirt, covered by a navy windbreaker with "WRPD" in large yellow letters across the back. She could see by the way his clothes fit that he did not shop in regular sizes.

Can I trust him? "Detective, maybe you can find some use for a little information I have. As you can imagine, the Placentia police want me as far from the crime as they can push me. I've run across something I'd like to investigate, but I know I shouldn't, and it might actually fall within your jurisdiction."

She paused, waiting to see if he was receptive. His raised eyebrows gave her the answer. "A medallion was recovered at the scene of the officer shooting, a dragon with a German saying on the back. That's one of the things that led the police to the Drachen Bruderschaft. I saw the same dragon recently, tattooed on Brandon Mayfield's arm, along with the word Drachen."

117

"You think Rick's son could be a white supremacist?"

"I think nothing, yet. I can't imagine why a gang would be interested in my case, but I was hoping to get a little information from Rick today when I interviewed him."

Wolfe grinned. "Even though you shouldn't be investigating the Drachen Bruderschaft."

Peri grimaced. "Can you blame me?"

"Not really, but I will join the PPD in warning you to stay away."

"Believe me, Detective, all I want is to resolve my own case. And see Skip open his eyes again. And have the police catch the shooters. Oh, and Officer Chou—I want him to be okay."

"You don't want too much, huh?"

An engine sound made them look up as a silver luxury SUV came through the gate, pulling over behind the squad cars. A familiar figure exited from the driver's side and strode toward them.

"Excuse me." Rick Mayfield's voice was stern. "What is going on here?"

CHAPTER 25

"Mr. Mayfield, do you know this woman?" Wolfe pointed to Peri.

Rick looked at her with no expression. "No."

She relaxed. He didn't recognize her from the town meeting. "My name is Peri Minneopa, Mr. Mayfield. We had an appointment today."

"What appointment?"

"Our appointment at noon. The one your assistant set up with me."

He stared at the detective, then at Peri, eyebrows scrunching. "I don't have an assistant. What number did you call?"

"I didn't call you. Someone named Ernie Valdez called me."

Peri held her hand out to the uniform who had cuffed her. He turned to the detective, who nodded, then gave Peri her cell phone. She scrolled through the numbers received and recited the one Valdez called from. The detective wrote as she spoke.

"That's not my number." Rick's words clipped in annoyance. "I don't have anyone working for me, other than Jenny, the receptionist at the real estate office. And I don't know any Ernie Valdez."

"Somebody called me, and lured me here." She smacked her forehead with her palm. "Somebody set me up."

"Set you up for what?" Rick looked even more confused.

"Mr. Mayfield, where have you been today?" Wolfe asked.

"At work, since nine."

"And you're here now, because?"

"I come home on my lunch hour, when I'm able to, to check up on my wife." His eyes darted to the detective, then Peri. "Leona's been under the weather."

The detective gave Peri a curious look, then took her aside. "Are you certain the body is not Leona Mayfield?"

"Positive."

He turned back to Rick. "Can anyone verify where you were today?"

"Sure. The office staff, then my clients. I was showing houses to them all morning."

Peri watched the detective. It was his move.

Wolfe stared at the ground, rocking slightly, before speaking. "Mr. Mayfield, there is a woman in your kitchen. Miss Minnopah identified her as Holly Duchamps. She's dead. Would you mind going in with our officers and verifying her identity?

"Holly?" Rick's knees buckled and he leaned against the nearest column. "Of…of course."

He pushed himself upright and stumbled toward the house, accompanied by two uniforms. When he returned, he was paler than before. One of the officers was at his elbow, guiding him. The policeman gave a small nod to the detective.

Rick's eyes widened. "Leona. Where's my wife?"

"My officers are still searching the premises, Mr. Mayfield." Wolfe took out a notepad. "Do you have a gun in the house?"

"What? Gun? Why, yes. I have a permit for a Glock. It should be upstairs, in the gun safe in my bedroom."

The detective looked at one of the officers, who brought over the bagged gun found in Blanche's SUV. It always astounded Peri to see the wordless interaction between the police. *Do they have ESP, or some kind of brain implants?*

"Mr. Mayfield, is this your gun?" Wolfe asked.

Rick examined the pistol in the bag. "No. Mine is a Glock. I don't know what that is."

The detective handed the gun back to the officer, who told him, "Number's been filed off."

Peri tried to hide her disappointment. A serial number, attached to a last-known owner, could clear her more quickly than checking for prints, checking for gunshot residue, and checking for an owner who was not her.

"What was your relationship with Mrs. Duchamps?" Detective Wolfe asked Rick.

The detective's words were still hanging in the damp air when a familiar Jaguar rolled up the driveway. Sean Jackson pushed himself from the seat and blustered toward them.

"Rick, I came as soon as I could." His huffing and puffing made him look like an angry bull, red eyes and all. "What's going on?"

"Sean, Holly's dead," Rick told him.

Detective Wolfe raised his eyebrows. "Again, Mr Mayfield, what was your relationship with Mrs. Duchamps?"

"Rick," Sean said, "I'd advise you not to answer that."

Wolfe whipped around to the large man. "Are you his attorney?"

The detective flicked his jacket away, exposing his holster and his badge. The move made Peri grin.

"No, but—"

"Then shut up." Wolfe gestured to one of the other officers. "Mister...?" He turned back to Sean.

"Jackson." Sean said.

"Mr. Jackson here seems to think he can add something to our investigation. Maybe you could take his statement while I interview Mr. Mayfield."

"Forget it," Sean said. "I'll talk to my lawyer first."

The detective shrugged. "Have it your way, but you've just put yourself at the top of our suspect list."

Sean's face paled, but he stretched himself a little taller. "Go ahead. I've got an alibi, and I don't even own a gun."

One more signal from Wolfe, and the uniformed officer took Sean by the elbow and escorted him to the side of house.

Peri touched the detective's sleeve. "How does he know she was shot, and when it happened?"

The detective didn't answer, but gave a slight nod. Guess Sean would have some explaining to do.

Rick gazed at the ground, then looked at the detective. "Holly is—was—just a friend and a business associate. Before you investigate any further, let me also say I have a very passionate wife. You could call her jealous. But I swear, there was never anything between me and Holly."

The old Rick who bedded Jared seemed unlikely to be a womanizer. Even if he was, Leona might have motive to kill Holly, but she wouldn't have motive to frame Peri for it. Maybe.

An officer appeared in the doorway. "Detective, we found Mrs. Mayfield. She's asleep on the patio."

Peri let a small harrumph slip, attracting the detective's attention.

"Miss Minnee-pa, if you'd step over to our CSU officer for processing, our interview is complete." Wolfe turned from her. "Mr. Mayfield, perhaps we could sit here on the porch and discuss the victim, and your sleeping wife. By the way, my partner just messaged me. There's a case in your closet. It's unlocked. No gun in it."

Peri walked over to the van marked Crime Scene Unit and awaited the officer in charge. While she waited, she texted Blanche with the news.

Hope your car doesn't have to be processed, her message ended.

Blanche responded within seconds. *Borrow Benny's Caddy next time.*

A young African-American woman in a blue uniform approached her, carrying a large kit. "Ma'am, I'll need to process your hands, sleeves, and shoes. I'll also need a DNA swab."

Peri submitted to being swabbed and wiped and sprayed. She tried to make conversation but the officer was focused on getting evidence and immune to questions about police work, sports, or her personal life.

"You're free to go, Ma'am."

"With my car?"

"No. We found a gun inside, so we still need to process that."

Blanche was going to hate this. "Without my car, how am I supposed to be free to go anywhere?"

The officer continued to write on bags and put them in a box. "Not my problem, Ma'am."

"Thanks." *For nothing.* Peri considered her choices. It was a long walk home. She took out her phone and called the only other person who could help.

"Hey, Benny, ready for your next assignment?"

CHAPTER 26

By the time Benny arrived, the police had finished processing everything and left. Rick had given Peri no opportunity for questions. He had the detective escort her to the sidewalk, then closed and locked his gate.

She leaned against the brick pillars, mentally slapping herself for not getting any answers, with the bonus of being tricked into being a murder suspect.

The more she replayed finding poor Holly, limp and staring, the more her stomach roiled. *Someone killed her to set me up. How was that worth someone's life?* She was fighting the urge to give up her license and go back to housecleaning when a 1960 black Cadillac Coupe de Ville sailed to the curb.

"I'm not happy," Benny said as she got in. "You know I don't like the freeway."

"I understand, and I appreciate you helping me." Peri gritted her teeth. *I'm not a bundle of joy at the moment, either.*

"I didn't take the freeway. I took Brea Canyon Road."

"Then why are you complaining?"

"I don't like that road, either. It's too curvy."

She swallowed a scream. It was easy to lose it with Benny. Between his OCD and his Asperger's, conversations with him revolved around his obsessiveness with Dean Martin, or his comfort, or his rules.

"Thank you, again, Benny. I really do appreciate you."

He pulled away from the curb and started back down the hill, through the town, and into the canyon. Peri was absorbed in her thoughts.

"Miss Peri." His voice startled her. "I want to help you with your cases."

"I know, Benny, and I'm sorry I haven't called yet with a job for you."

"No, it's okay. I need to tell you something." He seemed to struggle with words for a moment. "I can't work for you. I got another job."

"Another job? That's great. Where are you working?"

"At the Alta Vista Country Club. See, I had an idea for a golf day to raise money for Mr. Skip and the other policemen, but I wanted Phil and Nancy to do it."

"Wait. I saw an advertisement about a fundraiser at the club—did you do that?"

He continued as if she hadn't interrupted. "They said they want my help, since it's my idea. I have to decide what food everyone will eat. It's a lot of work."

"That's such a nice thing to do, Benny. I'm impressed."

"Sometimes Mr. Skip scares me a little. But I want him to be okay, and the other officer. Our police need our help."

Peri looked over at the man behind the wheel. She was more than impressed. For him to put aside his own needs and think of the community was outside his usual thought process. She was overwhelmed. Wanting to plan such an event meant the shooting had affected him deeply.

"Benny, I'd hug you if you liked that kind of thing."

"But I don't like it."

"I know." Her eyes misted. "Thanks for taking me home."

"When do you get your car back?"

"They said maybe tomorrow." She leaned into the seat. "I have got to talk to Rick Mayfield, whether he wants to talk to me or not. I hate to play the bitch card, but I'm sick of chasing my own tail. My office got trashed, someone set off the alarm at my house, and now I'm under suspicion of murder. This sucks. I wish—"

"Stop talking." Benny's voice was a shrill bark. "I need to drive my car and you are bothering me."

Peri closed her eyes, continuing the conversation in her head.

Once she was home, she heated last night's pizza and sat at the kitchen table, going over her notes. She had not visited the Fullerton police to see if they had identified any evidence in Jared and Willem's break-in. That went on her list of things to do, along with call Rick Mayfield and play hardball.

The detective said she'd probably get her car back within a day or two. Make that Blanche's car. In the meantime, she could call a rental company, but there was a better solution.

She called Allen, her mechanic. He was happy to loan her a reliable heap. While she waited for Allen, setting up an appointment with Rick Mayfield was next on her list. She dug through her black, borrowed bag, looking for the card with Rick's number, until one of the side pockets coughed it up.

As she pressed the numbers on her cell phone, the correct number automatically popped on the display.

"I've never called you," she told the phone.

Cancelling the call, she looked back at her history. The number on the card was in her database. It was the same number Ernie Valdez—if that was his real name—had called her from, to schedule the first faux-meeting. Rick had lied to her and the police.

Or had he? That would be so easily exposed, it didn't make sense.

She tried the number.

"Welcome to the Citizens for a Stronger Walnut Ridge," the recorded voice said. "Dedicated to building a safer, more responsible community, the right kind of place for the right kind of people. Press one to donate to our campaign. Press two for more information."

She pressed two, which led to a monologue on what was wrong with the country and how to make it right. All of it intimated that a city based on ideologies and restrictions that favored whites was desirable for everyone. Just as Peri decided Rick was worse than she thought, the recording said a surprising thing.

"Rick Mayfield is not the man to bring our city to greatness. As a matter of fact, his past shows that he is the least qualified candidate for the job. To donate to the campaign against Rick Mayfield, press one now."

She hung up, confused. A quick search for the realty company's website gave her another number for Rick. As she waited for the ring, she studied the card. It was for a local restaurant. Rick's number was written on the back.

Who gave me this card? I asked Holly... Closing her eyes, she visualized the scene, the people, the hands giving her the card. *Peter whats-his-name.*

At that moment, a somber voice answered the phone. "Rick Mayfield, New Vistas Realty."

"Mr. Mayfield, this is Peri Minneopa. I'd like to schedule an appointment to speak with you."

His tone dropped to an even less happy quality. "I'm sure you would, but I'd rather not talk to you."

"Rick, I'm sorry we got off to such a rocky start. I'm still reeling from finding Holly today."

"The police seem to think you might have found her alive."

"But. I. Didn't." She resisted the temptation to over-explain. "The police also know I received a call from you inviting me to your house."

"Not from me—"

"Look, Rick, let's leave today alone. The truth is, even if you had no intention of talking to me, I'd like to talk to you. I think you know I'm working with Jared Reese. Someone's been threatening him and I need your help to figure out who." She omitted the part where Rick might be the who, and tried to enlist him as an ally instead.

"Why should I care who's threatening someone from my old high school?"

"Because it appears the person threatening him is searching for a photo in his possession. A photo that, while invasive and embarrassing to him, would be a career ender for you."

The line was silent for so long, Peri thought he had hung up.

"How much does he want?" he finally asked.

"Want for what?"

"For the picture."

This was not what she anticipated. "What? No, no, it's not like that. Look, can we meet tomorrow and talk about what's going on?"

"Okay." He was silent again for a few moments. "How about tomorrow morning at ten?"

"Sounds good. Let's meet at my office, if you don't mind. I'm a little queasy about your place."

"Understood."

She gave him the address. As she ended the call, she heard steps coming up her porch. She opened the door to find Allen standing there, car keys in his hand.

"I can't thank you enough." She took the keys and strolled to the car, an older model station wagon. "I'll look like a mom driving this around."

"Good." He laughed. "Maybe no one will want to impound Mom's car."

CHAPTER 27

Her first stop was the post office. It would take an extra day, but she could mail Jason the flash drive, and hopefully keep her name out of it. As she walked to her borrowed car, she slipped on her driving gloves and stuck her hands in both pockets, unsure which one held the small drive. To her surprise, she felt a flash drive in each.

Pulling them both out, she stopped and stared at them. They were both black. She turned each over, trying to figure out why she'd have two. The drive in her right hand bore a dark red smudge.

A memory jolted her, of Holly's murder and running from the scene, scooping up her flash drive as she ran. *Not my flash drive.* She had picked up a piece of evidence.

Oh, no.

Although she had been a thorn in the police's side, she had never, ever removed evidence from a crime scene. She got into the car and buried her face in her hands. What to do?

It took several minutes to think of a plan. First, she would mail her flash drive to Jason for him to process. Afterward, she would check the contents of the drive she'd found, to be sure it was truly evidence, and turn it over to the Walnut Ridge PD. In between, she'd visit Fullerton.

After the post office, Peri drove to the Fullerton Police Department, a long, hacienda-style building with a clock tower. Detective Berkwits had told her he'd be available, so she gave his name at the desk. Within a few minutes, he walked around the corner and buzzed her in.

He looked shorter, somehow, and older. She decided it was because he wasn't wearing his hat, revealing a shock of wiry gray hair. His tan accentuated the freckles across his nose, and the bristled mustache above his lip was lighter than she remembered.

"How's everyone?" he asked, shaking her hand. His light southern drawl was the one thing she did remember, vividly.

By everyone, she assumed he must mean the two men in hospital beds. "No news. I'm going to visit as soon as I'm done here. I thought we could compare notes on the break-in."

"Sure. Let's go to my desk." He led her back to a room of cubicles and steered her toward one midway down the second row.

"I have to ask, Detective." She took a seat at his desk. "You aren't from around here, are you?"

"No, ma'am. Born 'n' raised in Brownsville, Tennessee." He laughed. "Great place to grow up if you ain't a scrawny Jewish kid."

"I hear ya. I was the tall, gangly beatnik in conservative Salinas." She pointed to the nameplate on his desk. "Sooner or later, misfits find their place."

"We sure do."

She pulled out her notebook while he opened his file. "Did you get any prints?'

"Yes'm, we did. The people who did this were not masterminds. And I'm guessin' you followed up on that receipt?"

"Same as you, right? Were the prints a match to Brandon Mayfield and Jessica Churchill?"

"Almost. We got prints for Jessica, but not for Brandon. Donny Jackson's paws were all over the house."

"Either of them in the system?"

"Juvenile cases, records sealed, on both of them."

Peri sat back, thumbing through her notes. "I guess if you're going to be a screwup, do it while you're a juvie. That way, your records are sealed and everyone is left to wonder what you could have done that's so bad."

Berkwits chuckled. "I guess, but most of the time they can't keep it together when they grow up. You gotta be focused to stop being a screwup."

"Donny Jackson?" She stopped at a page and read. "Mayfield's campaign manager is Sean Jackson. Any relation?"

"That's his daddy."

"Don't suppose he has any tattoos."

The detective looked through his file. "A few more since his high school photo."

She looked at the picture he handed her. Darker in skin tone, but everything else about him said Dear Old Dad. Round face, round, rheumy eyes, and the same lack of a neck. Standard tuxedo pose, with no visible marks, but the ear toward the camera had a small plug in it.

"Out of high school for four years, and no mug shot?" she asked. "I'm impressed."

"By the way." Berkwits spoke while still reading his notes, his voice soft. "I heard about that shootin' in Walnut Ridge. Bein' on the scene, that's rough."

"You have no idea." She wasn't sure whether he was digging for information or being nice. For the moment, she stopped being suspicious and voted for kindness. "I keep thinking, a woman died because someone set me up. It's hard to swallow."

"I bet it is. Why did you ask about the tattoos?"

She told him about the dragon on Brandon's arm, then sent him a copy of the picture from her phone. He wrote it down.

"Have you talked to this Brandon?" he asked.

"No. Believe it or not, I'm afraid to. If he's a member of the crew who shot Skip, who killed Craig, I don't know where I'd go with the information. I'm trying my damnedest to keep my nose out of that case. Of course, no one believes that, and with good reason. I've made a reputation, butting in to help solve police cases, and gotten in plenty of trouble for it."

She massaged her temples. "The detectives working the case are good at their jobs. I know they'll track down the killer. I also know they'd rather eat toads than accept my help. By accident, I found a piece of evidence they missed. Believe me, it was not intentional. I'm afraid I got angry and stubborn, and ended up giving it to the CSU guy because I liked him better."

He laughed. "As long as it made it into evidence, ain't nothin' wrong with that."

"I haven't told them about Brandon Mayfield yet, either. I'm going to try to give that info anonymously and I'm hoping they don't ask him to find out where it's from.

What if I tell them and they make Brandon off limits to me? My client wants this to go away. I want to do my job. Jared and Willem deserve their peace and happiness."

"You know, police departments don't necessarily like private investigators. They're typically not nice or ethical. And some guys don't like women in the field. That's two strikes."

"Right now I need some hits."

A phone rang. The detective pulled his cell phone from its holder and answered it. Peri rose to leave, but he gestured for her to wait. When he completed the call, he smiled. "How about observin' an interview? That was one of my officers. They just brought in Donny Jackson."

Fullerton PD's warm inclusion was a welcome change from Placentia's cold shoulder.

"I'd really like that."

CHAPTER 28

Berkwits escorted her to the viewing room. A tanned, beefy young man could be seen through the mirror, fidgeting at the table. Donny Jackson. He had added some piercings to match the plugs in his ears, a sleeve of tattoos on his right arm, and a dark soul patch to compliment his closely-shorn hair, but his round face and buggy eyes still marked him as Sean's son.

"Just so I'm clear, what is this guy's connection to your client?"

"It's kind of a 'six degrees' thing. Donny is Sean Jackson's son. Sean is Rick Mayfield's campaign manager. Rick is possibly harassing my client over a photo that could ruin his chances at becoming a conservative mayor in a conservative town."

"And why does your client have this photo?"

She didn't like what she heard in the detective's voice. "My client does not want to expose this picture or sell this picture or in any way threaten the other person with this photo. If anything, he keeps it as a sort of safeguard that the other party won't try to use it against him. Kind of a relationship cold war."

Peri watched his temples throb. She considered telling him about Donny's possible ties to Skip's shooting. She didn't really want to, since it might make Donny off-limits to her, but in the end, she had to do what was right. A police shooter trumped a stalker.

"While you're interviewing, you might want to dig into his associations with the Drachen Bruderschaft."

"Why would I do that?"

"Although I'd like to know who sent him to tear up Jared and Willem's home, his buddy Brandon has a Drachen tattoo, and I'd like the police to have every piece of evidence possible to find that cop killer."

"Understood." Berkwits smiled at her. "Let's see what we can get out of Mr. Jackson."

The detective walked into the interrogation room with a thick folder, and a pleasant expression. She was reminded of a father figure. *That's probably what he was aiming to do.* He pulled the chair around to the side, close and cozy.

"I hope you understand, son, we asked you down here to help us with a case. You're free to leave any time."

Donny looked up at the two-way mirror. "That's good. Cause I didn't do nothing, and if you think I did, then I'm a call my lawyer."

Peri shook her head. Donny was not a smart boy.

"No problem, Chief. I've been reading your file. You're a student at Fullerton College. What are you studying?"

"Just stuff. Trying to get my general requirements to transfer."

"Cheaper than four years at a university, huh?"

"Nah, the old man can afford it. Chafes his ass I'm not at Duke." Donny sneered.

"And yet he likes to keep you poor. We checked your bank account."

"So? I make do."

"Barely." He motioned to the folder. "You're in debt up to your ears, or you were. I see a large deposit to your bank account on Thursday, day after Jared Reese's house was vandalized."

"So?" The boy was still sneering.

"So where were you on Wednesday night?"

"I was in class."

The detective grinned. He held up a piece of paper. "It's a pity y'all didn't sign in on the attendance sheet."

"But I did."

"Actually, your friend Amy signed your name. See how her name and yours are written in the same hand? Oh, and to double check, we talked to Amy. She can't thank you enough. Twenty dollars jes' to sign you in— imagine."

Donny's smirk slipped away.

"I could be mean, here, Don, but I wanna help you. You seem like a nice guy. I'm gonna level with you. Not only do we know about the money and the false alibi, we got your fingerprints all over the Reese home, along with your girlfriend's. And I'm pretty sure we'll find those prints all over an office you trashed in Placentia."

"Oh, no, I didn't do the office, only the—" He slapped his hand over his mouth.

"Only the house," the detective finished.

With a little prodding at key points, the story spilled from him, that he and Jessica were hired to tear Jared's house apart, but Jessica did the office job with someone else.

"What were you looking for?" Berkwits asked.

"Looking for?" He appeared confused. "We weren't looking for anything. We were just supposed to trash the place."

Peri gasped. She was happy they couldn't hear her next door.

"Is that all Jessica was s'posed to do at the office?" Berkwits asked.

"I don't know about that."

"Who hired you to do this? Daddy?"

Donny sat back and glared at the detective. His face went from calm to troubled, but he said nothing.

"How'd they pay you?"

The worry lines on Donny's face eased. He looked over at the detective and shook his head. He leaned back, obviously finished with the interview.

Who was he protecting?

"Let's talk about your friends for a minute," Detective Berkwits said. "Is Brandon Mayfield a buddy of yours?"

"Sure." The boy seemed wary.

For a second, Peri considered leaving. If the detective was going to drill him for information on the Drachen Bruderschaft, it would stir her curiosity and she was doing her damnedest to stay out of the case. Of course, she reasoned, knowing more about Brandon might help her discover who was hassling Jared.

She stayed.

"He's got a real nice tattoo on his forearm." Berkwits reached down and pinned Donny's arm to the table, revealing the same tattoo Peri saw on Brandon. "Well, would ya look at that? A dragon, just like yours."

Donny's eyes narrowed. "So?"

The detective leaned forward, his elbows on the table. "Even says 'drachen' under it. Know what that means?"

The young man stared at him, saying nothing.

"I see your parents' names are Ilse and Sean Jackson." Berkwits opened a folder and leafed through it. "Mom belongs to the DAR. Dad belongs to the NRA. Grand old institutions. Conservative. Are you conservative like your parents, Don?"

He leaned further, inches from his face. "Or do you think they're not conservative enough?"

The young man said nothing, although the color deepened in his cheeks.

"Maybe the old folks are too complacent, huh? They've let this country go to seed. Too many people of the wrong color. And you get no support from the community, do you? We wouldn't even let you march in our parade this year." Berkwits stood. "I got to march, with other members of my temple."

Donny's face flushed red. He stood up, his fists clenched. "You have no right. No right. We can assemble. We can share our views."

"I have the right to protect citizens from hostile acts of any group, even if it's under the guise of freedom of speech." He stepped in close, towering over the young man. "And I have the right to arrest anyone who harms citizens."

Donny stood his tallest and leaned into the detective, a scowl on his face. "Fascists. Filthy mixed-blood murderers. What are you, Berkwits, a Jew? You've got no jurisdiction over me."

The detective's expression remained neutral as he took the boy by the shoulders and turned him to the wall, bringing his hands behind and closing them in handcuffs. "And yet, I seem to have just that. Donny Jackson, you are under arrest."

"What's the big idea? You can't cuff me. You said I was free to leave."

"Yeah, funny thing. You were, but now you're not. Now you're under arrest for breaking and entering, vandalism, and with your views, it'll probably be raised to a hate crime." Berkwits leaned into him. "You might want to call your lawyer now."

"Well, you can't use anything I've said against me." It was clear Donny thought he had one more Get Out of Jail Free card.

Berkwits laughed. "Oh yes, I can. If you want to volunteer information after I've told you you're not a suspect and are free to leave, then I get to use it all if'n I want. And I want. You can ask your attorney about it. Mention the name Beheler. He'll love it."

Peri grinned. *We all have the right to remain silent. Some of us lack the ability.*

CHAPTER 29

By the time she finished in Fullerton, visiting hours at the hospital were long over. Perhaps she could talk her way into Skip's room, but she'd done that once. It was not the kind of power one should abuse. Besides, she still had the flash drive from Holly's death to investigate.

She drove home and slipped into her favorite winter PJs. The hardwood kitchen floor felt cold as she made a bowl of popcorn. With the classic movie station in the background, she opened her laptop, plugged in the flash drive and prayed her anti-virus protection was up to date.

The stick had several folders on it. Peri chose the first one. The files all had a .jpg extension, indicating they were images.

She clicked on one. It showed two men, shirtless and embracing. One of them looked like Rick Mayfield, but she didn't recognize the other one. She swiped through the rest of the pictures. They looked grainy, as if they'd been scanned from old photographs, and they all showed a young Rick Mayfield with other men. Nothing was as graphic as the photo with Jared, but they were definitely not what a candidate would release to the press.

Is it possible Holly snuck into the Mayfield home to get dirt on the family? Why?

Peri reviewed the next folder. The pictures there were of Brandon and Jessica, in crisper resolution. Selfies of both of them, shots of Jessica in suggestive poses, of Brandon lounging with a beer in one hand and a gun in the other. Lounging on a bed in an RV trailer.

Holy hell, trailers. She flipped through the rest of the pictures. Most of them were close-ups of the two lovebirds, but the rest showed trailers in some kind of interior space. The flash had been used on these pictures. There was no sunlight or shadows.

Peri sat back. That Brandon was part of the gang was no longer shocking. But he knew about the warehouse, and had a gun. He might have been the shooter, or one of them. How was she supposed to get this information to the PPD? She'd tapped Jason twice now, even though once was anonymously. And she hadn't been as careful about this evidence as usual. Her cheeks burned, thinking of her mistake. Could it even be used by the police?

She needed to make amends with those detectives. Why wouldn't those yahoos realize she wasn't trying to get in their way? After all, she never got in Skip's way, at least not intentionally.

I haven't talked to Spencer, just Logan. Maybe Logan was exaggerating about his partner's opinion.

The movie in the background picked up. Tyrone Power was in a gun battle with someone. She remembered this film, *Johnny Apollo*. An upright businessman is jailed for some white collar crime and his son turns to robbery to earn the money to spring the old man.

It appeared Brandon had also gone over to the dark side, but she doubted he was doing it for his father. Perhaps he was doing it to get back at his family. Maybe

143

Rick would like to know what his son was up to. If the opportunity presented itself, she might tell him at their appointment tomorrow.

She opened the last folder. This appeared to be dedicated to Leona. No one got off easy with Holly. These were PDF copies of medical records and prescription orders. Leona had fallen many times. Broken arm, twisted ankle, and lots of back injuries. That made sense to Peri. Leona was so tall and slender, her back might be fragile.

Or had Rick abused his wife? However it happened, her reliance on prescription pain relievers was understandable. Most people would be sympathetic to her, even if they would judge her first.

Peri closed the files, and finished her wine and popcorn. The movie ended without a Happy Ever After, only a Happy Enough, Eventually. As she cleaned her mess and turned out the lights, intense sadness washed over her. Even if she solved this case and Skip woke up, nothing was going to back to normal.

She hoped Happy Enough would be enough.

CHAPTER 30

Walking into her office in the morning, Peri was glad to see Benny had picked everything up. She smiled, looking at the books. They were on the shelves, arranged by height and color. Author and subject matter didn't mean as much as visual cues did to her helper.

It took a few minutes to find the papers and folders, but she located them in the tall cabinet, stacked. At least they were out of the way until she could re-organize them.

In the meantime, she had an appointment with Rick Mayfield to prepare for. The cool weather meant she didn't have to run the air conditioner, but she did take off her jacket and sit down. Her temples had a moistness that threatened to turn into a hot flash if she wasn't careful.

Maybe it was nerves about interviewing Rick. Asking people questions had a way of going either very well or very badly, and she needed it to go well. She prepared her desk—a legal pad and pencil, her handy digital voice recorder—but her hands looked jittery as she arranged things. Placing them on the desk, palms up, she closed her eyes and attempted relaxation.

At promptly ten o'clock, she heard a knock at the door, followed by the turn of the handle. Opening her eyes, she watched Rick Mayfield enter, his expression grim. He did not look like a man eager to talk.

"Mr. Mayfield, thank you for coming." Peri rose and offered her dry, calm hand.

He gave her a perfunctory handshake and sat down. "How can I help you?"

"Let's get right to it. My client, Jared Reese, has been stalked, threatened, and had his house broken into. He'd like it to stop."

"That's what you said on the phone, but I still don't understand what it has to do with me."

"He thinks it might have to do with that photo."

Rick's face reddened. "Look, if he thinks he's going to blackmail me—"

"No. That's not it." Her patience was at its end with this subject. "Jared does not want money. He doesn't want anything, except to be left alone."

"Then leave me alone." He was not going to make this easy.

"Look, I don't care what you've done in your past, or who you used to be, or who you are now. You want to find religion and go hetero, it's none of my business." She flipped through the pictures on her phone, to the one she took of Jared's photo before she locked it in the safe. Pointing it at him, she said, "Jared doesn't want any money. He doesn't want this photo to go public. He doesn't want anything from you. He wants the stalking and threats to stop."

"What stalking? What threats?" His cheeks still red, he was glowering at her.

"Ever since your campaign manager called him, he's been watched, his truck broken into, his home vandalized—"

He raised his hand. "What do you mean, my campaign manager called him? I never told Sean to contact Jared."

"Well, he did. He told Jared to pack up and move far enough away to not attract any reporters who might find it interesting that you and he moved from Montana, were in the same class—you get the picture."

Rick's jaw tightened and slacked a few times. At last, he took a deep breath and his face softened. "I was a mess in high school. Hurting…angry…striking out at everyone else to try to make the rest of the world as miserable as I was. Part of it was being sent away from my family. Part of it was acknowledging I'm bisexual. I spent most of those years choosing young men who were as self-loathing as I was."

"What changed?"

"I misjudged someone. Instead of me bringing them down, they lifted me up. They taught me how to let go of the pain, how to embrace happiness, and to give instead of take. They turned me on to public service."

Peri lifted her eyebrow at him. His words might have swayed a revival tent, but she was unmoved.

"I know how this looks. I can't imagine what Jared told you, but if he said I was the cruelest, most sadistic son of a bitch on the planet, it was an understatement. I was vicious. If I was a dog, you'd have had me put down." He shook his head.

"Then I found Jesus, and the first thing He told me was to get some therapy. It saved my life."

147

Peri grinned. "I didn't know Jesus was so practical. Look, I don't care that you had relationships with men and now you don't. I don't even care if you want to keep your past private. I don't think you'll be able to do it, but if anyone spills your beans, it won't be Jared. You know him, or used to, at least. You know how private he was. He hasn't changed."

"Yes, I remember. When I decided to run for public office, I planned to tell everyone about my past." He winked. "You know how far a good salvation story goes with a Christian crowd. Then Sean Jackson approached me, volunteered to be my manager. He was so dynamic, I said yes without a thought."

"Sean didn't want you to come clean?"

"He thought we could suppress it. No one was coming forward. He was insistent, when he took me on as a client, that he run all interference."

"Does anyone else know about your past? Leona? Brandon?"

"Just Sean and Leona."

Peri sat back. "Are you certain your son doesn't know?"

"Why do you ask?" His voice was sharp.

"Because the Fullerton PD has fingerprints from Jared's break-in. Fingerprints they've identified, belonging to friends of Brandon."

"Why would Brandon know anything about this? Doesn't sound like he was involved."

"No, but he's a common denominator. He's their friend, your son. They attack a house owned by a former *friend* of yours. Lots of dots to connect. How much do you know about your son's activities?" She looked down at her phone, flipping through Brandon's pictures on her cloud.

"We're really close. I think I'd know if he was harassing someone."

Really close? "At the town meeting, I got the distinct feeling that you're a conservative candidate for mayor."

"There's nothing wrong with being fiscally responsible."

"I agree. I'm just saying, my perception is you are courting homeowners, and Christians, to the exclusion of a more diverse population."

"I'm not against diversity, but yes, I do believe this country was founded upon Christian values, and it's a fact most of the people who vote have a vested interest in their community, by being homeowners."

"How do your Christian values feel about gay homeowners in your community?"

He gave her a weak smile. "Love the sinner, hate the sin."

"Black homeowners? Mexican?"

He rolled his eyes. "Peri, really, didn't we already pass all those Civil Rights laws? If they're invested in the community, I'm invested in them."

"Maybe you should have a little talk with your son." She pulled up a picture of a sneering Brandon, holding a gun and a beer. "He seems to be hanging out with some dangerous people."

He stared at the photo for a long time. "Where was this taken?"

"I'm not certain, but ask him about that tattoo on his arm. Ever hear of the Drachen Bruderschaft?"

149

"We've had some problems with them in our town. Graffiti, drugs. One thing I want to do as mayor is make them want to be somewhere else."

"You've probably also heard about the shooting in a warehouse in Placentia last week. A warehouse full of trailers. Evidence suggests it was Drachen. These are pictures of your son in a trailer. It might be time for a come-to-Jesus meeting with your boy."

Rick paled.

"In the meantime, whether it's your campaign manager or your son, Jared would like to be left alone."

"I'd be glad to help, but I'm telling you now, I had nothing to do with anything Jared might have experienced." His face, still ashen, was stern. "I don't care if he has a photo of us. He can blow it up and hang it over his fireplace if he wants to."

"Pretty sure his partner wouldn't like that."

"He's got a partner?"

"Yes, they're getting married. Kind of high profile, in a way. Willem is a popular interior designer and Jared's a contractor. They've been profiled in Orange Coastal Magazine."

"I'm a little surprised he'd be so public about his lifestyle."

"Oh, that's mostly Willem. Jared tries to stay out of the spotlight—"

Willem. It suddenly made sense to her. They were well-known local businessmen, and the big wedding plans had all been at Willem's instigation. He was the extrovert. Their wedding announcement was probably the incident that triggered the stalking.

"Maybe if you made a statement, admitted to your past indiscretions. Sean would be mad, but whoever is threatening Jared would have no reason to continue. You might lose some voters, but you might gain others. And at least you could sleep at night."

"I sleep fine, thanks."

"Really? Even after Holly got shot in your kitchen?"

Rick glared at her. "That has nothing to do with Jared."

"And yet it kind of does." Peri held her phone up and flipped through the pictures. "Know where I got these? Holly had a flash drive when she died. These were on it."

"Where did she get them?"

"You tell me. Where did you keep your action shots?"

He blushed again. "There's a hard drive hidden in my closet."

"So Holly knew where to go."

"But why would Brandon's pictures be on my computer? And why not take the hard drive?"

"Because you would notice the hard drive missing." She tapped her pencil against her pad. "Brandon lives in an apartment, but does he have any computer equipment at your house?"

"No. When he sleeps over at the house, he brings his tablet along." His eyes widened. "We got Brandon his tablet for Christmas. When I set it up, I hooked it up with our cloud account. I assumed he'd change it to his own storage."

"I suppose he could store his stuff online. Young people tend to take stupid risks. Where do you keep your passwords?"

Rick grimaced. "On that hard drive."

They were silent. Peri stood and paced around her office. "So... here are pictures, hidden away, that could bury your political aspirations. Holly knows where they are. How?"

He lowered his head. "Holly used to work for our real estate company. She's been to the house a number of times. She pretty much knows where everything is."

"Wow. Everything?"

"I mean, we opened our home to her, didn't hide anything. Leona talks. A lot."

"You said Holly used to work for you. Why did she leave?"

"Leona." He rubbed his temples. "She accused Holly and me of an affair. Naturally, Holly took offense and quit."

"I'm assuming she took offense because it wasn't true?"

"Of course it's not true."

"So, maybe, she took the files to discredit you, ruin your chances at being mayor?"

"You're the investigator. You tell me."

She frowned. "I don't know, but in the meantime, what can we do to make Jared feel safer?"

"I'll talk to Sean." He stood. "He's on my payroll. If I say stop, he has to stop."

"Thank you." She shook his hand. If Sean was responsible for Jared's problems, it sounded like Rick could stop it all. She debated whether to tell Rick she planned to turn Brandon's photos over to the police. In the end, she voted no. Brandon was his son. What would

Rick do to protect him? "I guess we're done here. Thank you for your time, and your honesty."

A few minutes later, she walked out into the late morning sun. She'd forgotten she was in the loaner station wagon and spent a few minutes trying to find her own car. At last, she saw the faded silver Volvo and remembered.

"Damn, I gotta get Blanche's car back." She started the engine. "But first, a visit to Skip."

CHAPTER 31

She called Jared on her way to the hospital and gave him an update.

"At least we know who tore up your place," she said. "And it sounds like Rick Mayfield wants to work with me."

"He's really changed, I guess."

"I think so. He was actually talking about telling his constituents about his bad-boy past. Turns out the boy wasn't looking for the photo, but I'd like to know that the girl wasn't, either."

"I can't wait to tell Willem."

"Okay, well, I'll keep you in the loop with whatever else I find out. Have a good day."

Peri parked in the hospital lot and went into the lobby.

The receptionist smiled as she checked in. "The girls are visiting," the woman whispered.

"Thanks." Peri pushed through the doors and marched down the hall, preparing herself for a tense visit with the family. Officer Markel was at his post. "Always good to see a friendly face guarding Skip."

"You know, sitting here has taught me a lesson. I used to call my mom once a week. Been calling her every day lately, just to say hi."

She patted his shoulder, and entered the room.

Daria sat at her father's bedside, holding his hand. She appeared to be talking to him. Amanda stood at the end of the bed, back to the window, and chewing on her thumb. Her posture was straight and rigid. There was no particular expression to her features, but her resting face looked unhappy. As Peri entered, she pulled her fingernail away from her mouth.

"Good morning, Amanda, Daria." Peri gave Amanda a warm hug. The young woman's frame felt stiff at first, but as Peri kept hugging, she softened a bit. Peri gave her one more affectionate squeeze, then turned to embrace her sister.

"Look, Peri, they took him off the ventilator. I think he looks good, don't you?" Daria asked.

It was hard not to see more color to his cheeks, even more activity behind his eyes. Peri tried to be objective, but she needed to believe in miracles.

"Yes, I think so," she told Daria. "What did the doctor say?"

"She said the swelling's gone—" Daria began.

"We do not owe Peri a diagnosis," Amanda said.

Her sister stood and faced her. "Enough. You are being perfectly horrid to a nice woman. A nice woman who loves Dad, and who Dad loves."

"If they're so much in love, why aren't they married?"

"Amanda." Peri tried to reason with her. "We're older, independent people. We don't feel the need to combine our houses or certainly our finances."

"Well, Drew says unless you've committed yourselves in a public ritual, you're nothing but Saturday night's date."

"Drew says, Drew says." Daria's voice rose, in tone and volume. "Drew is an ass, and ever since you've been with him, you've become the same. Pompous, superior, unbending, so sure of yourself, you're positively stupid."

"Stupid?" Amanda's voice matched her sister's. "Well at least I'm not flitting from lover to lover, like some kind of 70s hippie slut."

"Sure, slut-shame me, that's what Drew would do. For your information, I haven't had that many lovers but if I had, I wouldn't be ashamed. I'm in charge of my own sexuality, unlike you. How does Drew like it—in the dark, under the covers, missionary position? Or have you even had sex yet? Maybe he wants to save it for when you want children."

Peri stood back and watched. The argument was getting louder and angrier, each sister bringing more of their baggage into the mix.

"Girls, excuse me," Peri softened her own voice, to make them listen. "I don't think we need to fight about our core beliefs."

"This is all Dad's fault. He had to divorce Mom and move here!" Amanda was yelling.

"First of all, Mom divorced him," Daria yelled back.

"And went crazy after that," Amanda said.

"SHUT. UP." The male voice was hoarse and raspy, yet commanding. All three women snapped to attention. They glanced at the doorway, but no one was there.

Peri looked at Skip. His eyes were open.

"Just shut up," he repeated.

They all gaped at him. He was still motionless, but his eyes were animated, scanning them.

"Somebody get the nurse," Peri said. No one moved, so she grabbed the call button and pressed it.

"Peri." Skip raised a shaking hand toward her.

She rushed to his side, taking his hand, kissing his face, his lips. His lips kissed back, making the tears pop from her eyes.

"Sorry." She wiped at her face. "I'm so relieved."

Behind her, she heard a slight cry, then the sound of heels clacking. She looked over to see Amanda had gone.

Daria shrugged. "I'll go get her."

Peri moved from Skip's bed. "No, I'll get this, you hug your dad."

She was leaving the room as the nurse arrived. Pointing, she said, "He's awake. Did you see where Amanda went?"

The nurse gestured right, so Peri headed that direction, toward the cafeteria. She found the young woman at a table in the large, empty room, her head bowed.

"Amanda." Peri sat down across from her. "We're all happy your dad is awake."

She was crying when she raised her head to glare at Peri. "He said your name first."

Peri's mouth opened in shock. "I—I'm sure it's only because I was the first one he saw."

"No, he doesn't love me." Her face had already begun to mottle, and her eyes and nose were swollen. "He never cared, not even enough to stay in town when he left Mom."

Peri's first instinct was to deny the statement, but Skip's daughter needed to be heard. "I'm sorry you've felt like this, Amanda, especially for such a long time. You must be so hurt."

Amanda mopped tears from her face.

"I can tell you your Dad talks about you all the time. He shows me the pictures your mother used to send. Now that you're a grown woman, he'd like to have more from you. I think the last picture he has on his desk is from your high school graduation."

"Well, maybe he should ask me." Her voice cracked.

"You're right, maybe he should. Now that he's awake, you two should talk."

Amanda slumped forward, sighing long, heavy breaths. "When he left for California, I wanted to die. We were close, so close—how could he leave?"

"I know, it sounds impossible." Peri searched for words to soothe her without crucifying Skip. "Look, I met your dad a few years after the divorce, and I never asked him about it. What I do know is he moved out here because there were more career opportunities for him, and his great regret was he had to be so far away from you."

"Really?"

Peri took Amanda's hands in hers, squeezing them. The young woman squeezed back, making Peri smile. "Yes. He loves you, Amanda. Why don't you go talk to him? I bet he'd love to hear your voice."

When they returned to the room, Peri slowed, to allow Amanda to enter first. She looked in to see Daria hugging her dad. Amanda approached slowly, shuffling. Peri watched Skip's hand raise toward Amanda, palm up, beckoning her on the other side. Amanda grabbed his hand and joined her sister, leaning in to kiss him.

Officer Markel tapped Peri's shoulder. "Chief Fletcher is on his way."

The doctor swept past her into the room, went immediately to the bed, and checked Skip's vitals. Peri came in behind her. Skip was smiling, and they had lifted his bed to a semi-sitting position.

"Peri," he said.

She blinked away her tears of joy. "How are you feeling?"

"Tired."

The doctor continued to prod and listen, then told him, "You'll be tired for a while, but your signs are all good. Welcome back."

"What's the last thing you remember?" Peri asked.

His brow creased. "I was dreaming of snow. It was cold and bombs were going off. Awful." He smiled at her. "You're so pretty. I forgot how pretty you are."

She couldn't help but smile. Daria and Amanda stood back and let her near the bed. Amanda still looked a little stiff, but she managed to grin. Peri leaned down and kissed Skip.

"I've missed you," she told him. She rested her cheek against his and sighed with relief. "Thank God you're back."

"Hey, Skip." Chief Fletcher's voice growled a hearty greeting.

Peri turned away to let the stocky, gray-haired man greet his detective.

"Excuse me," the doctor said. "We can't have this many people in the room."

"I need to get some work done," Peri told her. "I'm sure Chief Fletcher has some questions." She gazed at Skip. "I'll be back later."

CHAPTER 32

On her way to the car, she called Blanche, Benny, and Jared, all of whom were excited to hear Skip was awake and alert. She then phoned Detective Wolfe to find out about Blanche's SUV.

"We've finished processing, but it's Sunday." His deep bass made her heart flutter, against her wishes. "Don't you want to wait until tomorrow?"

"Not really. It's my friend's car and I want to get it back to her as soon as possible. Besides, I have some evidence for you."

"Evidence?"

"Okay, don't be mad. When I discovered the body, I accidentally found a piece of evidence." She explained finding what she thought was her own flash drive.

"I can understand that. What I don't understand is why didn't you turn it over to us as soon as you realized it?"

"I'm so sorry. As much as I get involved in police cases, I've never done anything like this, taken evidence from a scene. When I realized what I had, I wanted to make certain it had something to do with Holly or the Mayfields before I turned it over to you. Again, I'm truly sorry. I'll bring the drive by right now."

"That would be nice." He did not sound happy.

"Skip came out of the coma." She hoped good news would make him a little less cross.

His reply was not enthusiastic. "Well, that's something."

She took the back roads to the Walnut Ridge police station. The freeway was faster, but city streets gave her time to think about her case, adding up all the information she had collected, including her interview with Rick, and the files Holly was stealing.

By the time she pulled into the station's parking lot, she had more questions than answers. Detective Wolfe waited for her at the receptionist area and buzzed her in. His face told her exactly how he felt about seeing her. He was silent as they walked back to his office.

"I really am sorry. I also had a talk with Rick today. I confess, none of it makes sense, but I'm happy to share everything with you."

He still looked unimpressed, but a slight upturn in the corner of his mouth indicated he might be getting over it. She handed him the bag containing the drive.

"I suppose your fingerprints are all over it."

"Shouldn't be. I used gloves each time I handled it, except for when I picked it up from the floor, and I tried not to grab it hard. It got me a lot of mileage with Rick Mayfield about my client, but it left me with more questions." She told him about all the folders and their contents.

"I can't say I'm happy about you taking evidence from the scene, especially when it has the kind of information the police could use. Fortunately, we were so busy processing fingerprints, DNA, and GSR, we wouldn't have had time to look at a flash drive until now."

"Again, I apologize. I've never done anything like this, and wouldn't have done it on purpose." She sighed. "You've got to believe me, I'm beyond mortified. I can't imagine what Logan and Spencer are going to say when they hear."

"It does sound like an understandable accident." His scowl softened. "I suppose they don't have to hear about it. From your description, I'm not sure how any of these folders specifically help us, evidence-wise, except to look for someone she might have either been blackmailing, or someone paying her for blackmail intel."

"At first, I thought it was about Rick's campaign, but this is February. I mean, wouldn't you pull something like this around filing time?"

"This is filing time for Rick. Walnut Ridge is having a special election in June. That's why we've been digging around Rick's personal and financial life. Turns out, he's come into a pretty big windfall."

"How big? And is it legal?"

"Huge, and very." Wolfe opened the file and read. "Rick made a real estate deal with a corporation for a big chunk of land his father willed to him."

"This might be more about money than politics," Peri said. "How well known is this news?"

"That's what we're focusing on. Who knew what, and how badly do they need the money?" He picked up the phone and spoke quietly into it, then turned back to Peri. "I'll have our CSU get the files off, see if there's any trace on the drive."

"While you're at it..." She pulled the card with Rick's number from her tote and put it on his desk. "You might want to look at this. One of the city council members gave me this card the other night. The number written on this card is the same number that called me to the Mayfield house when Holly was killed, but it's not Rick's number. It goes to a disturbing recording about voting against Rick and bringing 'real American values' back to Walnut Ridge."

The detective picked it up by the edges. "Which council member?"

"Peter somebody. I don't remember the last name."

"Marshall?"

"Yes. Peter Marshall. My prints are probably all over it. I didn't know what I had until I tried to call Rick. I admit, I thought Sean Jackson was a suspect. He knew how she died, before anyone told him. Now, I'm looking at this Peter guy, asking myself why he'd give me a bogus phone number."

Wolfe shook his head. "Turns out, Jackson has a police scanner."

Peri laughed. "Sorry. I thought those were for shut-ins."

"Bought it a few weeks ago, which I consider a little coincidental. We're reviewing the tapes to see if what came over the radio matches what he knew, so he's still a suspect. Along with Donny Jackson, and now Peter Marshall, and let's throw in Rick's immediate family, too."

Peri ran her fingers through her curls. "I might have thought about Brandon first, member of a gang and all.

Holly seems pretty unremarkable for a blackmailer, but you never know."

"Yep. In our business, lots of unremarkable people do strange crap." He stared at her.

"I assure you, I'm unique in my unremarkableness. Am I still a suspect?"

They were interrupted by the door opening. The same woman who had processed Peri at the Mayfield home entered. Wolfe handed her the drive and the business card. "Thanks, Arleta. See what you can get off these."

He turned to Peri. "By the way, the evidence in your car does not support the initial circumstances."

"That's good news. I'm assuming you'll be looking at my financials, and my LUDs."

"Already done. You're right, Miss Minneopa. You're uniquely unremarkable." He stood and held out a sheet of paper. "Hand this to the guy at the lot. You can get Ms. Debussy's car back."

"Thank you, Detective. I hope your CSU didn't dismantle too much of it. You've seen my finances. I can't possibly pay to have it put back together the way Blanche likes it."

He escorted her out the building and pointed to a small, fenced lot across the street. "Arleta was as gentle as she could be. I don't think she even cut out the carpet. There was a little Luminol sprayed, but a good detailing will get that out."

Peri sprinted to the lot.

First stop, the car wash. Then Beebs' house, then back to see Skip. I need to hear his voice again.

CHAPTER 33

Apart from a heavy coat of powder that exposed multiple fingerprints, Blanche's white SUV appeared intact. Peri exchanged the paper for the car keys and drove away, vowing never to borrow her friend's car again.

At least Blanche should be happy there are no bodily fluids on her seats.

As she headed down Grand Avenue to the freeway, she noticed a black SUV behind her. It would not have made an impression, except it kept passing other cars in a rapid and somewhat reckless way, making her aware of the flash of black swerving in and out of her mirror.

She was trying to move into the left lane and enter the 60, when the vehicle roared up next to her, the tinted window of the back seat hanging right across from her position at the steering wheel. Her first thought, of the window lowering and shots being fired, jabbed fear through her veins. She slowed down, to let the SUV pass.

The big black car slowed also, keeping Peri pinned in the right lane. Her notion grew stronger, making her grip tighten on the steering wheel, and her foot shake against the pedal.

"You. Are. An. Ass." Her body was trembling, but her blood was hot. "If you mess with this car, Blanche is going to kill you. And then me."

If I survive.

Past the onramp, the black SUV turned into her, causing her to veer away. Afraid of being T-boned, she kept steering right. On it came, toward her side. She slammed on the brakes, trying to maneuver around it. Traffic, however, was uncooperative. Cars from behind whipped around them, honking, anxious to get away.

She cranked her car further. Not an ideal move, but the only one still available to her that would keep her moving forward. The black car turned hard into her, pushing her along the dusty shoulder without actually touching, until she stopped at the chain-link fence.

Panic throbbed up and down her spine.

It was no relief when two large men emerged from the front seat. They were in white shirts and army fatigues. She tried to memorize as much about them as her terrorized heart would allow. White guys. One had a mustache and a light brown crew cut. One wore a Dodgers baseball cap. Both had multiple tattoos, around their necks, up their arms.

Peri saw the flash of a dragon on the inside of one wrist, and remembered Beebs' words about having six bodies on her slab, courtesy of the Drachens. Benny's description of the man who visited her office. White shirt, check. Fatigues, check. Tattoos, for the win.

She could hear her pulse beating in her head.

Dodger Cap knocked on her window. She gathered her bravery and stared at him, lifting one eyebrow in a question.

He spoke through the glass. "Mr. Smith would like to talk to you."

John Smith, the name Benny gave me. She kept her eyes on his cap, focusing on the bar of the "L" that crossed the "A." *I bet the Dodgers don't want this kind of advertising.*

Her mind raced through the catalogue of how to avoid being abducted. No one had a gun out, so perhaps she was part of their catch and release plan.

"My website has a contact form," she told him.

His look of confusion quickly cleared. "Mr. Smith would like to talk to you *now*."

She held up her phone. "I can give you my card. He can call me."

Mustache nudged Dodger Cap aside and gestured toward the black car. With a gun.

"Mr. Smith wants a private audience." He pointed the gun at her. "Leave the phone."

She lifted her hands, showing him the phone again, then placed it on the passenger seat. Before she opened the door, she pressed the Emergency dialer and Send. She jumped from the car and slammed the door, before Mustache could hear anyone answer her call.

With any luck, they'll at least send a patrol car this way.

Sandwiched between Dodger Cap and Mustache, most of the sunlight disappeared from Peri's view. She couldn't even see her own shadow as she walked to Mr. Smith's SUV, and her probable doom.

Don't get in the car. She'd heard this advice from multiple experts, and she believed it to be good. It occurred to her that running toward the freeway and screaming might garner some attention from the other drivers. She wheeled about, in a sudden dash for freedom.

Her rib cage collapsed, along with her lungs, as Mustache struck her midsection with his gun. She doubled over, trying to catch her breath. Dodger Cap held her from falling to her knees, gently leaning into her.

"Are you okay, Ma'am?" He provided a stable frame to keep her upright until the pain had passed.

Peri nodded and unfolded her spine in slow motion, feeling her ribs to see if they were still intact. Everything seemed to be in order. Mustache turned her shoulders back toward the SUV, and they continued on. This time, the hard barrel of his gun in her side discouraged her from running.

Dodger Cap reached forward and opened the back door. He was definitely the gentleman of the two. He didn't have to strong-arm a lady to get results. She looked into the darkness. A figure sat in the shadows, behind the driver's seat.

Peri hesitated, wishing for a TV miracle, where a police car screams into view and the bad guys scatter. No sirens. She took a deep breath and stepped inside.

The shadowed figure leaned into the light. She noted his dress, a polo shirt and slacks. If she hadn't been in the back of an SUV driven by thugs, she'd have mistaken him for a Best Buy employee. His blond hair was neat but not shorn. Unlike his associates, he was not covered in tattoos. He had two tasteful designs on his forearms, the Marine emblem on one, a dragon on the other.

A voice could be heard, along with a crackling noise, from the radio. Peri focused on the words. It was a police scanner. Maybe they gave Sean Jackson one, or Donny, as a gift for joining their crew. *Nice way to keep abreast of the latest news, about who's chasing who.*

She glimpsed movement through the windshield. The hood was now up. Clever. It looked like a classic scene, one guy with car trouble, and another one pulled over to help out. Even the police might not stop for that. She turned back to her captor.

He held out his hand. "Peri Minny—Mennypaws? I'm John Smith."

CHAPTER 34

She extended hers in return, observing the way he turned their handshake slightly so his hand was on top. This was an old-school power move, subtle but still effective.

"How do you pronounce your name?" he asked.

"Minn-ee-OH-pa."

"That's a Dakota word." He studied her. "You don't look native."

Racial chest-beaters. She hated them. What exactly did he do to be white? What did any of us do to earn our DNA?

"If you're asking my ethnicity, it's pretty obvious, my folks were both Scandinavian. Their families spent time in the Minnesota area, where they appropriated a Native American last name. Or that's the story I was told around the dinner table. What kind of stories did you hear?"

Smith appeared unruffled. "We're not here to discuss our purity. We're here to discuss the theft of my reputation."

"As John Smith or Drachen Bruderschaft?"

"We have a legitimate organization, one that does not run afoul of the law—"

"You mean, except when you sell drugs or weapons or spread your graffiti all over the county?"

"If you will allow me." His eyes narrowed. "Our organization does not run afoul of the laws that have been established for the protection and decency of our citizens."

"So you only sell drugs to non-whites, and guns to whites, and it's not graffiti, it's advertising. I get it."

"For someone sitting in my car, on my turf, who would only be missed by a guy in a coma, you are awfully mouthy."

Peri stopped talking. He was right, she had no family to miss her. Blanche would weep. Benny would be upset. But Skip would grieve. At least Smith wasn't keeping watch over him. Otherwise, he'd have known Skip was awake.

She softened her tone. "Sounds like you want to give me a message and turn me loose like some carrier pigeon. Why me? I'm no cop, and I'm not investigating the shooting."

"Call it what you like, there is a group calling themselves by our name and engaging in activity without our participation. We chose you as our messenger because we know the ties you have to the police department."

"Let me guess, you didn't shoot those cops."

Even in the shadow, his teeth gleamed as he smiled. "We wouldn't have needed to."

"Lawrence Kelly wasn't one of yours?"

"Technically, no. Kelly had been in our ranks, but he was a bad fit for our organization."

She stared into his blue eyes. "So you took away his Bruderschaft card, changed the locks, and turned him loose?"

He held her gaze. "Sort of. He was supposed to do one more assignment to complete his service with us."

The picture dawned on her. "To find out who the fakers are."

"It's entirely possible he wasn't shot by the police."

"I see. So, Brandon Mayfield. Real or fake?"

Smith leaned back, smiling and silent.

"Jessica Churchill? Donny Jackson?"

She suspected he wouldn't answer. He didn't.

"All right, maybe you can tell me this. How do I, or the police, tell the fakers from the real thing? Otherwise, it seems to me, the police are going to spend all their time trying to link you to the cop shooting." She folded her hands in her lap. "And you know how it goes with anyone accused of shooting one of their own, let alone four."

He didn't say anything for a long time. Peri listened to the whoosh of traffic on the 60. She tried to imagine a scenario where she'd avoided the black SUV and got away. If only she was brave enough to dent Blanche's car, maybe she could have crashed her way out.

"Fair enough," Smith said at last. "We might as well cooperate. I certainly don't want my people to be mistaken for cop killers."

He held his arm out to the light. "Look closely at the tattoo. If you look in the airspace around the tail's swirl, you'll see a capital B. And the word, Drachen, is between the dragon claws, like he's holding it."

"And what do the fakers have?"

"From what Kelly said, their tail doesn't form a B, and the word extends past the claws."

"Why would they get something like that wrong?"

Smith sat back. "Who knows? I know they didn't use our ink gal, so whoever they went to wasn't aware of our brand. Maybe they didn't care. Since they aren't actually in our group, it wasn't important they get the tattoo perfect."

"And do you know how they've been using their misbegotten fame?"

"Mostly, I hear they use it as bravado. A little graffiti, some petty theft. The warehouse was their first big job. They traded on my reputation to get those trailers with all that heroin."

"Heroin?"

He smirked. "I see the PPD doesn't keep you in the loop if your boyfriend isn't around."

Peri pushed her anger down, if only to keep from slapping him. Then she remembered what Skip said when he awoke from the coma.

He dreamed it was snowing.

"I get bits and pieces," she said. "I'm actually surprised by you. I'd think you'd have your own special way of dealing with the wannabes."

"Normally, we do like to handle things in-house. But we didn't want to be on the hook for a cop killing."

"Not one you didn't do."

Smith frowned. "Let's be clear. I have never killed a cop or even shot at one. I have great respect for law enforcement. It's not their fault the laws are wrong."

"You sound pretty enlightened. Of course, you only elude them when you're choosing which laws you don't have to obey."

"Miss Minneopa, we are going to have to agree to disagree, and end our discussion here, before one of us loses their temper." He whistled, bringing Mustache to open the car door. "Thank you for your indulgence."

Moments later, she was back in Blanche's car and the black SUV disappeared. She grabbed her phone from the seat and looked at it. The emergency call hadn't even gone through. That's when she noticed the warning—no cell service. The perfect place to hijack someone.

She allowed herself a few moments to tremble violently before starting the engine. John Smith and his henchmen were gone, but she still felt their presence. She stepped on the gas, hard, to get away from this place.

Driving down the freeway, she looked at the clock. Four p.m. on a Sunday meant the car wash was closed. She called Blanche and told her what happened.

"Oh, dear God, Peri, are you okay?"

"Yes. It was frightening at first, but once I figured out he was using me as a messenger, I was okay."

"You know I told you I'd go to the chief if you started investigating the shooting."

"How am I responsible for this? The guy sought me out. And I might have avoided him, if I wasn't so worried about wrecking your car."

"Next time, take the dents and get the hell outta there. What are you going to do now?"

"My plan is to go to the station and try to give information to those two bonehead detectives who think I should be barefoot and pregnant. After that, I'm going to stop by the hospital and give Skip a kiss or two. But first, I'm heading to your house to give your car back."

"Sounds like a plan. I'll have the wine ready."

"Did I ever tell you I love you?"

"Get your ass to my house." Blanche ended the call.

This whole thing has been an uphill battle. Peri pulled into the Debussy neighborhood. *But I've got to keep climbing.*

CHAPTER 35

The detectives weren't in their office, and neither was Jason. Peri was equal parts disappointed and relieved. She'd like to attempt a truce with Logan, and she'd never said two words to Spencer. The information she'd received was important, although she would have preferred getting it in a less terrifying way.

As she passed Chief Fletcher's office, she was surprised to see him at his desk.

"This is Sunday. Why are you here?"

"Hey, Peri." He waved her in. "Irene's out of town this weekend, so I thought I'd get a little paperwork done. It's always the worst part of the job."

She sat down across from him. "I was looking for Logan or Spencer. Something happened today they need to know about."

He put down his pen. "You haven't been doing anything you oughtn't, have you?"

"I wish people would give me a little credit. You told me not to get involved in the shooting. I understood and agreed. Everywhere I turn, I end up with information, not because I'm looking for the killer."

"What part of your case took you to the warehouse?"

She hung her head. "One false step. One. And I wasn't looking for evidence. As a matter of fact, I assumed I wouldn't find any. Jason is really thorough. Here's the thing, Chief, there are key things I could be telling your detectives if Logan would stop pissing me off."

"Pissing you off how?"

"I'm pretty sure he hates all PIs, plus he's one of the multitude of people who think I'm an idiot for not marrying Skip. Which may be true, but if we could get past all this, I keep stumbling across info, stuff I've shared with every other police agency within twenty miles. I'd like to share it with him."

"Why didn't you come to me?"

"Because I know coming to you will look like I'm going over their heads. If I was disliked before, that would move me into enemy territory."

"True enough. At the moment, they're out trying to interview the leader of the Drachens. Someone reported his vehicle pulled over at the 60 and Grand earlier."

"And I could have told them all about it." Peri leaped from her chair. "That's the whole problem. I was with Smith at the 60 and Grand. He ran me off the road and held me hostage while he told me the warehouse job was done by a group pretending to be the Drachens."

Pulling out her phone, she showed him the tattoo on Brandon Mayfield's arm and pointed out the differences Smith had outlined, telling him about her encounter as she did.

"That reminds me." She flipped through pictures until she found one of the medallion from the warehouse. "So this looks legit." She showed Fletcher. "I have no idea whose this is, or if Brandon was there that day. Maybe Smith was lying, and the Drachens were in the warehouse. Or this belongs to the dead guy who, according to Smith, was there to find out who the fake Drachens are. I'm betting you'll get more answers from Brandon Mayfield than John Smith."

"Yes." Fletcher looked down at his notes, picking up his cell phone as he did. After a few swipes with his index finger, he held it to his ear. "Spencer? Have you found Smith yet? I need you to come back to the station. No, let him go. I've received some information."

Peri watched him talk. She couldn't decide whether to stay and work through her difficulties with the detectives or go see Skip and let the chief handle it. Skip's face appeared in her mind, grinning as he looked down at her, eyes sparkling. She imagined what he'd be saying to her now, warning her to stay out of all this trouble.

By the time the chief ended his call, she'd made her decision.

"Would it be alright if I left? I'd like to get to the hospital before they kick out the visitors. If the detectives want me to answer any questions, you've got my number."

"You bet. Tell Skip we all said hello."

CHAPTER 36

Placentia-Linda was only a couple of miles north. Peri drove down Kraemer Boulevard, past tall houses nearly hidden behind block walls on either side of the wide street. She was in the hospital parking lot within five minutes.

Officer Markel was at his post, as usual.

"Don't you ever go home?"

He laughed. "You and I must have synchronized our schedules somehow."

"Are his daughters still here?"

"Nope. I overheard them. One of them has a fiancé. He's coming into town. They had to get ready for him."

"Ready? What would they need to get ready?"

"As much as I could hear, there was carpet cleaning, grocery shopping, and something about moving things around."

"Moving things around? I don't know if Skip'll like that."

Markel gestured toward the door. "Go ask him."

She grinned and entered Skip's room. There was a gentle murmur from the TV. Without looking at it, she could tell from the sound it was a basketball game. It heartened her to hear it. Skip loved the Lakers.

He was propped up in his bed, looking a little drawn, but otherwise healthy. As she came in, he turned to her and grinned.

"Hey, Doll."

She sat down on his bed and leaned in to kiss him. He embraced her, holding her for a long time. Peri melted into him, pressing her cheek against his. "I missed you."

Skip scooted sideways in the bed and turned her around. She snuggled next to him, his arm around her shoulder.

"I've missed you, too," he said.

They relaxed together, watching the basketball game.

"How's your day been?" she asked.

"Quiet. How's yours?"

"There's so much I need to tell you, but I don't know if I should."

"Tell me you're not working my case."

Peri sat up and frowned at him. "Everyone thinks I have to be up to my armpits in your case. It's not true. What is true is my case seems to be butting up against yours. It's weird, but I'm trying my best to solve a stalking case and I keep coming up with evidence that fits the warehouse. I hand it over to the detectives and they get mad at me. Believe me, I'm not trying to butt in. Not this time."

He pulled her back down to him. "I believe you. I'm too weak not to."

"I swear, if I wasn't so worried about you, we'd be having a fight about this." She nuzzled his neck, wallowing in her gratitude.

"I didn't know this was a private party." An unknown male voice interrupted.

Peri rose up and saw a serious young man, standing in the room with Skip's daughters. The look on the man's face said he intended to intimidate her with his disapproval.

Bite me. If I didn't back down for gang members, I'm certainly not fazed by your tsk-tsk face.

"Amanda, Daria, it's good to see you." She stood and held out her hand. "You must be Drew."

His arched eyebrow, and the way he sneered at her outstretched palm, cooled the room by twenty degrees. After an awkward pause, he extended his hand. She took it, turning her palm down, mimicking John Smith's power handshake. It was a cheap move, but it was time to launch a good offense if she had any plan to stand up for herself, and her relationship with Skip.

"Sorry we're late." Daria moved forward to hug her. "Drew wanted to get acclimated to the town." Her sarcasm announced her feelings for her sister's fiancé, in the most negative way.

Amanda stood between them, looking like a rabbit waiting to bolt. Peri felt a wave of sympathy. Here stood a young girl in love, or at least she thought she was, with a young man who was the oil to her family's water.

"Well, I'm glad you're all here." Peri moved from Skip's bedside. "I know you have a lot of visiting to do."

Turning to Skip, she saw a pained expression in his eyes, and hurried back to him. "What's wrong?"

He pointed to his chest. "Hard to breathe. Hurts."

Peri grabbed the nurse's call button and pressed it in short, furious blasts. In moments, a nurse ran to the room.

"What's the problem?" She went to Skip and got out her stethoscope.

"PE?" Peri asked.

The nurse looked at her and gave a small nod, then pulled out a radio. "I'm going to have to ask you all to leave."

"Why? We have the right to be here." Drew puffed his frame larger. "I'm a lawyer, and I know—"

"I don't care what you know right now, Sir, we have work to do and you can't be interfering or distracting us."

The nurse moved toward them all, her arms outstretched as if herding geese. Peri turned and did the same. Drew faced them for a few seconds, but was soon caught up by the two women's efforts, combined with Daria and Amanda on each arm, encouraging him to exit.

As soon as they were in the hall, a woman Peri recognized as Dr. Marx ran past them, into Skip's room, followed by a nurse. The doctor wore an expression of concern.

Peri leaned against the wall, hand over her heart, reminding herself to keep breathing and not pass out.

"What's going on?" Drew was still bellowing his arrogance. "I demand—"

"You demand nothing." Peri walked into him, pushing him back. He was probably six feet tall, but her five-foot-nine-inch frame stretched to the occasion. "Skip may have a pulmonary embolism. That's a blood clot, either to his lungs, or maybe on the way to his heart. They may need to operate."

Daria gasped before she broke into tears. Amanda went to her sister and enfolded her in her arms.

Drew did not back down. "Probably your fault. All that…" He waved his hand about. "Canoodling. And how do you know so much, anyway?"

"Actually, the wound in his leg plus extended bed rest is more to blame than any canoodling. This is the first day we've canoodled in a long time. And I know so much because a pulmonary embolism killed my dad. You get to be quite an expert when you lose someone that way."

She finally won. The young man shrank back, speechless, then turned to the sisters, leaving Peri alone to peek into the room and see what they were doing. The doctor was leaning over, obscuring any view of Skip. Within seconds, the nurses rushed from the room, pushing Skip's bed with them. Dr. Marx followed, pausing briefly at the group.

"We're taking him for X-rays. Why don't you folks go to the waiting room? I'll keep you informed."

"Waiting room?" Amanda asked.

Peri pointed. "This way."

They stared at her, so she added, "I have been here a few times."

In what seemed more of a foyer than a room, Daria and Amanda sat down, huddling close. They were praying. Drew paced for a few laps before he finally sat next to Amanda.

Peri had learned by experience, this would take longer than any of them thought it would. Hospitals tend to do that. She made a quick call to Chief Fletcher and Blanche to let them know what had happened, then turned to the trio.

"Anyone want coffee?"

Drew scowled at her. "Why would we want—"

"Yes." Amanda rose as if poked with a cattle prod. "Mind if I go with you?"

CHAPTER 37

As they headed to the cafeteria, Peri glanced at Amanda. She recognized the pursed lips and faraway look on the young woman's face.

"You look a lot like your dad when he's thinking about something."

Amanda smiled a little.

"You also remind me of myself at your age. I was in love with someone who was very different from me. I thought our differences made us one complete person."

"What happened?"

"I married him."

"But you're not—"

"Still married? No, we divorced, after two years and four months." Peri paused, considering how to speak. She didn't want to chase Skip's daughter into her boyfriend's arms. Young People's Spite Disease could be fatal.

"I think opposites can get along wonderfully, if both people respect and honor each other's differences." Peri took a cup from the tray and filled it with coffee. "In my case, my ex-husband did not respect my opinions, or my feelings."

They moved to the cashier and Peri took out her wallet. Amanda followed with two mugs, one for her, and one for Daria.

"Then why did you marry him?" She asked as they walked.

Peri sighed. "I was in my twenties, all my friends were marrying, and it seemed like an exciting thing to do. I hope that doesn't sound shallow."

Amanda shook her head. "Not any more shallow than my friends."

They were almost back at the waiting room, when Amanda stopped, touching Peri on the arm. "Do you think I should marry Drew? I really do love him."

"I'm sure you do." Peri took a big breath, hoping she was not going to put her foot in it. "All I can tell you is, the man you end up with should respect and honor you for who you are. If you find that you're turning off your own thoughts because he'd be disappointed, I fear you'll be unhappy, if only because I see so much of your dad in you, and he'd never stand for that."

In the waiting room, Drew rose to meet them. "What took you so long?"

Daria took her coffee and sipped, rolling her eyes at Peri as she did.

"Has the doctor been here?" Peri asked.

"No." There was a whining quality to Drew's response.

"Then why does it matter how long we've been gone?" Amanda asked.

The sudden hush was so deep, even the clock stopped ticking.

"I guess it doesn't." Drew broke the silence. "I was just wondering."

Peri looked at Amanda. Her lips were still pursed, but from her eyes, it looked like her mind was not straying, as much as it was calculating. Maybe Amanda was rationalizing how to stay with him, or maybe she was figuring out how to get him back on the plane tonight.

In either case, I need to butt out.

After an hour of quiet—at times awkward, and at other times merely uneasy—Dr. Marx appeared around the corner, her face hard to read.

"Your father had a pulmonary embolism." She kept her focus on her chart. "That's a blood clot, usually beginning in the legs, that has traveled to the lungs. In the worst cases, it puts pressure on the heart, and can be fatal."

Amanda and Daria turned to look at Peri.

"Fortunately, your father is here, with people who recognized his condition immediately. We're giving him a blood thinner that should keep more clots from forming. The existing clots should dissolve on their own, but for the next few days we'll be monitoring him carefully."

"And if the drugs don't work?" Daria's soft voice sounded frightened.

"Then we go in with a catheter and remove the clots. But let's see what the drugs do first."

"Thank you, Dr. Marx," Amanda said. "I'm sure you understand, we'll all feel better when this is over. But thank you for responding and taking care of him so quickly."

"He'll be back in his room in a few moments, and you can see him." The doctor gestured toward Peri. "But thank her, too. If she hadn't recognized what was happening and called the nurse right away, things might have gone differently."

The doctor rushed off and left them to stare after her.

Peri moved around the corner and texted the Chief, filling him in on the latest news. When she returned to the group, the doctor had left. The three young people stayed in their places, looking at each other. Peri had to remind herself to breathe. She watched Drew, standing apart from everyone, his hands clenching and unclenching. After a few moments, he walked to Amanda and put his arm around her shoulder.

There was a small tug as he attempted to draw her away from Daria. Amanda resisted, then took Daria's hand, and the trio wandered back to the chairs to sit down.

"I need to make some phone calls," Peri told them. "Have either of you talked to your mom? She might want to know what's happening."

"She would." Daria pulled away from her sister. "I'll get this, 'Manda. You sit here with Drew."

Daria accompanied Peri to the patio outside. "What did you say to her?"

"Me? Hopefully, I gave her the advice I would've found helpful at her age."

"I'm not a big Drew fan, but honestly, Peri, what I've been hating is seeing my sister become someone else, someone who doesn't laugh or talk or 'get' me anymore. I don't mind losing her to love. I do mind her losing herself." Daria turned away, but not before Peri saw tears in her eyes.

"Ah, Daria, you'll find in this life that sometimes you do lose your way, even lose who you are. It's part of growing up and trying on different versions of yourself until you find the one that fits."

Peri's only sibling, Dev, crossed her mind. He couldn't even be bothered to keep her informed of his latest address. She frowned. "Don't judge Amanda too harshly. Just be there for her."

Daria nodded and walked to the far corner of the patio, pulling out her phone.

Peri had finished her call to Blanche when her phone vibrated. It was Benny. He had been next on her list.

"Miss Peri, where are you? I haven't seen anybody for a long time. Jared and Willem are not working on my house."

"Benny, this is Sunday. Jared and Willem deserve a day off. I was going to call you to tell you what's happening with Skip." She relayed the news in as simple a way as possible, without sounding patronizing.

"What can we do now?" he asked.

She sighed. What could any of them do? "Pray. All we can do is pray and hope for the best. I think even Dino would agree."

"Yes, Dino would pray. Oh, and tomorrow, we are choosing the food for the fundraiser. We will choose good food and sell lots of tickets and raise money."

"Sounds great, Ben. Tell Phil and Nancy I said hello."

Peri ended the call, feeling exhausted to the point of having to sit down. She lowered her body into a wrought-iron chair. It was stiff and hard, but at least the patio furniture didn't have rain-soaked cushions on it.

She was aware of fingers on her shoulders, rubbing. Daria was giving her a massage. Peri patted the girl's hands.

"Thank you, Sweetie. I'd cry right now, but I don't want to show Skip's injuries any weakness."

"I know, right? It's like, if I let myself feel the fear, it might invade the room and make Dad's condition worse."

Peri smiled. "Are we being superstitious?"

"Do we care?"

"No." She stood and hugged Daria. "Shall we take our positive juju back into the room and see if your dad is back?"

"Yes. Dad can use all our powers. Even Drew Downer's."

Peri linked her arm with Daria's and led her back inside, hoping their combined magic would bring Skip back to them.

CHAPTER 38

At 4 a.m., Peri dragged herself from bed and put on a full pot of coffee. Worrying about Skip had kept her awake late but she couldn't go back to sleep. She turned on the old movie station and opened Jared's file on her computer. Reading through her notes sometimes helped her see what she'd overlooked.

Sleep deprivation made that unlikely, but the task kept her from focusing on Skip until 8 a.m., when she could take a shower and get dressed.

By 9 o'clock, she was at his side, watching him sleep. Considering what he'd been through, he looked pretty good. His face was not as gray as it had been when he was in the coma. He looked peaceful. She couldn't resist touching him, and carefully laid her hand on his. He sighed in response.

Get well, Skipper. She pointed her thoughts to him, willing him to recover. She'd never been particularly spiritual. She prayed only when she was in trouble, with a quick "thank you" breath as soon as the problem had passed.

Visualization was not in her repertoire. *Still, the power of positive thinking couldn't hurt. Who was that pastor who preached it?* No matter. She was aching to do something to bring him back to health.

Closing her eyes, she pictured Skip awake, sitting up in bed. It was a little hard to do at first, but soon she could imagine him standing and walking. Smiling, walking around the bed and out the door and—

Bang!

A door slammed in the hall and Skip's hand gripped hers, smashing the bones together, crushing flesh. She yelped and pulled away. Skip jerked awake.

"No-no-no," He repeated as he panted, sweat popping on his forehead.

Peri grabbed his shoulders. "Skip. Skip." She kept calling to him.

"I was—" His eyes widened as he looked around the room, his vision roaming unfocused.

A nurse ran in and placed her hand on his moist forehead, then moved down to take his pulse. "Are you okay?"

Peri became aware of a machine's frenzied beeping, and realized Skip's heartrate must have spiked through the ceiling. Officer Markel appeared behind the nurse, hovering as if waiting to be called into action.

Skip grimaced. Peri couldn't tell whether it was from pain or annoyance.

"It was a bad dream." His red-rimmed eyes had a look she'd never seen before. Lost, asking her for help.

She took his hand again, afraid to say anything. For the first time in their ten years together, he looked like he might break down sobbing. He wouldn't want strangers to see that.

The nurse reset the machine and checked his vital signs again, reassuring them that dreams can be intense enough to drive up vital signs. Satisfied, she left.

Officer Markel stood, waiting.

"I'm okay, Ara," Skip told him.

"If you need me, I'm right outside the door."

Peri watched the officer leave, closing the door behind him. As soon as they were alone, she reached across to take Skip in her arms and comfort him. He pulled her close, as if he was clinging to her for survival. She laid her cheek against the top of his head, cradling his face in the bend of her neck. His skin felt moist.

"Ah, Honey." Her words nearly choked her. "This has been a lot for even you to manage. A gunshot, a fall, an embolism. Not to mention losing your friends."

"I'm okay." His voice was low and muffled. "I've seen trauma in other guys. I know what to expect."

He pushed her back and sat up. "Doll, I don't want this to come from the situation, and I understand your point of view. Always have, and I respect it. But now, more than ever, I really want us to be married."

She took his hand and kissed his palm. "You know, I've been promising God if you'd wake up, I'd do anything—even marry you."

He laughed.

"But you know my fears about living together. We tried it before."

"Yeah," He nodded, "and I've been thinking about that. What if, instead of trying to move into an existing home, we sold both our homes and bought one that was for us?"

"It's a big leap." Peri sat back. Her breath had caught in her chest and was having a hard time making it out of her lungs. "I have an idea. Let's wait to discuss this until you're out of the hospital. When we're actually ready to start making plans."

He grinned. "Is that a qualified 'yes'?"

She leaned down and kissed him. "I'd give it about ninety percent."

"You know what happened the last time you did this." Drew's voice scolded, as Peri looked up to see Amanda and Daria follow him into the room.

"Why is me kissing my girlfriend so tough on you, Drew?" Skip asked. The flat, just-the-facts, business tone made Peri smile. This was the Skip she knew and loved.

"Sadly, I have to leave you all." Peri rose. "I have a case that needs closing." Turning to Skip, she winked. "See ya, Skipper."

"See ya, Doll."

"Skipper? Doll?" Drew asked as she walked past him. "What is this, the forties?"

Peri opened her mouth to answer, then looked at Amanda, who had crossed the room to sit by her father. Daria was already talking to Skip, asking him how he felt and describing what she and her sister did the previous evening.

If they don't care what you're blathering about, neither do I. She gave Drew a pasted-on grin and left.

As she returned to her car, Skip's proposal ran through her mind and she ran her fingers through her hair. A jumble of feelings, good and bad, wanted and unwanted, rolled over and over in her. There was only one thing to do to re-focus her attention on her job.

She called Blanche and told her about it.

"I'm afraid. He may not even be out of the woods with the embolism."

"I know, Kiddo." Blanche's smooth contralto was soothing. "PE is scary, but he's in the best place to have it, where he can get immediate attention and monitoring."

"You're right. In my head, I know you're right." Peri held the phone with her shoulder while she buckled her seatbelt. "In my heart, I'm reliving that day with Dad. One minute we were standing around talking, then I heard the pain in his voice, then nothing. I had no idea what was happening. The ambulance was too late. When I saw Skip's face, heard his whimper, it was all I could do to not scream."

"You probably saved him. How's it going with the girls?"

"Better, I think. Amanda seems to be softening, a piece at a time." Peri started to say more, but her phone beeped. "I got another call, Beebs. Gotta go."

Jared was on the line. "Peri, I don't want to seem worried, but I can't get hold of Willem."

CHAPTER 39

Benny stood in the middle of a room at the Alta Vista Country Club. He swayed left and right, rocking in his loafers. One hand kept combing across his hair. The other was in his pocket, rubbing his talisman, his glass ashtray from "Some Came Running."

I am supposed to see Jo-Anne to taste the food. Phil and Nancy were supposed to be here. Nothing is happening the way it is supposed to.

Jo-Anne was busy when he arrived. Some other woman escorted him into the room. She gestured for him to sit, but he didn't. *Some other woman. That's wrong. Too many people.*

Phil and Nancy could not come with him. Phil said they had an emergency. Plumbing leak. *Who cares about plumbing? I hate emergencies.*

He even called Peri. All he got was her voicemail. When he talked on the phone, someone needed to be on the other end. *I hate voicemail.*

This room was too cold. He frowned. *This day is not a good one.*

"Benny, good to see you." Jo-Anne swept into the room and shook his hand before he'd even had time to choreograph it. "Our chef will be bringing our tasting in one moment."

Oh, no, no. A line of sweat popped on his upper lip. *We cannot sit here together. I don't know what to say.*

"I'm sorry Phil and Nancy couldn't come, but I understand they had an emergency." Jo-Anne's voice sounded too loud in the room.

"Yes. Their sink was leaking."

"I hate plumbing problems, don't you?"

"I don't know. I don't have plumbing problems. But I don't like problems."

The door opened and a woman appeared, pushing a cart with silver domes atop. Benny could smell the garlic, basil, and oregano as it entered.

"Benny, this is our chef, Samantha Hollis." Jo-Anne moved to the door. "I'm going to step out and let you two work the menu."

The woman thrust her hand at him. She wore a chef's coat, black and pristine. Her hair was pulled away from her face, showing dark roots to her copper-red ponytail. "Benny, you can call me Sam. Do you like red sauce or white?"

He scowled. This was not the way the appointment was supposed to go. He felt this new woman's hand in his, clamping around his palm and pumping twice before withdrawing. Jo-Anne was supposed to be serving the food and Nancy was supposed to be talking about it and the three of them were supposed to be eating it. Benny looked at his right hand, then at her.

He could see her brown eyes and her smile, but only for the mere second he allowed himself to skim over her features.

Samantha Hollis. *Wait. Sam Hollis?*

"Did you want red sauce or white?" she repeated.

"Your name." Food had left his mind. "It's the same as Dean Martin's character in *Texas Across the River.*"

"Yeah, I know. My dad was a big Dean Martin fan." She grimaced. "He also wanted a boy."

"I like your name. It's a good name. I love Dean Martin. I used to have a lot of his things, but a stranger set my house on fire and some of them burned. I'm buying more, though."

Sam looked at Benny for a long time. His skin felt itchy being stared at, and he could feel his face warming. He shuffled away from her, until his leg hit something solid. Turning with a little hop, he saw it was the table.

"Sorry, Mr. Needles, I didn't mean to stare. You remind me of someone I used to know. There was a boy in my class when I was little."

"What happened to him?"

She shook her head. "I don't know. I was an Army brat. We moved every year."

He was disappointed, but didn't know why. It bothered him, so he focused on the floor, still frowning.

"So, about that sauce?" she asked.

His head popped up and he looked at the cart. The aroma of food returned to the front of his mind and made his stomach gurgle. "I like red."

What followed was an hour-long session of tasting four entrees, two salads, and three desserts. With each course, Benny had to taste every dish multiple times, in tiny bites, and go back and re-taste once he had made a selection. At the end, he sat back in his chair and sighed.

"That was hard."

"I'm impressed, actually," Sam said. "I typically don't have clients who want to make certain each course complements the others."

Benny shrugged. "It's what Dino would do."

He hopped up, wanting to leave, then stopped himself. *Dino would say goodbye.*

"Thank you, Sam." He held his hand out again. "This will be a good fundraiser."

"I agree, Benny. We'll keep in touch. By the way, I like Dino, too."

He peeked up to see her smiling. It made him feel like smiling. *Maybe this was a good day, after all.*

Driving home, his eyes were droopy and he had to push his foot on the accelerator to keep his car going the speed limit. He was tired. Tired from making the meal choice, tired of having his house torn apart—even having the police officers shot and Peri worrying about Skip exhausted him. Too much change. Too many things happening.

Life needed to stay the same.

At home, he called Willem. Willem didn't answer. He called Jared next. This time, he had better luck.

"Jared, when are you and Willem coming back to fix my house?"

"Benny? I'm sorry, I thought Willem would have told you. I have to be at our house this morning for our insurance rep to come by, then I'll...Wait—isn't Willem there?"

"No."

"That's odd. He left an hour ago. Said he was going to pick up some coffee, then go over and show you sketches."

"I was at the country club. I had to choose food."

"Well, maybe he saw you weren't home and ran some errands. It's still odd he didn't call you. I'll try to get hold of him, and I'll definitely be at your house as soon as I'm finished here."

"Okay." Benny ended the call. It wasn't really okay, but he was stressed and tired. He couldn't say anything more.

He went into the kitchen. Although he had just tasted all of Sam's food, he was still hungry. The portions were small, much too small to fill him up. He picked a box of wafers from the pantry and poured a glass of milk. After lining up ten cookies in a straight row, he set the glass in front of him, chose the end cookie, and dunked it three times. As he chewed, he looked around the kitchen.

Willem was going to make this place look like Dino was part of everything. It was exciting. *I wish it was all finished now.*

He heard a car pull up, so he went to the living room to see who it was. Willem's bright yellow Camaro convertible rolled to a stop. Benny started toward the door, then saw a dark van pull across his driveway.

A man wearing a ski mask and dark coveralls jumped from the passenger seat, ran to Willem's car, and tried to open his door. It must have been locked, because Moonie jumped from the back seat and barked at the man. The man pulled a gun out and pointed it at the dog. The next time he tried the door, it opened.

"Oh, no, no, no," Benny turned away from the window, then turned back. "What should I do?"

He could see Willem in the driver's seat. He was screaming, and the man next to him was trying to drag Moonie from the car. The man looked mad.

Benny called 911, shrieking. "A bad man is taking my friend. You have to stop him."

"Calm down, Sir. Who is taking who?"

"No, whom. Who is taking whom."

"Sir, what is your emergency?"

"They're taking him. My friend Willem and his dog."

"Who is taking your friend?"

This was not helping. Benny had never called 911 before. He assumed they would send help right away.

"I have to go help Willem." He ended the call.

After locking the front door, Benny snuck out the back. He looked around the corner, down the driveway. The man with the gun yelled at Willem, who was still crying. He watched the man reach in and yank Willem from the seat. Willem had Moonie's leash in his hand. The dog followed him, tail between her legs, barking and growling.

Another ski-masked man grabbed Willem from behind and dragged him toward the van. Moonie jumped at the first man and grabbed his leg. The man was screaming, and Willem was screaming. Benny put his hand over his mouth to keep from screaming with them.

Willem pulled at the dog's leash. Benny could hear him say, "Moonie, leave it." Moonie let go of the man's leg and went in the van with Willem and the other masked man. The first man limped to the driver's side of the Camaro.

Benny snuck into his car while the man was getting in the Camaro. The van drove away, then Willem's convertible backed out and drove toward Morse Avenue. As the man pulled out, Benny saw him take off his mask and put on a pair of sunglasses. Benny rolled his sleek black Cadillac out of the drive and followed them.

I'm going to help my friend.

CHAPTER 40

Peri shook her head. *What the hell? Willem gone?* "When did you see him last?"

Jared's voice was on the edge of panic. "This morning, which doesn't seem like that long ago, but he was supposed to be at Benny's house."

"Is he not answering his phone? Have you checked with Benny?"

"I did earlier. What has me worried is Benny was supposed to be home, too. I'm at Benny's house now. His car is gone, but the garage door is open and the back door is unlocked. The last time I tried Willem's phone, someone answered and I heard weird noises, then nothing."

"Hmm." She tried not to frighten him further. *That does not sound normal.* "Do you know Willem's license plate number? Let me see what I can find out."

She wrote down the information and ended the call. Her mind leapt back to Skip, and she shook her head. When it rains, it monsoons.

Crap, where could Willem and Benny have gone?

Peri did a bit of quick digging, using her cell phone. There were no recent police reports involving either

Benny's or Willem's car. That was good news. The next step was to visit Benny's and see if there were any clues.

If Benny had a cell phone, I could try calling him.

Jared's company truck was in front of Benny's home when she pulled up. He must have been watching for her, because he came out as soon as she parked, an expectant look on his face. She hated having no news for him.

"I thought perhaps I might find some clues as to why Benny would have left things undone," she said.

"Okay…Guess I'll keep working and wait to hear."

"Have you tried Willem's number again?"

"Goes to voicemail." His eyes narrowed and blinked, as if shaking the fear away. "I've left several messages."

She rubbed his shoulder. "We'll find him."

Walking around the back of the house, she looked at the open garage door. As careless as he could be about his house, Benny was meticulous about his Caddy. She approached the garage in a slow, sweeping manner, searching for anything out of the ordinary. Nothing jumped at her, so she went to the back door and let herself in.

The kitchen was not as dirty as she had seen it in the past. After the fire, she had convinced Benny to hire a cleaning lady to straighten up his house every other week. That woman was an angel to tackle Benny's place. An open box was on the table, along with a line of vanilla wafers and a glass of milk.

"So, Benny was sitting at the table." She talked to herself as she moved about the room. "He got up, walked out the back door, got in his car and left. Why?"

She heard a car pull up outside, so she went to the window and looked. It was a patrol car. She recognized the officers, Driver and Powell. Peri went out to meet them.

"We got a call from this residence," Officer Driver got out of her car. "Dispatch had a hard time making out the words—the caller rattled off something then hung up."

"Thought you should check it out anyway?" Peri asked.

Officer Powell shrugged. "We got here as soon as we could. We're a little short staffed."

Peri held up her hand. "I know. Sorry, it wasn't meant to be a dig."

"From what we could understand, a bad man was taking his friend and we needed to come stop it. But that took several listenings to decipher."

Jared had joined the group as Officer Driver explained the call. He looked at Peri.

"Benny." Peri pulled at a weed standing tall along the fence. "I'd have to hear the tape, but those sound like his words."

"Taking his friend," Jared said. "Willem?"

"Possibly." Peri turned to the officers and brought them up to speed. "I'm betting Benny saw Willem being kidnapped, and decided to try to follow them."

"If they kidnapped Willem, where's his car?" Jared asked.

"Possibly forced him to drive it somewhere." Officer Driver stared down the street. "You wouldn't want to leave the victim's car until you wanted people to know he was missing."

"Do you know of anyone who might want to kidnap your, your...?" Officer Powell left the word unsaid.

"My fiancé." Jared sounded edgy, as if looking for a fight.

"Your fiancé." Officer Driver's voice was calm and accepting. "Anyone with a grudge?"

Jared stared at Peri, so she spoke up. "I've been working on a case for Jared. It started with stalking, and quickly escalated. I have some possible suspects, but nothing concrete yet."

"Give us some names," Officer Powell said. "In the meantime, we'll put a BOLO out on both cars, and contact our detectives."

Peri turned to Jared. "I think Willem's high-profile status in the community is what started this brouhaha. If this is somehow tied to the election, they can't hold Willem for four months."

"You don't think they'd kill him?" Jared's voice cracked with worry.

She shook her head. "Then you become the very public, very grieving widower. The election staff doesn't want you in the news at all."

"Then what?"

"I don't know." She looked at the officers and shrugged.

"For right now, Mr. Reese, we'll treat this as a ransom." Officer Powell adjusted his hat. "We think you should go home and wait, difficult as that sounds. We'll contact the Fullerton police and I'm sure they'll send an expert."

Peri shook the officers' hands. "Thank you for your help. Hopefully this can be sorted out soon, without frustrating the PPD."

Peri guided Jared back to his truck. On the one hand, she couldn't imagine Benny putting his own life in any kind of danger. On the other hand, he'd been acting so out of character lately. Perhaps organizing the fundraiser had made him bolder.

"Do let me and the police know if you get a ransom call," she said.

"What if they tell me not to call the cops?"

"They always tell you not to call the cops. I don't see how a ransom would work, anyway. They want you to shut up about Rick Mayfield's past, but you can threaten to reveal all if Willem isn't released. They're counting on you to be too afraid to react."

The tall young man straightened his broad shoulders. "I may be afraid, but if they're counting on me to be a sissy boy, they've counted wrong."

She patted his arm. "Keep in touch."

Peri hurried back to her car. There was one place to start looking, and that was with Rick Mayfield.

CHAPTER 41

The first place Peri looked for Rick was the Mayfield house, calling him several times to tell him she was coming. Her calls kept going to voicemail. When she arrived, the iron gate to the driveway was locked. She pushed the call button until a woman's voice answered at last.

"Is Rick Mayfield at home?" Peri asked. "This is Peri Minneopa. I need to speak with him."

There was a pause, and the woman said, "Come in."

The gates rolled open and Peri drove up the circular drive and parked, her car's nose facing downhill for a fast getaway. *I am not getting caught in the kitchen with a dead body again.* A cool breeze whipped around her as she got out. She looked at the sky to the west. Dark clouds were moving in from the ocean, and she could smell the salt in the air.

She walked onto the porch and rang the bell.

Leona Mayfield opened the door. The black top and leggings she wore made her look even thinner. Her eyes darted about, lighting on Peri's face in brief bursts before continuing their wild trip.

"Mrs. Mayfield, I was hoping to speak with your husband. Is he around?"

Gayle Carline

"No." Her languid voice was just short of slurring. "Please come in and have some coffee."

Peri followed her into the kitchen. At the sight of the island, she hesitated, remembering Holly's body lying next to it. "I really need to talk to him. Do you know where I can find him?"

Leona selected a mug from the cabinet and poured coffee into it. She offered it to Peri. With an upbeat push of her voice, she said, "No, I haven't seen him all day."

"Oh, well, do you expect him home any time soon? I've tried his number but it goes to voicemail."

"Sugar?"

"No, thank you. About your husband—"

"Yes, my husband. Got up this morning, left our house, haven't seen him again." Leona poured herself a cup, then added a liberal splash of bourbon to top it off. She held the bottle out. "Bourbon?"

"Thanks, no." Peri frowned. "And you have no way of contacting him?"

Leona laughed. "Nope. No. Nada. No way to call."

"I've called his number several times, but I thought you might have a private line."

"No. Nothing private about us." She laughed again. Each time, Peri grew more uneasy.

"Mrs. Mayfield, how much of your husband's life before marriage do you know about?"

The grin spreading across Leona's face sent prickles up Peri's backbone. "You mean all his boy toys? I knew. Still know. The boys and the girls. Rick's not gay, you know. He's insatiable. It's a wonder he gets any work done at all. If he could, he'd spend his entire day humping anything with a pulse."

210

This was not the story Rick gave her. "How do you feel about that?"

Leona reached for the bourbon and held it up as a salute before pouring another dollop in her cup. "I'm fine with it."

"I don't understand. You're independently wealthy, in good health. Why don't you divorce him?"

"Because I was *in love*." She gestured wildly and took a deep swig. "When you're in love, you don't need a pre-nup. If I divorce him, I hand over half of everything."

"Surely half of everything is enough to live on."

"Comfortably so. But I will not be...what's the female version of cuckolded? I will not be she-cuckolded by my husband then lose even a penny to that man-whore."

"What did you think of Holly Duchamps?"

She made a dismissive, hmpfing sound. "You know, I went to school with sweet little Holly. Everyone thought she was the nicest girl ever, but I knew the truth. She stole my boyfriend in seventh grade. Tried to steal Rick, but I was onto her little game. I couldn't stop her from borrowing him, but she couldn't keep him."

"It didn't bother you she ended up dead on your kitchen floor?" Peri motioned in the direction of the island.

"Cost a fortune to clean it up." She shrugged. "But if you're wondering if I killed her, the answer is no. Could have. Didn't."

"How about Rick? Think he's capable?"

"I told you, he's a lover, not a fighter. Or a killer."

"Sean?"

211

Leona licked her lips. "Maybe. He's certainly willing to do anything to get Rick elected."

"How about your son?"

Leona lunged for her, falling against the edge of the counter. "Brandon? How dare you? Brandon is my son."

Peri reached out and managed to set her upright. Leona pushed her hands off and grasped the countertop with one hand, smoothing her hair with the other. "Get this perfectly straight. When I say my son I mean mine. There's no Rick in him."

"You mean he's not Rick's child?"

"Oh, he is in name. He was conceived with a sperm donor. It seems all Rick's shenanigans have left his little sperm too tired to swim." She laughed again, this time louder, longer, and creepier.

Peri's stomach rolled over. If she talked to this woman any longer, she'd be throwing up in the rose bushes when she left. She put her mug on the counter. "Well, thank you for your time, Mrs. Mayfield. I appreciate it. If I run into Rick, I'll let him know you'd like to hear from him."

"Not really, dear, but you can tell him that if it makes you feel better."

Peri moved toward the front door, her escort closing in on her. "Goodbye, Mrs. Mayfield, and good luck with everything."

"You, too." Leona reached out with talon-like fingers and grabbed Peri's shoulders, pulling her into a clinch, complete with air kisses. The smell of bourbon on the woman's breath nearly made Peri gag.

As Leona released her, Peri reached for the door and yanked it open. She trotted to her car, trying not to run, and driving away with a lot to chew on.

Leona gave a completely different version of Rick than Peri saw when he came to her office. People rarely saw themselves objectively. Sometimes they even lied. The truth about Rick Mayfield was somewhere between his version and his wife's. Peri did not get a creepy-sex vibe when she spoke with him, but psychopaths were good at hiding.

One thing was for certain, though. Leona was a sad, certifiable whack-a-doodle.

CHAPTER 42

Rick's real estate office seemed like the next logical place, although Peri felt like every second on the road was wasted because she wasn't any closer to finding Benny and Willem.

Benny. The poor little fish was so out of his water, she wouldn't be surprised if he ended up needing more therapy than Skip for post-traumatic stress. And if anyone harmed him, she'd hunt them down and beat them into bloody extinction.

I suppose I've adopted him. My little brother. My little, demanding, pain-in-the-ass brother. At least he wants to hang out with me, as opposed to my biological brother. Talk about a pain-in-the-ass.

Dev had moved as far away from the family as possible, as soon as he could. He had to be dragged to their parents' funerals. If Peri needed to get in touch with him, she had to hunt him down. She hated to think of how much time she'd wasted, chasing someone who didn't want to be around her.

She pulled into the New Vistas Realty Company parking lot, scanning for Rick's SUV. No sign of it among the Mercedes and Beemers. There was Sean's dark-green

Jaguar. Was Sean behind the wheel that night she cased Rick's house? Did he follow her to Blanche's?

The clouds dumped rain as she stepped from her car. Ordinarily, she did not let precipitation bother her. Today, her nerves got the most of her, causing her to sprint to the safety of the awning.

Once inside, she saw a room full of desks, some peeking from half-walled cubicles. To her left, in the foyer, sat a young couple. At the front desk, an even younger, well-dressed blond man with glasses asked Peri if she required help.

When she asked, he said Rick was "out with a customer."

"He's not answering his phone."

The young man had a blinding white smile. "Did you leave a message?"

"Yes, several." Peri didn't add "you moron" to her statement. "It's important I speak to him."

"Well, I'm sure he'll call you when it's convenient."

She nearly snapped that she didn't care about convenience, she needed him to tell her if he'd seen Benny or Willem and where. The truth was, she suspected Brandon was involved. As she formulated her next thrust for his parry, she saw a familiar face.

"Sean." She called out to his campaign manager.

The red-faced man turned toward her. "How are you? What can we help you with?"

"I'm desperate to get in touch with Rick."

Sean pulled out his phone and pushed at the screen. "I'm sure he's got it set to vibrate or something."

He held the phone to his ear a moment, then pressed the screen again. Going around the reception desk, he looked at a calendar book. "We're all required to log our client appointments and leave a number. Safety, you know." He ran his finger along the lines. "Here we go." Once again, he pressed some numbers on his phone, then held it to his ear.

A phone rang, in the office. The trio looked around, then the woman sitting in the foyer opened her purse. She produced a ringing phone and answered it. Sean looked at her.

"Excuse me, are you Rick's one o'clock appointment?" he asked.

"Yes, my husband and I have been waiting here for quite a while."

Peri's heart sank. "Did Rick tell you he was going to be late?"

"No." The woman said. "We've been trying to call him, but it's going to voicemail."

Peri turned back to Sean and spoke in low tones. "My client and my assistant are missing and believed to be kidnapped. Rick's not home, he's not here, and he's not answering his phone."

"Wait, you don't think Rick is the kidnapper?" Sean's red face got a little redder.

"No, I don't, my favorite suspect seems an unlikely one to kidnap his own dad."

"Brandon?" Sean looked at her and tapped his fingers on the desk. "I'd agree with you, if Rick and Brandon got along better."

"Not a cozy father-son relationship?"

He moved farther away from the other realtor and gestured. "Kevin, why don't you help this couple?"

Peri followed Sean to a more private area. "How much do you know about Brandon's involvement with gangs?"

"More than I care to know and less than I probably should." He shook his head. "That boy is going to be a career-killer for his dad."

"And your son, Donny?"

"I know Donny's involved, but it's not what you think." He leaned close to Peri's ear. "Donny's been working for the Feds as an informant. He's trying to get intel on the Dragon Brothers."

She considered this. Although it was possible, Donny hung out with Brandon, making him one of the fake Drachen Bruderschaft. He had no access to the real deals, as she had been introduced to them. It was more likely that Donny was lying to dear old Dad.

It also seemed unlikely that Sean believed it, but he seemed to be swallowing the story. Peri considered letting it drop. Ultimately, she couldn't.

"By the way, have the Fullerton police released Donny yet? Is trashing someone's house part of being undercover?"

The man's ruddy face deepened into burgundy.

"I don't know what you've heard, but Donny isn't in any trouble with the police. That's what I told them when I posted his bail."

"Maybe, but his fingerprints were all over the furniture. And he admitted trashing my client's house, my client whose fiancé is now missing, along with Rick, who coincidentally went to high school with my client. Donny wouldn't tell the detective who hired him for the job. Who do you think he's protecting?"

Sean took a big breath, the veins in his neck like a roadmap. He looked like he was going to explode. As his fists clenched and his jaws tightened, he closed his eyes and stepped back, relaxing his shoulders. Another necessary trait for a spin doctor: emotional self-control.

His body returned to its peaceful, lumpy state. "I told you, he's working with the Feds. He's not going to blow his cover for a couple of fairies."

"Are you including Rick Mayfield in that description?"

"Of course not. Rick's not missing, but if he turns out to be, I'd look at that loser son of his. But you don't need to worry." He pitched his body forward, looming over her. "I'll take care of Rick."

He was trying to make her back up, and back off. Stretching tall, Peri stepped into him, causing him to lean his balance away from her, and take a step to keep from falling.

"If you don't mind, I think I'll let Detective Wolfe and the Walnut Ridge PD handle it. They're the professionals." She turned toward the door, noting that everyone in the office was watching. "Let me know if you hear from Rick."

Sean frowned. "Of course, Miss Minny-what was the name again?"

"Minneopa. Here's my card." She left, not bothering to look over her shoulder and see him toss it in the trash.

CHAPTER 43

Peri held her phone as she got in the car. *Who to call?* Benny lived in Placentia, Willem in Fullerton, Rick in Walnut Ridge. *Which police department has jurisdiction?* She eenie-meenied her way to Placentia, the last one she preferred to involve, mostly because the detectives already considered her the scourge of the earth.

Screw it. She repeated one of her mom's favorite sayings: "I'm a bad girl and I'm okay with that."

Since the detectives were already unhappy with her, she dialed Chief Fletcher's number and brought him up to date.

"Either Rick is holding Benny and Willem somewhere, or someone else is holding all three of them." Peri told the chief about her visit to Rick's wife and to Sean. "Leona seems pretty out of it, and Sean still thinks his son is working for the Feds, but I guess it's possible one of them had something to do with it."

"Possible." Fletcher sounded noncommittal. "I'll give Walnut Ridge a call and see if we can work together, have Logan and Spencer check them out."

He ended the call, causing Peri to melt into her driver's seat and close her eyes. *I do not need this.* Worrying about Skip was a full time job. Piling everyone else on top made her feel like she might implode. She couldn't sit and do nothing. That wouldn't do.

She looked up the bank where Brandon worked, and called. Surprisingly, he was there. Peri started the car and drove south, formulating a plan.

Her anger drove her to want a face-to-face, cards-on-the-table meeting with the boy. If he wasn't behind this, she'd be surprised, if only because everyone kept telling her what a total screw-up he was.

On the other hand, she had no actual proof of any wrongdoing. Even the photos of him with guns and booze weren't enough to actually place him in that warehouse.

She hoped he wasn't the one who killed Daniels and Gomez. If he was and she got her hands on him, she wasn't certain she could keep herself from killing him.

Perhaps surveillance was a better option. She drove into the parking lot of the bank branch, found Brandon's Audi, and parked where she could see it. Adjusting her seat back to a reclining position, she waited.

Sitting and watching was usually boring. Today it was unbearable. Peri kept adjusting her position, rotating from one hip to the next, crossing her legs, stretching her arms behind her.

Something needed to happen. Benny and Willem needed to be found. She did not have time for this, looking on as people streamed in and out of the bank. Suits, sweats, even a few pairs of shorts on this cold February day. Where was the fast forward button when you needed it?

Brandon came out early, before closing. Peri made certain she was not visible as he trotted to his car. He didn't act guilty—there was no furtive glancing, no hesitance about his movements—but he did look hurried. He swung into his small car with the ease of youth. After a few moments, he pulled out and wound through the shopping center, turning left onto Bradford and heading back toward Fullerton.

Peri followed slowly, at a distance. Brandon did not seem to be on high alert, but there was no reason to push her luck. It was easy to hang back and still see his little red car, zipping around traffic that mostly obeyed the speed limit.

The first stop was his apartment. Peri turned left at the street behind him as he parked. She doubled back and saw his car, still there, so she hid behind a truck, a block away. When he came out with a duffle bag, she got worried. Was he running?

She let him get to the end of the street before she made a move. He turned right on Chapman Avenue, heading east. Peri stayed well behind him, worrying he'd either get too far ahead and she'd lose him, or he'd spot her and change his plans. She managed to stay with him all the way down Chapman until it crossed under the 57 freeway in Placentia, then got stuck behind a bus while he turned right on Placentia Avenue. At that point, she had a hunch.

If he didn't get on the freeway, Brandon was on his way to the warehouse.

She eased her car down Crowther, hovering around the speed limit and checking out the warehouses on her right. It was Monday and she expected more activity, then remembered it was President's Day. Whatever he was doing at the warehouses, he'd picked a nice quiet day to do it.

As she suspected, Brandon's car was in the parking lot of the warehouse where the shooting had occurred. Peri drove on to the next parking lot. When she pulled into the space, she saw a familiar car, parked evenly between the lines.

Benny's black Cadillac.

She jumped out and ran to it. It was locked. No Benny inside. Reining in her feeling of dread, she surveyed the scene. There was a background hum of traffic, and a whisper of wind. The sky looked as if it might rain again. She couldn't spot any doors ajar in these massive buildings, nor anything amiss. Her spooky meter was at full throttle, making her shudder.

Peri walked around the building to look at the warehouses in the next lot, where Brandon's car was parked. The side door to the one with the trailers was cracked open. *So we're back to the scene of the crime.*

She darted to the door, running on the toes of her tennis shoes and making no noise. Two voices inside were intertwined, matching levels of what sounded like frustration, anger, and a pinch of whining. One of the voices was known to her.

Benny.

Listening for a moment longer, she was able to pull their words apart. Benny was saying, "I never called you. I don't know what you're talking about."

The other voice came back rapid-fire. "Don't act like an idiot. Someone called and told me to bring this money if I wanted to see my dad alive."

"Who's your dad?" Benny's voice was reaching its soprano range.

"You know who my dad is. Rick Mayfield."

Enough of this. Peri stepped from behind the door and went inside.

CHAPTER 44

"Benny, I've been looking all over for you. You really need a cell phone."

The two men stopped their argument and turned to her. Brandon's right hand moved toward the left side of his belt buckle.

"Whoa, there, Bugsy." She put her hands out, palms toward him.

"Who's Buggy?" Brandon asked.

Peri allowed herself a small headshake. "Guy who owns the Shell Station on the corner. Anyway, easy on the gun. I'm guessing it's your dad's Glock."

Brandon looked down at his jacket. "How'd you know?"

"What would else would you be reaching for? A Kleenex?" She pointed to his hand. "You might want to rethink where you holster that thing. I know more than one guy who accidentally shot his balls off."

The young man scowled. "I know how to handle a gun."

"Yeah, yeah, like everyone else who picks up a piece. Don't come crying to me when there's an accident." She became aware of someone tugging her sleeve. She turned to see Benny, looking like he was going to jump out of his skin and do a skeleton dance around her.

"Miss Peri, they kidnapped Willem!"

"And my father," Brandon told her.

"One at a time. Benny, let me get his story first." She had a feeling her friend's tale would take longer. "Brandon, how much do you know about your dad's abduction?"

"Not a lot. I was at work and I got a phone call. It was a man's voice. I didn't recognize it. He said to meet him here with twenty-five thousand dollars and he'd release my dad."

Peri stared at him. "Pardon me for saying, but that doesn't seem like a lot of money for a ransom. Surely your family has more than that."

"Yeah, that's what I thought, too, but then I started wondering if they knew how much cash I could get my hands on."

"You keep that money in your apartment?"

"Not usually." Brandon looked down, a faint pink growing up his neck. "I took it from my folks' safe. It's not what you think. My mom's been, well, acting funny lately."

"I just left your mom, Brandon. Funny doesn't cover it."

The young man sighed and let his shoulders drop. He looked burdened, like he was carrying a load of information he'd like to give away. "She's been saying the weirdest things. Awful stuff. I thought it was the booze, then she tried to send me out to get her a fix. A fix. Heroin. I took the money so she wouldn't have it available. Maybe if she had to go to the bank to get more, it might at least slow her down."

His story touched her. "So, you arrived here with the money, but no one was around."

"Right. I got here and saw the door open. I went inside. That's when I met this joker."

"I am not a joker," Benny said. "I am a serious person. A serious person. You grabbed me."

"Look, I said I was sorry. I came in here, saw you, thought you had kidnapped my dad, and—"

"And there was a general misunderstanding." She turned to Benny. "What do you have to say about any of this?"

"It is not my fault. Not my fault they took Willem and his dog and his car from my house."

"No one's blaming you. Did you follow them here?"

"Kind of." He stared at the ground and mumbled for a second. "Willem was in my driveway, then the van came. There were men with guns and Moonie bit one of them and then they put Willem and Moonie in the van and everyone drove away."

"And you followed them."

"Yes. I followed the black van and Willem's yellow car down Kraemer, but at Chapman, the yellow car turned right and I had to decide. I hate to decide. I followed the van."

"That was a good choice," she said. "Follow the van because that's where Willem is."

"Yes. People are worth more than things."

Benny stopped talking, as if that was the end of his report.

Peri encouraged him onward. "And the van came here?"

"Oh. Oh, yes. The van came here, and I parked in the other lot because they have bigger spaces and I didn't want anyone to scratch my car. Then I walked to this place and the van was gone, but the door was open."

Peri tried to keep her heart from falling into her stomach. The odds were good the driver of the van had spotted Benny. Those 1960 fins were difficult to overlook, even if they were black. Still, did they have enough time to pull over, stash a body in the warehouse, then leave?

If they did, she was hoping the body was still alive.

"Did you search the warehouse, Ben?"

He shook his head.

"I think it's probable they turned around in this lot and went somewhere else." She gestured at the space. "But we should search the warehouse, in case they dropped anyone off in here."

"If they did, wouldn't we hear them?" Benny asked.

Peri and Brandon traded glances.

"Not if they were tied up and gagged," Brandon said.

"Try not to touch anything," she told the pair, pulling a pair of disposable gloves from her pocket. "If we find someone, the police will want to dust for prints."

They each took a different direction. Peri made her way through the trailers at the back of the building. The light was hazy, sneaking from the windows above. She got out her cell phone and turned on the flashlight app. The extra light helped to see under the trailers. She tried all the doors, but they were locked, so she shined the light through the trailer windows to see if there was anything inside.

Each time she pointed the flashlight into a trailer, she held her breath. Eight trailers, eight investigations, no bodies. Walking back to the door, she breathed a little deeper in relief.

"It would have been nice to find someone trussed and alive, but I'm glad we didn't end up with anything worse."

"What could be worse?" Benny asked. "They have Willem."

"Hey, don't forget about my dad." Brandon sounded irritated.

"Yes, yes, I know. They've got everyone and we've got nothing." Peri paced, feeling the heat rise up from her chest. She had passed annoyance and was on her way to angry. "Ben, I don't suppose you got a license plate or any details about that van, did you?"

"Of course, Miss Peri. It was a black Chevy van, commercial style, older model." He recited the license number.

Peri beamed and hugged him, causing him to stiffen and wince.

"Sorry, but I sometimes forget your attention to detail." She got out her phone. Looking over at Brandon, she paused. Who to call first? "We've got too many cities involved here."

Skip would have helped her sort it out, if he wasn't lying in a hospital bed. Chief Fletcher was the next one in line for her trust, now that Craig Daniels was gone. She pushed her grief away once more and pressed the chief's number.

CHAPTER 45

"Stay there, Peri," he told her after she had explained everything to him. "I'll call Walnut Ridge and Fullerton, and bring them all in. Logan and Spencer will be there in about ten."

She tried not to groan when she answered him. "Thanks, Chief. We'll wait here."

He wasn't fooled. "I heard that eye roll. Play nice."

"Yes, Chief." She ended the call and turned to the two men. "The police will be here shortly. Brandon, Walnut Ridge is going to work with you."

He looked unsure. "The caller said no police."

"They always say no police. What else are they going to tell you? Unless you think you can do this on your own, I wouldn't listen to them."

He stared at the ground. She hoped he'd cooperate. With any luck, he wouldn't figure out the police would want his phone. There are probably texts and pictures he'd rather not share with law enforcement.

Benny was fidgeting, walking to the door and back, hands in his pockets, taking dramatic breaths.

"What do you need?" Peri asked him.

He looked at his watch. "I'm supposed to be at Phil and Nancy's. It's play time with Matt Helm."

She pressed a few numbers on her phone and handed it to him. "Here. Tell them what's going on. They'll understand. I'm sure you can play with Matt the cat later."

He took the phone and held it to his ear, grimacing at her for some reason. *Maybe he doesn't like me being so casual with the cat. I suppose I need to call him Mr. Helm.* She turned her attention to Brandon.

"So, about your mom…"

The young man shrugged. "She's in bad shape. Dad wants to send her someplace. Donny's old man says no."

"Why does Sean Jackson get a say in your personal lives?"

"Because Sean Jackson is supposed to get Dad elected."

"How do you feel about your dad being mayor?"

"I guess it's okay. I kinda wish he wasn't running. Between his regular job and being mayor, I don't know how he'll have any time for Mom, or…"

"Won't he give up the day job?"

"Oh, no, that's not how it works. Mayor isn't a full-time paid gig."

"Getting back to your mom and my discussion with her, how much of what she says is fact and how much is drugs and booze?"

"Depends on the day and her mood. Try me."

"Dear old dad. Straight arrow or sex fiend?"

Brandon frowned. "He's prolly no angel, but he's got a pretty full schedule. I'm not sure when he'd have time to be doing everything she says he does."

"Think he was doing Holly Duchamps?"

"No. Definitely not her."

"How can you be so sure?"

"She was too busy with Pete."

"Peter Marshall? The other candidate?"

Brandon laughed. "Sometimes I earn a little cash cleaning up after these public hearing events. I've seen them, sneaking off to a side room. Walked in on them once, for a laugh. Damn, that's a sight I'll never unsee. He's got the biggest, whitest ass—"

Peri held her hand up. "I don't need the visual. I hate to ask this, but, your mom said you weren't biologically Rick's."

"You have to understand, ma'am, it's not only the drugs. Mom's always been a little frail, mentally. Dad's done everything to convince her. Even had my DNA tested, for God's sake. I'm a Mayfield, through and through."

More wheels clicked in Peri's brain. "Sean said you weren't close to your dad."

"Sean Jackson's a dick, like his son."

"I thought you and Donny were tight."

"We were. Then he decided to play gangsta."

"I thought you were playing gangsta with him." She pointed at his arm. "What about the *drachen* tattoo?"

He turned his arm over. It was blank. "That? It was temporary. Donny's got the real thing. So does Jessica. They're together now."

"They are? What was that thing last week, where you two left me in the parking lot with the cops?"

"Yeah, she asked for my help. Old times' sake, and all that. I was a sucker."

"Brandon." A strong baritone echoed through the warehouse. Peri turned to see Sean Jackson striding over to them. He engulfed Rick's son in a bear hug. "I heard

231

over the police scanner. What's this woman been telling you? She was at work today, trying to make it look like your dad had kidnapped someone."

"I never said that—" Peri protested.

"A bunch of people have been kidnapped, including my dad." Brandon shook the duffle bag at him. "I got a call to deliver ransom money, except when I got here, all I found was that guy."

"You heard on the police scanner?" Peri asked. "But the report would have gone out less than ten minutes ago. You couldn't possibly get here from Walnut Ridge in that amount of time."

"I didn't say I was at home. I was in Brea, doing some business."

It still didn't sound right to her. "And I'm pretty sure their report wouldn't have mentioned Brandon by name."

Sean frowned. "So I got a phone call. So what?"

"Care to tell me who called you?"

He stared at her, silent.

"So, Donny, then," she said.

His expression didn't change, but his eyelids fluttered. "Well, you should be happy to know, the police will be here, soon."

"Police? No." He grabbed Brandon's arm. "Come on, son, we need to get you out of this."

Brandon pulled away. "Screw you, Jackson. I'm staying. My dad's been kidnapped. I need to help him."

Sean's face got redder. "This is not the time to decide you love your old man after all."

"This is exactly the time, and when didn't I love him?" The boy backed toward the door. "What's this spin you're putting on things, that Dad and I aren't close? It's a lie and you know it."

Peri's mind ticked faster as she tried to reconcile this Brandon with the one she'd been shown through everyone's lenses. Everyone except his father, who had insisted his son was a decent young man.

Several loud pops were heard outside, and Brandon fell, grabbing his shoulder as he did.

"Duck!" she yelled and pushed Benny to the floor, then ran toward the door and peeked out to see the back end of a yellow Camaro fishtail out of the lot. She stepped from the doorway as a familiar black SUV swung in, missing the sports car by inches.

CHAPTER 46

Logan and Spencer pulled into a parking space. She ran to the driver's side door.

"Shots fired, from that car." She pointed at the yellow car speeding away. "It's Willem Chen's. You should have the license."

Spencer reached for the radio from the passenger side. "Anybody hurt?"

"Brandon Mayfield's been shot. I don't know how badly."

Peri rushed into the warehouse with Logan, who left Spencer to handle the BOLOs. She ran to the young man. A ruby puddle was forming underneath his shoulder. She knelt, dimly aware that Logan was kneeling next to her.

"I got shot." Brandon's eyes looked glassy. He was going into shock.

"You're going to be fine." This might not be true, but she couldn't stand to say anything else. Looking up, she said, "We need a tourniquet."

Logan stood and yanked Sean's tie from his neck, then handed it to Peri.

"Thanks."

She fastened the tie around Brandon's upper right arm. It looked as though the bullet had passed through, but the arm was pretty torn up. Logan had knelt again, helping her to tighten the tourniquet to slow the blood loss.

"It probably veered off the bone," Peri told Brandon. "Saved it from entering your chest cavity. That's a good thing."

Brandon looked up at her, gritting his teeth as his body shook.

A siren screamed into the lot and paramedics were in the warehouse within moments. Peri backed away. The boy grabbed for her, and missed, so she stepped forward and took his hand.

"You'll be fine. These guys are going to help you more than I ever could."

Squeezing his hand one more time, she let go and turned to join Logan, who was on his phone. She waited for him to finish.

Spencer walked inside. "Perimeter is secure. What's she doing here?"

The way he pointed made Peri want to cut his finger off, but she'd promised the chief to play nice.

"Look, I'd rather not be here," she told them. "I'd much prefer it if my case didn't cross the same territory as yours. In the meantime, would you like my statement?"

Logan nodded and got out his notepad, while Spencer walked toward Benny. Peri explained everything, from Willem's kidnapping to tailing her number one suspect to the warehouse, trying to state facts without adding any supposition.

While she spoke, she kept an eye on Spencer and Benny. Within two questions from the detective, Benny went from stuttering milquetoast to full-throttle Dino. Neither of his personae seemed to thrill the detective.

Spencer returned as she had finished her statement. He gestured toward Benny. "What's up with him?"

Peri stifled her urge to be bitchy and stated facts. "Benny's afraid of the police. He's obsessed with Dean Martin. He has Asperger's. He's got a good heart and a great memory."

"He's a nutcase."

"That *nutcase* can give you the make, model, and license plate of the van that kidnapped Willem." She tried to keep the bite from her tone, but she couldn't help barking a little.

Logan and Spencer shared a look, then Spencer went back to Benny, notebook in hand. Logan turned to Peri. "Thank you for your description of the events. It was very detailed."

She cocked her head and gave him a "You're welcome" nod.

"By the way, how's Skip doing?"

"The PE gave us a scare, but he seems to be improving."

"Pat and I always intend to stop by and see him. We'd like to be able to tell him something."

"I know you would. We want those bastards caught."

Logan scowled. "Look, we're trying our best to get enough evidence to arrest some—"

She stopped him. "Stand down, Detective. At no time did I say you weren't doing your jobs. Trust me, I know how hard it is to work a case that doesn't have a lot of meat on its bones. I feel like I'm chasing my own tail with this client."

The gurney with Brandon rolled past them and she pointed. "At least yours doesn't keep getting worse."

They watched the EMTs wheeling the young man out. Sean walked next to him, cell phone at his ear, speaking in a low tone.

"I wonder if the gun used today was used at the shootout." Logan turned to Peri, his expression wooden. "If we get a match, would that info help you?"

"Yeah. It would." She tried not to register her surprise. "And by the way, young Brandon there was carrying a Glock. If he doesn't still have it, I'd check the chubby guy on the phone. He's a political handler, you know the type."

With typical detective shorthand, the detective called to his partner and nodded at the trio approaching the ambulance. "Spence—Glock."

Spencer trotted over to appropriate the weapon. He found it in Sean's jacket pocket, held it up for Logan to see, then turned to talk to Sean. The conversation went from asking Sean to come into the station and give a statement, to being threatened with lawyers at twenty paces.

"You might want to check that against the bullets and casings you got from the police shooting," she told Logan. "Although I'm guessing it'll be clean."

"Thanks." Logan stared at the ground, shaking his head. "I know I've been a prick. But you keep feeding information to the department. You haven't exactly been sweetness and light, but you're still willing to help."

Her brain was full of a thousand words to explain how it all worked, that she couldn't hold back anything that would help the police, and especially when it might

237

help them find the shooters. Instead, she reasoned, less is more with Detective Logan.

"I'll always help the department."

Detective Spencer joined them. "BOLOs out on both vehicles. Bonham's on his way here to process. Just how much did you guys disturb this place?"

Any momentary good will evaporated with his accusation, but she kept her voice steady. "We were looking for someone who might be tied up, and gagged. Hopefully alive. I made sure not to touch any of the trailers I pointed my light into. Most are locked, so I didn't go inside." She pulled latex gloves from her pocket to provide proof they wouldn't find her fingerprints.

Logan touched his partner on the sleeve, still looking at Peri. "Why don't you and Benny go on? I'll have Jason call you when he knows something."

Benny was standing near the door, waiting to jump out.

"Come on, Ben." She walked to him and pointed. "The detectives say we can go."

He was pouting. "You pushed me back there."

"I'm sorry." She escorted him to the other parking lot. "Someone was shooting and I didn't want you to get hit."

"Now my pants are dirty." He unlocked the trunk of his Caddy and pulled out a towel, which he shook at her. "I have to carry this all the time now because someone may be sitting in my car and may be dirty. I didn't think it would be me."

"Oh for Pete's sake." Yelling or sniping would do no good. *But I've been so pleasant with the detectives. I can't stay on the Happy Train forever.* She took a deep breath. "When are Phil and Nancy expecting you?"

The distraction worked. "They said I can come tomorrow."

After spreading the towel on the driver's seat until it covered the leather and was free of wrinkles, he sat down and started the engine.

"Thanks for your help today." Peri got into her own car and leaned her head back on the seat, pressing her fingers against her closed eyes. Her phone played its jaunty incoming tune. It was Jared.

"What's the news?" His voice had a slight tremble to it.

"The good news is, we have the license number of the van that took him." She caught him up with the recent events. "Turns out Benny followed them, but lost them at the warehouse."

"Good to hear he's okay."

"Have you heard from anyone who might want money?"

"No. The police are here, monitoring all the phones." He sounded so lost.

"Want me to come over?"

There was a silence, then a small, "Yes."

"Let me grab something to eat and I'll be there in twenty."

"Just come over. I can feed you."

Poor Jared. If Skip was MIA, she'd be frantic. "Be right there."

CHAPTER 47

Peri pounded her steering wheel as she drove to Jared and Willem's house. She needed to be out looking for Willem. And who took Rick Mayfield? Where did they take him? Holding the client's hand while he freaked out wasn't in her job description, but Jared tugged at her heart.

Old age was softening her.

Jared opened the door as she came up the walk. She gave him a squeeze and a light kiss on the cheek. It seemed like the thing to do.

"No word from any kidnapper?"

He shook his head. "Why would they take him?"

"Not sure, but I have some theories." She followed him past the living room, where a man in a suit was sitting in the midst of recording equipment, waiting for a call.

In the kitchen, Jared pointed to the table, where he had set out a buffet of pasta salad, cold chicken, and rolls. "Is this enough?"

"More than." It had been many hours since she'd eaten. She filled a plate and sat down. Jared poured them both iced tea and took a seat across from her.

"These theories. Any of them end well?"

"Certainly." She brought a forkful of pasta to her lips. "At first, I thought this was all about you and Rick, which it kind of is, but kind of isn't."

She kept talking in between bites of food. "The problem started when Rick got interested in politics and Willem contacted the media to show off your wonderful partnership, both professional and personal. I'm thinking, if just one of those things had happened, you'd have been safe."

"How so?"

Peri took a long drink of tea. "I think Rick Mayfield is on the level. He really has turned his life around, regrets his past, and wants to move on, honestly. His campaign manager is the one holding all the strings, trying to work the family like puppets. Brandon told me Rick wanted to get help for his wife, who's addicted to just about everything, but Sean Jackson said no.

"If you and Willem had remained under the radar, perhaps no one would've bothered to notice that you and Rick went to the same school. No one from the press, especially."

"Trust me, I'd have been happy to stay under everyone's radar. But Willem's been pushing us to increase our visibility. We've always been involved in the community, but now we belong to a bunch of organizations, plus he got us that coverage in the magazine."

"Exactly. It's all about the timing."

"So why take Willem, and what will they do with him?"

"I think someone took Willem to keep you from talking. Which means they'd keep him alive—and safe."

She ate the last bite. "But why they took Rick, I don't know."

She got up and paced around his kitchen. "There's a lot I don't know and it's making me nuts. Why kidnap Rick? Why lead me to the impression Rick's son is some kind of outlaw gangster-wanna-be? Turns out, the tattoo was temporary, and he was probably joking around in those photos. Although, I'm sure he's no angel."

"What young man is?" Jared picked up a bowl from the buffet and covered it in plastic.

"You're right. Maybe he got in over his head. Happens." Peri joined him in cleaning the table. As they worked in silence, she wracked her brain for another way to find Willem and Rick. It worried her no one had called Jared with any demands.

Her phone jingled, so she answered it. Detective Logan was on the line. "Thought you should know Brandon Mayfield is in surgery. His humerus took a lot of impact, splintered quite a bit. There's a team working on him, trying to save the arm. Jason's processing the bullet now."

His call nearly knocked her over. "Yes, thank you."

She shook her head in astonishment. As she looked down, she heard another phone ring. Jared ran to the living room. The agent pressed a button, then handed Jared the phone. Peri stood by the two men, looking for a sign of good news.

"Hello?" Jared's voice sounded an octave lower, as if he willed his nerves down into his diaphragm. Another person's voice could be heard, high and loud. Jared stood and shouted, "Willem? Oh my God, Willem, where are you?"

Peri noticed the agent writing in his notebook. He was wearing earbuds, listening to the call. She wished she could hear more than Jared's side of the conversation.

"They what? Okay, calm down." He paused. "Calm down. It sounds like she's safe right now. We'll figure this out."

After another pause, he said, "I'm on my way. I love you, too."

He ended the call and turned to leave the room, but the agent stood and grabbed his arm.

"One moment, Mr. Reese. Our detectives will take you. We don't want whoever did this to ambush you."

"Could someone fill me in?" Peri asked.

"Sorry, Peri. Willem said they let him go. Dumped him on the lawn of the Bradford House, but they've still got Moonie. They told him they were going to keep her until the June election. If I kept my mouth shut about Rick, they'd return her. If not…"

"Four months? Well, I guess it makes more sense than holding Willem that long."

Jared looked worried.

"Of course, we're going to try to get her back before then. Unless there's something else you're worried about."

"When we adopted Moonie two years ago, we didn't know anything about her past, except she'd been in a home where they fought dogs. She had no scars, and her ears were intact. Perhaps they were planning to breed her. Anyway, she was fear aggressive. We almost weren't allowed to have her, but Willem had such a way with her, she's always been putty in his hands."

"But kept away from him for four months…"

243

"I don't know what she'll do to them." He frowned. "Or what they'll do to her."

The agent interrupted them. "Excuse me, Mr. Reese, but the police are here."

"Could Peri come with me?" he asked. "I'd feel better if she were there."

The agent nodded. Peri took Jared's hand and they went out to the waiting detectives' car.

They had a friend to rescue.

CHAPTER 48

The dirt on Benny's slacks called to him as he drove home. These were his very best tan slacks with the knife-sharp crease and the cuffed hems that broke perfectly at his shoes. He almost ran a light, and turned left instead of right, forcing him to drive around the block. Dirt was distracting.

Once home, he walked into the kitchen and saw the cookies, still waiting for him. *Oh, no, I need to finish the cookies. And my milk is warm. This is not good.*

He jigged between the kitchen and his room for a few moments, until he took a breath and decided on a plan. First, he would change clothes. Second, eat the cookies. Third, take his dirty things to the dry cleaner. That would work.

His closet made him proud to be a Dino lover. A range of suits, from black to herringbone, pleated slacks, sports coats, and a variety of shirts with prominent collars to wear open or with a silk scarf. All had been custom-tailored to fit his rather particular physique. He even had a tuxedo.

Choosing a pair of grey slacks, with a black and grey striped shirt and a black cardigan, he changed and went downstairs to his next task. He had poured a fresh glass of milk when his telephone rang.

"No, no, this is not good. My milk will get warm." He fussed with the glass as the ringing continued, then stuck it in the refrigerator and picked up the receiver. The person calling got a snippy "hello."

"Mr. Needles? It's Sam Hollis from Alta Vista, hope I'm not catching you at a bad time."

"Yes, it is a bad time. I need to eat my cookies now."

"Oh, I'm sorry. Would you like me to call you back?"

No one had ever asked him if anything was convenient, or offered to let him finish a task before they gave him something else to do. Miss Peri was his friend, but she would have told him to wait on the cookies and listen to her.

But hearing Miss Hollis say her name made him grin. It was like hearing from Dino.

"No, Miss Hollis. My cookies can wait."

"I know we had chosen the dessert, but I'm afraid I didn't write down the details. Did you want the crème brulee served with berries, or plain?"

"We want it plain, unless you can guarantee the berries will be raspberries and not strawberries. Only raspberries would taste right with the chicken parmigiana."

"That's right. Let me make that note."

"Okay." He waited for a few seconds. This was the hard part of talking on the phone, telling when people were finished.

"You know, we never talked about drinks," she said at last. "We normally serve coffee and iced tea, and allow guests to pay for soft drinks or alcohol. Is that the way you want to keep it?"

He let out a small whine as he breathed. One more decision. Why couldn't Phil and Nancy decide this? They go to these things.

I don't know. What would Dino do?

"You could ask your friends if you don't want to decide right now," Sam told him.

"Yes. Yes, that's better." He smiled. Not only did she have Dino's name, Sam was a nice person. She understood.

"Okay, then, Benny. Let me know and I'll see you on Saturday."

"Okay." He hung up, still happy. *It's good to have someone want to see me on Saturday.*

Gathering his dirty clothes, he decided to visit the dry cleaner first. The cookies would be his reward for finishing his chores. He walked outside and opened his car trunk, to store the dirty things. They were not going to mess up his upholstery. As he turned to get into the driver's seat, something fluttery caught his attention. He went to the rose bushes and looked down.

It was a beige piece of fabric, stuck in the thorns of a bush. There was a dark stain splashed over it. Benny jumped back. "Eew."

I bet it blew away from the garbage truck. I hate the garbage truck. They don't pick up anything they spill. How am I going to get rid of this? It's icky. Full of germs. He went to the garage and looked around. *Maybe I could get the shovel and cover it with dirt.*

"No," he said. "It wouldn't rot. It would stay there."

The edges were torn, and the stain was dark. He could barely look at it. He'd have to find a bag and something to pick it up with. Back in the kitchen, he found a pair of tongs, and an empty plastic bag. This would do.

The tongs barely held the fabric, but he managed to grasp it long enough to put it in the bag. Then he threw the tongs down and shuffled about in disgust.

"Eew, eew, eew."

He was on his way over to the trash can, to deposit the bag and the tongs, when he stopped. *Wait. There's something about this scrap. It's not from the garbage truck. Maybe it came from the neighbors.*

He walked to the curb and looked up and down his street. On one side was the Lutheran church. Across from him was a strip mall with the post office, a bank, and various other businesses. His closest neighbors, to his right, had a tall fence they built after his mom died.

Benny's brain started to churn, returning to Willem's kidnapping. Willem was fighting the men who were dragging him away. He held up the bag and studied it.

His phone rang again. He could hear it in the house. Rushing for the door, he stood with the bag in his hand. It couldn't come in the house with him. At last, he put it beside the door, and scooted inside.

"Benny, it's Peri."

"Miss Peri, I have something." He told her of his find. "Moonie bit one of the men. Maybe this is a piece of his clothes."

"Could be, Benny. I called to tell you Willem is safe, but they still have Moonie."

Benny was a little afraid of the big dog. *Everyone else loves her.* "Then you need to save her."

"Yes, we're working on that. Why don't you take the fabric to the police station? Ask for Jason and tell him what you've got."

She might as well have told him to put a dead body in the back seat. "It's gross. I can't carry it in my car."

"You said it's in a bag."

"Yes, but it's gross. I can't carry it in my car. You can come get it and take it to them."

"I'm busy right now, plus I'm not the one who found it. That's important to the police. You can do this. Put it in the trunk and take it to Jason."

He scowled. "My dirty clothes are in my trunk. The ones you got dirty."

"I am sorry your clothes are dirty. Double-bag the scrap. Hell, triple-bag it, put it in a strong box, lock it in a safe. Just please do this for me. The more evidence we have, the easier it will be to find out who kidnapped our friend and his dog."

When she said that, he knew what he had to do. "You're right, Miss Peri. Willem's my friend. I need to help him."

He hung up the phone and rooted around until he found two more Albertson's bags and a re-closeable storage bag. After securing his evidence, he placed it as far away from his clothes as possible, then got in his car to run his errands.

First would be the dry cleaners, so his clothes spent as little time possible with the ickiness that was a bloody scrap. Then he'd go to the police.

As he pulled onto Kraemer Boulevard, he scratched his head and sighed. Friendships were hard. At least when he didn't have any friends, he didn't have to help anybody.

CHAPTER 49

The fifteen-minute trip from Fullerton to Placentia's Bradford House in rush hour traffic seemed to take forever. After a cursory interrogation, Detective Berkwits seemed content to let Peri and Jared have their silence in the back seat. Jared still held Peri's hand. She squeezed his every once in a while, to let him know it would all be okay.

It had to be okay.

They pulled into the back parking lot of the historic home, joining two patrol cars and a second SUV. A stately reminder of the prosperous citizens who founded Placentia, the two-story Victorian home was maintained by a committee and available for tours, picnics, and the occasional classical music concert. It seemed almost appropriate as a drop-off for kidnapped decorators.

As the SUV stopped, they could see Willem sitting on the back steps. Peri watched it like a movie—Jared exiting the car, Willem's recognition, running, and their embrace. She inhaled deeply and sighed, feeling as if she had been holding her breath for hours.

"I'm so relieved," Jared said, Willem kissing his neck and collapsing into his arms. "I don't know when I've been so scared."

They held each other for a few moments while the detectives stood by, seeming reluctant to intrude. Peri studied their faces. They were good at playing deadpan, but their crossed arms and shoulders pointing away was a clear gauge of their comfort level.

It's only love, in all its forms. This was hopefully the worst these two would ever have to face. She moved closer and tapped both men on the shoulders until she got their attention.

"I know you've been through a lot, Willem, but the detectives need to ask you a few questions."

"Yes, absolutely. If I can help them at all." He turned to Jared. "They've got her in a crate, sedated. Our little Moon-Pie. My heart is breaking."

Detective Berkwits led him over to his SUV for questioning while the officers searched the grounds for anything the kidnappers might have left behind. Peri gave Jared a quick hug and wandered toward the house.

She was stopped by Detective Logan. "What do you know?"

"Not that much. I was at their house when Jared got the call. He asked me to come."

"I thought you were supposed to call us when you had something." Detective Spencer had joined their twosome. He exchanged a sour look with Logan, which was not lost on Peri.

"And here I thought I was supposed to stay out of your business." She had endured enough from Logan's partner, and she'd only met him twice. "By the way, which case are you on? Because this is the case of my client's fiancé being kidnapped, not our policemen being gunned down."

"Enough." Logan's voice was guttural. He turned to Peri. "We checked Rick's Glock against the shooting. No matches. His son's fingerprints don't match anything we collected there."

She took a big breath, relieved. Not that she wasn't willing to believe Brandon was involved in the shooting, but because after talking to him, she hoped he wasn't.

"What about Donny Jackson?" she asked.

"Got a match with his prints in the warehouse. Too bad he made bail—we haven't been able to locate him."

"Benny should have dropped some fabric off for you."

"Yeah, we got it. That might actually prove interesting. Jason's initial analysis is it's Type AB-negative. We've got another AB-negative sample from the warehouse. If it's a match then we know our kidnapper was one of the shooters."

"And our cases are linked." Peri scowled. "It's good for you guys, but it makes it hard to pursue my case when it's stuck on your case's heel."

"Guess it sucks to be you."

"Lighten up, Spence." Logan's response startled even Peri. A phone rang, and Logan reached in his pocket. He moved away from the group to answer.

"Think you've got my partner all twisted over to your side?" Spencer had not finished needling her.

"Look, I don't care if you like me, hate me, or anything in between. I have a job to do, which doesn't require your permission or your blessing. Detective Logan appreciates I've been sharing my intel with the PPD. You don't have to." She shouldn't have said this much to him. Justifying her lack of a need to justify herself revved her anger. "As far as I'm concerned—you can suck it."

Spencer's eyebrows flew up as his mouth fell open. He pointed a disapproving finger at her and was about to speak when Logan interrupted them.

"The yellow Camaro's been found at Chino Hills State Park. Rick Mayfield was unconscious in the driver's seat, a gun in the passenger's."

"Where are they taking him?" Peri asked.

"Placentia-Linda. Want to come?"

Peri looked around to see if he was talking to another detective. No, he was talking to her. She motioned to Jared she was going with Logan. As she approached the SUV, Spencer stepped in front of her and grabbed the passenger door.

"I ride shotgun."

Peri rolled her eyes. "Yes, Detective."

"Knock it off, both of you," Logan said. "Hope Rick Mayfield can tell us something."

Peri fastened her seatbelt and looked out the window at Willem and Jared. "Maybe he can tell me where Moonie is."

CHAPTER 50

Peri followed the detectives as they made their way through the hospital's reception area and into the emergency room. The smell of antiseptic and cleaning solution grew stronger.

A nurse greeted them and led them to a corner bay. "I'll tell the doctor you're here."

Logan turned to Spencer. "Why don't you see if the Mayfield boy is out of surgery? We need to interview him."

Peri opened the curtains and entered the bay, followed by the detective. Rick Mayfield lay on the bed, moaning, his eyelids fluttering. She studied him for signs of lucidity. Feeling a presence, she turned and saw a doctor, on the young side, tan and blond as any surfer.

"Afraid he'll still be out for a bit." His voice was upbeat and Australian. Not what she was expecting.

"What's in his system?" Logan asked.

"Barbiturate of some sort. Not a lethal dose, but enough to put him off his feet for a bit."

Peri suppressed a laugh when the doctor said "barbiturate." His accent made it into "bah-bit-U-rate," reminding her of the commercial where they were "tossing shrimp on the bah-bie."

"He seems to be waking up." She pointed. "Or is that a byproduct of the drug?"

"No, by the looks of it, he'll come to in the next hour. You're welcome to stick 'round, of course, detectives."

Peri looked at Logan, expecting him to scowl and correct the doctor. He gave her a small grimace, but said nothing.

"Detective, why don't I stay here and keep watch over him, while you check on your partner?"

Logan agreed and walked off to find Spencer. When the doctor left, she took a seat at Rick's side and waited, checking her cell phone for any news. Blanche texted her, asking what was happening, so Peri filled her in. The phone vibrated. She looked down to see it was Benny.

Moving out of the ER bay and into the hall, she kept her voice at a whisper. "What do you need, Benny?"

"Miss Peri, did the police analyze that fabric yet?"

"How should I know?" She regretted her sharp tone. "Sorry, I'm in the middle of something. They've only done preliminary tests. So far, they know it's type AB."

"Who has that kind of blood?"

"I don't think they have tied any names to the blood types yet."

"Well, look for the guy with the bites on his leg."

Peri could hear moaning coming from the bay. "That's a great idea, Ben. Look, we found Willem, and he's fine. Rick Mayfield is unconscious. I'm hoping he can help me find Moonie when he wakes up. Now, I need to get back to work."

There was a silence on the phone, then a somber, "Okay."

Great. Nothing says guilt like that long pause before Benny says 'okay.' She tried to lift his spirits. "You're a good helper. Thank you so much."

Ending the call, she returned to Rick, whose eyes were open, if unfocused.

"Ooohh, wha-wheh-ooh." He was still not forming intelligible words.

She pulled the chair closer to him. "Rick, it's Peri. Peri Minneopa."

"Huh? Menno-pla?" His response didn't inspire hope.

She tried again. "Rick, you're in the ER."

"Okay."

"Did you take the drugs, or did someone drug you?" Her patience for a waking drugged man was thin.

"Sure."

Enough. She leaned over him.

"Rick!" She shouted, and slapped his face.

His eyes flew open. "What?" He gazed around the room, then settled his stare on her. "You're the, the private eye."

"Yes, I'm Peri. Do you know who you are?"

"Rick. Em-Mayfield. Where'm I?" He looked at his arm and saw the IV. "Whass 'is? Wha-happen?"

"What's the last thing you remember?"

He frowned. "Lass thing…I 'member it was dark."

"Well, yes, dark. Let's back up from that. Before the darkness?"

"Pretty car. Yellow."

Yellow car? "Was it a Camaro?"

"Don't know. Brandon's girlfriend's there."

"Ah, Jessica. Do you remember where?"

"Off 57, by college. Hotel." He squinted. "She smile at me, then I felt sting in my neck."

"Why were you at the hotel, Rick?"

His speech was clearing, slowly. "I got a call. Brandon in trouble. Needed me to meet him."

"Did you speak to Brandon?"

"No, jus' Jessica."

"After the sting, what happened?"

He appeared to struggle, his brow furrowed. "Hands pushed me into a…space."

"A space? Not the Camaro?"

He shook his head. "No. Large…dark."

She had an idea. "Maybe a van?"

"Maybe. Everything was fuzzy, but I hear a whooshing sound. Could have been a van door sliding."

"Did you hear anything else?"

He closed his eyes. "A gasp. And maybe…maybe a growl?"

"Willem and Moonie." Peri sat back in her chair. "Jessica's accomplice probably came up from behind, shot you full of drugs, and set the stage."

"Stage for what?"

"I think this is where I come in." Detective Logan pulled the curtain back and entered.

CHAPTER 51

"He's awake now." Peri stood, offering him the chair. "How's—" She stopped herself before saying Brandon's name.

"They've saved the arm, but it's going to be a long process. Had to do some heavy grafting, hoping no infection sets in." He turned to Rick. "Mr. Mayfield, I'm Detective Logan of the Placentia Police Department. We need to talk."

Logan sat down beside him, removing a notepad from his pocket and jotting a few words down. "When we found you, you were unconscious and had a heavy dose of barbiturates in your system. Did you take the medication willingly?"

"No, I don't like drugs." Rick looked at the IV in his arm. When he spoke again, his voice sounded weary. "My wife is an addict. I'm so tired of fighting them, so tired of fighting her."

"What are your last memories?" Logan asked.

Rick related what he'd told Peri. Logan nodded, writing. At one point, he took out his phone and looked at it, then put it back in its case on his belt.

"You're running for some office in your town, aren't you?"

"Yes. Mayor. Although I'm starting to think it's not worth it."

"Know anyone who would like to sabotage your run?"

Peri touched the detective's sleeve. He turned and looked at her, raising his eyebrows.

"Either sabotage or guarantee your election," she said. "Would anyone in your circle of friends and family go overboard to fix the race? Either getting you elected, or forcing you to withdraw?"

Rick stared at the ceiling as he spoke. "Probably long lines, on each side. Sean Jackson is my campaign manager. He's been aggressive at spinning my life, keeping my past buried, my wife from going to rehab, trying to make me look wholesome to conservatives.

"The mayor has endorsed me strongly. Every time I make a statement, he's there at my elbow, telling everyone how great I am. I enjoy his confidence in me, but it's getting overwhelming and it's only February.

"Leona doesn't want me to be mayor. Hell, I don't know what she wants. I want her to be clean. She's afraid of the withdrawal. Right now, I don't think she's lucid enough at any one time to plan anything. And, of course, Peter Marshall has tossed his hat in the ring. He's kind of an odd duck. Been on the council two years, pretty quiet, but votes against everything. The rest of us can't even figure out whether he's conservative or liberal."

"And how about Brandon?" Peri asked.

"So far, he hasn't said anything, one way or another. I know he's disappointed his mom's not getting help. It's possible he blames me. I guess he's right. I don't have to listen to Sean, I could get Leona the help she needs and take my chances with an election."

"I think you could pick up the sympathy vote," Peri told him. "But I'm not in your jurisdiction."

"Here's where we are, Mr. Mayfield," Logan interrupted. "We found you in Chino Hills State Park, in the parking lot near the Discovery Center. You were in a stolen yellow Camaro. There was a gun in the seat with you."

He looked up at Peri. "I got word from my CSU the gun was used in a drive-by shooting that injured your son, Brandon."

"What?" Rick sat up in bed, then grabbed at his forehead and sank backward.

"Lie back, Mr. Mayfield." Logan eased him back. "Your son is fine, although he will have a long recovery."

"Why didn't you tell me? When can I see him?"

"Let me check on that." Peri went to the nurses' station. A young woman, in a flower-print top and blue cotton pants, was studying a monitor.

"Is it possible to talk to the doctor who treated Mr. Mayfield?"

A familiar blond appeared from behind one of the curtains.

"Wow, it's like a magic act," she said.

The nurse laughed. "Dr. Canby, this woman would like to talk to you."

Peri explained what was happening. "I don't know whether his son is going to be staying in the hospital, or if you are going to want to keep Rick, but if there was some way for them to share a room, or wheel one of them to see the other, it would comfort them both."

The doctor and the nurse glanced at each other, and the doctor gave a small nod. The nurse picked up the phone. "Let me see what we can do."

An hour later, Brandon lay in a bed in the recovery room, his father by his bedside in a wheelchair. Peri watched Rick caressing his son's hand as he slept. Detective Spencer had rejoined his partner, who tapped Peri's shoulder and motioned for them to leave the area.

Once outside, Logan spoke. "I'm seeing this go down one of two ways. Either Rick Mayfield was so strung out on drugs he took the gun and shot wildly, accidentally hitting Brandon. Or the entire thing was staged to make it look like he shot Brandon."

Peri concurred. "The gun that shot Brandon—any matches to the warehouse gunfight?"

"Yes. Same gun that killed Craig and wounded Chou. It's a cheap knockoff, gang-banger piece. Nothing I'd expect Mayfield to get his hands on."

"Not the older," Spencer said. "But the younger?"

"I'm not convinced Brandon's running with the gang," she told them. "Although everyone except Rick is trying to make me believe he's a bad seed. The facts are, he's got a steady job—in banking, for Pete's sake—he and his dad both claim to have a close relationship, and why would he provide a cheap gun to shoot himself? Especially when he has access to Daddy's Glock."

"Well, we've got a team at the hotel parking lot, and one at the Discovery Center," Logan said. "They're keeping everything intact until we get the CSU over. Jason's on his way to the hotel. Karen from Brea is collecting evidence at the park."

The gears in Peri's mind cranked forward. "If I promised to stay out of their way, could I get permission to go the park and check some things out?"

Spencer grimaced, but Logan agreed, so she left. After she stopped by Skip's room for a quick kiss, she headed out, calling Benny as she did.

"I've got a job for you."

CHAPTER 52

"I don't like the hospital."

"You didn't even have to go inside," Peri told Benny. "Thank you for picking me up."

"Did you wash your hands?"

"Yes. And Skip said to say hi."

Benny was quiet for a moment. She saw a little blush in his cheeks.

"I need to visit him?" This was more question than fact, and Peri recognized what he was asking. He had difficulties knowing what societal rules were, sometimes. *Hell, most of the time.*

"Not everyone is cut out to visit people in the hospital. Some people are afraid of germs, some are afraid of doctors, or maybe they had a bad experience. Skip knows you wish him well. I mean, you're putting on a fundraiser for him and the other officers. That's a really big deal."

"This Saturday. Don't forget. And you need to dress up."

"Absolutely."

"Can Mr. Skip come?"

"I don't know. It depends on what the doctor says."

"I hope he can come. And Officer Chou."

Peri smiled. In his own way, Benny always tried to do the right thing, but this was above and beyond. "Me, too."

When Benny dropped her off at Jared and Willem's house, the lights were on inside. She'd planned to go in and see if Willem could remember anything that would tell her where to look for Moonie. She knew they were worried sick, but it was getting late and they'd been through a lot. Willem might be more helpful after some sleep.

It was too dark for her to comb through Chino Hills State Park for a missing pitbull. She got into her car and hurried home. Time to do some investigating online. Perhaps by tomorrow, she'd have a narrower search radius.

CHAPTER 53

The words "southern California" and "wide open spaces" don't often go together. Nevertheless, Chino Hills State Park and its neighbor, Carbon Canyon Regional Park, offer over 14,000 acres of undeveloped hills and valleys. Route 142, aka Carbon Canyon Highway, winds through the land, giving the public easy access to pristine nature for family fun, as well as less reputable activities.

Peri wasn't certain if she'd find Moonie there, among the nearby residents, or nowhere at all. But Rick Mayfield had ended up at the park's information center, and his journey began in the van with Willem and his dog. It was the best starting point she had.

By 9 a.m., she was in the parking lot outside the Discovery Center. It was her favorite kind of day, cold air with warm sunshine.

The gravel crunched under her boots as she headed for the crime scene. Karen, the CSU from Brea had collected evidence the day before, and there were a few strands of tape remaining around one of the trees. Peri began at the yellow tape, looking over the ground, the plants, everything, seeking some evidence of a dog's presence.

She crept along, scanning all levels, moving away from the tree at a snail's pace. The rain had left soft ground, good for footprints. The area of the crime scene was made obvious by the lack of boot prints within it. Moving through the scene, she walked further away from the parking lot and into the brush.

The air smelled of wet dirt and fresh vegetation. She breathed deep and looked back at the Discovery Center. The glass and wood building had a deck around it, and sharp angles at each corner. A patch of sage caught her attention. The stems were bent, as if trampled.

Under the back of the building, she found something unexpected. Feces. It could have been from a wild animal, but it looked distinctly like it was from a dog. There was a faucet attached to the building, and the ground around it had puddles, more than the other rain-soaked areas. Deep marks in the mud looked like a box of some kind had been there.

A scene began to take shape.

She could imagine Moonie, sedated, and soiling the crate. Her kidnappers would not want to drive around with the smell, so they somehow pried 60 pounds of dog out onto the sage, rinsed the crate, and then had to push the dog back in.

She took pictures of the scene, in case she needed to get the police involved. Leaning into the trampled sage, she found something to verify her suspicions. There were patches of short, white hair attached to the stems. They had to belong to Moonie. There was also a large, mud-crusted paw print, pointing away from the parking lot and into the wild brush of the park.

"Crap," Peri told the universe. "What if Moonie escaped?" She walked toward the print, snapping pictures, and scanning for the next clue. She argued with herself, wanting to continue to track and wanting to call in someone with experience. But who would that be?

I'm not a freakin' girl scout, but I can follow footprints and fur.

Happy the rainy season meant more prints to find, she kept searching through the sage, and other indigenous plants, most of which had briars. A few feet ahead, there was a lighter print. It was another paw, with a deeper depression on the toes. She might not be a scout, but she knew what that meant. Moonie was on the run.

An American Pit Bull Terrier running loose would strike fear in most people. They wouldn't see Moonie's silly smile, or her love of belly rubs, or her intense desire to find Willem. They'd see a loose fighting dog. If she was lucky, someone would call the authorities. If she was really lucky, the authorities wouldn't shoot first and apologize later.

"Damn it, Moonie. Where did you go?"

She kept moving forward, looking at each bent sprig or broken branch for some evidence the dog had run by. Another print headed toward a trail, which was good and bad. Good because the brush was getting thick, slowing her efforts. Bad because, despite the rains, there were people still using the trail, meaning more prints to try to decipher, and more potentially disastrous encounters for Moonie.

At the edge of the path, she was rewarded with four solid prints, in a more-or-less rectangle. Moonie stopped here—but why? Peri searched around the trail for the next print. It was difficult to find dog paws among the shoe treads.

She bent over, examining edges, and heard movement ahead. Glancing up, she saw a runner approaching.

"Excuse me." She was still focused on the tracks. "Have you seen a dog running around? White, medium-sized?"

The man stopped. "You mean the pitbull?"

"Yes!" Peri grinned. What a relief. Then she noticed the man's shoes. Converse high-tops. Why would anyone run in Converse high-tops?

She straightened to look at him as his fist connected with her jaw. The impact sent her off the path and into the mud. Running footsteps moved away from her. She pushed herself up, shaking her head and feeling her face, if for no other reason than to see if her head was still attached.

Rising, she ran back down the path after her attacker. The sound of an engine made her look to her right. Parked along the roadside, a black van spit gravel from its tires as it blasted east, toward Chino Hills.

"Aw, damn it," she told no one, and scrambled up the slope to see where the van had been parked.

She scoured the gravel for any signs of feet or other clues, trying to focus, but reliving her encounter. The man had been dressed in shorts and a long-sleeved tee-shirt. She had only a cursory look at his face, not enough to be able to close her eyes and reconstruct it in her mind. Hitting the note taker app on her phone, she spoke into it, not wanting to lose her first impressions.

"Tall, stocky. Baseball cap, Dodgers, but not Ball Cap guy from the Smith encounter. Tan complexion. Round face, maybe familiar? Facial hair, maybe a dark soul patch. And a helluva sucker punch."

He had been running down the path alone. The worst scenario was he found Moonie but she was no longer worth holding for any ransom. Best case was he didn't find her. Or he did find her and she wasn't happy to see him.

She continued to search the parking spot. Gravel was not that conducive to collecting evidence, but she did see an oil stain. It was shiny and black, without any rainbow coloration that would indicate it had gotten wet in last night's rain. With any luck, the van was leaking oil. Peri pulled up Detective Berkwits' phone number and called him.

"I found the van." She explained her morning, including the punch, and told him of her plans to keep searching.

"Be careful, Peri." His soft southern drawl comforted her. "We'll contact the San Bernardino and Orange County Sheriffs. They have jurisdiction over the park. Hopefully, if someone finds the dog, they can detain her without incident."

Without incident. Peri remembered Jared's comment about Moonie's original temperament, and her attachment to Willem.

She returned to the path, praying all the way.

CHAPTER 54

I have to be here. Benny stood in the middle of the door at Placentia-Linda Hospital. The lobby was decorated in pale, neutral tones. *This is good.* Only a few people sat in the chairs, reading. *This is better.* Still, the microphone hissed every time an announcement was made. *That is bad.* And his nose fought the odors, especially the smell of sick people, masked by the scents of heavy cleaning agents and artificial air fresheners. *That is worse.*

Dino would be able to do this. Be strong like him.

He spent a few seconds kicking himself for arguing with Jo-Anne at Alta Vista. If he hadn't insisted two tables be reserved for Skip and Kenneth, complete with a space for their wheelchairs, Jo-Anne wouldn't have insisted he get proof the two policemen would be at the banquet.

Miss Peri wasn't answering her phone, so he had to come down and find out for himself.

Benny wanted to take a big breath, the way the Nickels taught him, to calm himself, but he didn't want to breathe in the aroma, or the germs. He blinked a few times, before returning to the receptionist. The only thing to do was let Dino take over.

"I was wondering, I need to, I'd like to see a couple of my friends today," Benny-Dino said. *Smooth as silk.*

The receptionist gave him their room numbers, then pointed through the double doors, giving him a quick description of where to turn, left and right.

"There are signs." She moved away to answer the phone.

He looked at the double doors. Once through them, and he would have to keep going. His step faltered, and he stopped, backed, and stopped again.

Looking at his shoes, he summoned his hero. Dean could not abandon him now. As he looked down, he glimpsed his earbuds. *Of course, that's what I need.* He plugged them in and turned on the music.

"You're Nobody till Somebody Loves You," escorted him through the doors.

He hurried down the halls, his loafer heels clicking along the tile floors, until he reached Skip's door, where the policeman sitting outside made him screech to a halt. Heart in his throat, trembling, Benny turned off the music and forced one foot at a time until he stood before him.

"Benny Needles to see Skip Carlton."

The officer stood and beamed, offering his hand. "Mr. Needles, am I glad to meet you."

Benny looked at the large hand and reached his own out, hoping this wasn't some kind of trap to spring forth and catch him.

"The department heard what you are doing for our officers, and we are honored," the man in uniform continued. "Our guys have insurance, but it doesn't cover everything. Your fundraiser is not only good for them, it's good for city morale."

"Can I see Skip now?"

The officer pointed and stepped aside. "I'm sure he wants to thank you as well."

Skip was sitting up in his bed. Benny let his eyes wander, catching glimpses of his friend without staring at him. There were others in the room, too. Two women and another man. This was too many people in the small space. He frowned.

"Benny," Skip said. "I'm glad you came. These are my daughters, Amanda and Daria, and Amanda's fiancé, Drew."

The little man regarded them briefly, then turned back to Skip. "I came to ask you something."

"Yes?"

He kept glancing at the three people, scowling. *They need to leave. This room is small.* He looked at his shoes.

Skip tapped Daria's hand and nodded toward his visitor. She smiled. "Amanda, Drew, let's take a break. I think they have something to discuss."

Benny grinned as they left, until he heard Drew say, "What's with that guy, anyway?"

"Don't waste your energy on him, Ben," Skip said, his voice firm. "He doesn't understand much of the way the world is. What's up? By the way, I heard about the fundraiser. Thank you. You're quite a guy."

The grin appeared on his face again, even if he still stared at his loafers. "I want you to come to the banquet, Mr. Skip. Can you come to the banquet?"

"I'd love to, if they'll release me from the hospital. It's up to the doctor."

Benny's head bobbed up. "Then we need to ask the doctor."

The squeak of rubber soles made him turn to see a nurse enter the room. She walked around Benny, holding a chart, smiling and greeting the two men.

"Sharon, this is my friend, Benny Needles," Skip said. "He's the one organizing the benefit."

"Nice to meet you," she told him. "I've got my tickets."

"Can Mr. Skip come to the banquet?"

She read the chart, and reached down to take Skip's temperature. "Well, I'm not the doctor, but Skip is doing very well. If he's not released by Saturday, perhaps the doctor can arrange for a brief trip to attend a banquet."

"Good, then you'll be there."

"I said maybe, Mr. Needles. We still need to ask Dr. Marx."

"Can you ask him now?"

The nurse continued to take measurements, reading numbers off a machine attached to Skip's arm. At last, she turned to Benny. "Let me see if I can find her."

She left the room, leaving him alone again with Skip.

"How's Peri doing?" Skip asked. "I saw her yesterday, but we didn't talk much about what she's working on."

"Miss Peri is trying to find Willem's dog." He gave him a brief version of the latest news.

"I'm glad Willem is safe, but I hope Peri stays safe, too."

"Why wouldn't Miss Peri stay safe? She is looking for a dog."

"Because some people have guns, and they aren't careful, and they shoot other people. And sometimes they shoot dogs, especially when they think the dogs are mean."

Benny laughed. "Moonie isn't mean. She's hairy and smelly and I don't want her in my house and I don't want to pet her because her mouth is always open and it's full of dog spit. But she's not mean."

"She's a pitbull, Ben. Some people think they're all mean."

"Well, no one will shoot Miss Peri." He stood up straight, scowling. "I will protect her."

"Thank you. I know you help her as much as possible."

A tall, dark-skinned woman in a white coat breezed into the room. "What's this about breaking you out of the hospital?"

CHAPTER 55

Each minute Peri spent finding some evidence of Moonie made her question her decision. The dog was running, while she practically crawled after her. She could feel the distance stretching out between them.

"My problem," she mumbled as she found one more possible print, "is I'm too damned stubborn."

Adjusting her direction to account for the angle of the dog's paw, she waded through some kind of tight clump of bush with burrs that clung to her khakis. As she pulled her way out, a thorn snagged her sweatshirt, tearing a hole.

She paused to look around and get her bearings. *Oh, well, I needed new clothes.*

It had been an hour since she last checked her watch. The sun was higher and the air warmer, but she kept the sweatshirt on to protect her arms. Popping out of one more thistled patch of brush, she came upon a small trench that had relabeled itself a stream after the rain. A full set of paw prints heartened her. Their placement and depth led her to believe Moonie had jumped the little creek.

If it's even Moonie I'm tracking.

She hopped the water and found the landing prints. There was a full trail of them in the soft mud, leading away toward a grove of live oak. Peri kept her eyes to the ground, moving quicker. Her sight adjusted to the shade as she entered, and she hoped the dog had used this arbor to rest. For the first time, she called out.

"Moonie? Moonie? Here, Sweetie."

Her foot kicked something solid. Someone was here, but it wasn't Moonie. And he wasn't in any condition to answer. The man lay face down, a small, dark hole in his back. The ground underneath him looked too dark for just rainfall. Peri recognized him without turning him over. His tattoos identified him as John Smith's associate, the one she called Dodger Cap.

It hit her hard—that man who punched her, the one running away, wore a blue cap. Dodger blue.

She pulled out her phone and dialed 911. *Well, I've got the Fullerton, Placentia, and Walnut Ridge police involved in all this. Why not the OC Sheriff and San Bernardino as well? I'm collecting the whole set.*

Coming from the grove, she tried to tell the dispatcher where to send the police. It would have been easier if she knew where she was. The dispatcher, while doing her best, couldn't understand Peri's description of her location.

"I'm in Chino Hills State Park. I can see Route 142 from where I am…east of the Discovery Center…I don't know if I'm in Orange County or San Bernardino…I don't know… maybe they can drive by real slow and I'll wave?"

Eventually, the dispatcher agreed to send out someone, even if it turned out to be the wrong jurisdiction. Peri stood next to the trees, looking right and left for signs of flashing lights, listening hard for a siren.

The sound she heard was not a siren, but a whine. She walked around the outside of the trees to the south. There she found what used to be a white dog. Moonie was covered in mud, crouching next to a log, shivering. She wasn't moving. Her leash was caught in the cracks of a large gnarled branch that had fallen.

"Moonie, baby!" Peri rushed to her.

As she neared, the dog stood and faced her, her tail stiff and the hairs on her neck rising. Peri heard a guttural growl from her, a definite warning, and stopped. Although she hadn't owned a dog in years, she was raised with more than one, and could recognize the body language for "if you insist on coming closer, I shall insist on biting you."

She sat and angled her body away from Moonie, speaking in a soft, low voice. "Hey, Moonie, girl. Good girl. Good Moonie."

From her periphery, she saw the dog relax and sit back against the log. Peri inched her way backward, in slow and methodical movements, until she was within the dog's leash radius, stopping and waiting when she heard Moonie growl. The entire time, she kept a lulling monologue going.

"Such a good girl, Moonie. Willem misses you. Want to go home and see Willem and Jared? Good Moonie. Good, good girl."

It seemed to take forever, but eventually Peri was rewarded with a cold nose under her palm. She eased her hand back, under Moonie's chin and along her jaw, and massaged, hoping she'd be remembered as a friend. The dog groaned and sank down, laying her head in Peri's lap.

"That's our good dog." A sudden burst of tears surprised her. "I'm so glad you're okay."

Peri looked up to see flashing lights coming. She took a deep breath and told the dog, "The police have to come and look at that man under the trees. I need you to be a good girl now."

Moonie looked up, her black eyebrow lifting and her mouth open in a wide grin.

"Are we good?" Peri stood and waved at the car. A blip of a siren told her they'd seen her, so she untangled Moonie's leash and gave it a small tug. Moonie stood and walked with her without hesitation.

Together, they strolled to the front of the grove. While Peri waited for the officers to park and climb up the hill, she dialed Willem's number.

"Have I got good news for you."

CHAPTER 56

To Peri's surprise and relief, the dog stood by her without even looking at the police as they approached, then walked into the grove quietly. As they neared the body, Moonie pulled back on her leash, whining and growling. The younger of the two policemen turned toward her, his hand on his service revolver.

Peri hurried to reassure him. "It's okay, Officer. She seems to be anxious about the body. Maybe it's the smell of death, I don't know."

"Is she your dog?"

"No, she was stolen from my client." She reached for her ID, then realized it was in her tote, in the car. "I'm a P.I. I was trying to find Moonie here, when I stumbled across the body."

"Do you know him?"

Peri hesitated. Technically, she didn't know who he was. Truthfully, well, they'd met.

"Not really. But sort of. I don't know his name, but I do know he's a member of the Drachen Bruderschaft. Chief Fletcher of the Placentia PD can probably explain it better."

The officer's partner had turned the body over. "Gunshot. Through and through."

They looked at Peri, who held her arms out. "You can search, but I don't own a gun."

"Why don't we step away from the body, Ma'am," the young officer said.

They stood in the sun while he called for CSU and the homicide unit. She needed to call a few people herself, but didn't know who came first. This was like Police Department roulette. She played Eenie-Meenie again.

As usual, Placentia won.

The police hadn't told her not to call anyone, so she pulled out her phone, happy to have Chief Fletcher in her Favorites file. He answered on the second ring. Peri explained where she was and what she'd found, as fast as she could. She could see the young officer looking at her. It looked like the wheels in his brain had begun to turn, and they were not turning in her favor.

"Ma'am—"

"Gotta go, Chief." Peri ended the call. "All done. No more calls."

Within fifteen minutes, the peaceful park became a cacophony of chaos. The CSU officer and homicide detectives arrived, with Willem and Jared on their heels, and Detectives Logan and Spencer in the not-too-far distance. Peri could see the irritation on the young officer's face as Willem ran up, squealing.

"Moon-Pie, my darling baby!" He knelt down and let the muddy dog leap onto his shoulders and smother him with wiggly, lapping kisses.

"Sir, really, I need you to step back," the officer told him.

Willem did not appear to hear. Neither did Jared, who joined Willem in the Moonie cuddle-fest.

"Sirs." The officer moved toward them, obviously irked.

"Officer." Peri interrupted him. "Maybe I can help."

He frowned at her. She smiled back.

"I know you're doing your best to keep the whole process methodical and undisturbed, and now there's an army of unnecessary people in the middle of it."

"Maybe if you hadn't called the whole county, I wouldn't have to control it."

"I'm sure that's right. However, like you, I have a few jobs to do. My first job was to let my client know his dog was safe. My second job was to let the Placentia PD know a person of interest was found dead."

"Person of interest?"

"I'm a P.I. working with the police." She wondered if she should have said she was "annoying the police" as she watched two stocky men hike up the hill.

Logan and Spencer arrived, a little red-faced from the climb. "Who is he?"

"I don't know, but he and his buddy ran me off the road the other day, so I could have a sit-down with John Smith." She told them everything, including being punched by the runner. "The guy looked a little familiar, but he hit me so fast, I can't describe him. I do know he was wearing a blue ball cap, like the dead man had on when I last saw him alive. John Smith was looking for the Drachen fakers. Maybe they're trying to do more than fake their membership. Maybe they're trying to take over."

Spencer looked doubtful. "How do we know you didn't do this?"

Peri cocked an eyebrow. "Seriously? And what would be my motive? I've already told you, I don't think Smith and his crew did the cop shooting."

"Lay off," Logan told his partner. "I don't see her for this job. She wouldn't shoot a man in the back, especially if she was trying to get information from him. And if he's the one who shot our guys..." He looked at Peri with the smallest of grins. "Hell, I'll give her a medal."

"I can assure you all, I had no desire to meet this man again. Once was quite enough." A brief memory of her interview with John Smith flitted across her mind. *Would it be worth it to talk to him again, to see if he knew who might want his associates dead?* Arms came from nowhere to scoop her up in a hug.

"Peri, my angel, I can't thank you enough." Willem spun her around before setting her feet back on the ground. "I don't know what I'd have done if you hadn't found our girl."

She looked at Moonie, who was sitting in her usual, casually-askew position, basking in the scratches she was receiving from Jared. "I'm so glad she's safe. When it looked like she'd escaped, I thought I'd never find her. I'm not exactly trained in tracking."

"She must have been frightened, to run like that," Jared said.

"Don't worry, baby," Willem cooed. "We'll stop by the store on our way home and get you a brand new collar and leash. And maybe some new toys. Definitely some treats. Poor thing, you're probably starving."

Logan strolled over to the trio. "Technically, they were kidnapped in Placentia, so we'll be handling the case."

"Will Jason have time to process all this, and can he share results with Fullerton?" Peri asked. "Even though I'm sick of my case and your case meeting up, I have a feeling they've got an awful lot in common."

"And I confess, I'm beginning to think you're not bad at this job," Logan said.

Peri nearly staggered. Logan actually trusted her. Now she had to get Spencer on board.

CHAPTER 57

After she drove home, Peri changed out of her muddy, briar-riddled clothes, then zipped off to see Skip. Familiar faces met her at the hospital entrance. Rick Mayfield and his son, Brandon, were at the curb. Rick was standing by Brandon, who was in a wheelchair. A nurse waited with them.

"Rick, Brandon, I'm glad you're both doing better," Peri said. "Is Leona picking you up?"

The two men traded quick glances.

"No, I thought it would be better if Sean picked us up," Rick said. "This has been hard on her."

"I can imagine. Well, take care of yourselves."

A familiar Jaguar pulled up. Two male voices were arguing inside, hidden by tinted glass.

She looked at Rick, who shrugged. The driver's door opened and Sean got out. There was a smile on his face, but his eyes held something else—annoyance. "Good to see my favorite candidate and his favorite son are on the mend."

"Take care," Peri repeated, then continued toward the hospital door. Behind her, car doors opened and bodies shuffled into seats.

She heard Sean say, "Donny, for Chrissake, get in the back. Brandon can't use his arm."

A familiar voice huffed, "So what's that to me?"

She turned to see Donny slide into the back seat. It was only a glimpse, and he was wearing a sweatshirt with the hood pulled on top of a hat with a brim, but two things caught her attention. One was a dark soul patch. The other, caught briefly in the sunlight, was a Dodgers logo on his baseball cap.

The automatic door opened, but she stood in front of it, watching the Jaguar slide from the parking lot. She closed her eyes and pictured the jogger on the path. His face had seemed familiar. What had he asked her?

"You mean the pitbull?" Same inflection as, "So what's that to me?" Same voice as in the police interrogation room.

She kept herself from running down the hall to Skip. With a nod and smile to the guard, she strode in, barely noticing Skip's three visitors.

"Skip, I think I know who kidnapped Willem and Rick and Moonie, and shot Dodger Cap, and I think his DNA may match the shooting scene, too."

"Hi, Peri." Daria's voice brought her back to the moment.

"Daria, Amanda, sorry, hello Drew, I'm afraid I'm a little caught up in what I just saw. Forgive me for being a little excited."

"What is this, some kind of 'Murder, She Wrote' script?" Drew's mouth twisted into a sneer. "Maybe we should call you Jessica Fletcher."

"What? It's only that..." Peri looked up at him. "You know what? Shut up, Drew."

Amanda gasped.

"Sorry, Amanda." Her gaze flicked to the young woman, before turning back to Drew. "First of all, I'm a licensed P.I. who's been chasing ghosts all week, so this is a huge break. Second, I'm taller than Jessica Fletcher, and blonder, and a helluva lot meaner. Third, shut up."

Drew scowled and stomped from the room. Daria laughed, and Amanda gave her sister a soft slap on the arm.

"I'll be back." She rose, but there was a twinkle in her eye as she chased after Drew.

Skip reached out for her hand. "Hey, Doll, what'd you find out?"

She sat down and let the case spill, concluding with her ID of Donny Jackson as the runner in the park.

"What a jerk. He hit me in the face, with his fist." She rubbed at her jaw, still tender. "Probably gonna bruise."

"I'm just glad you weren't hurt worse."

She leaned in and kissed him. He put his arms around her, holding her tight.

"I have news, too," Skip told her, as she sat up. "Benny came to see me today."

"Benny? My Benny? Needles?"

Skip grinned. "He didn't stay long, and it wasn't a fascinating conversation. But he absolutely had to know if Kenneth and I could attend the banquet Saturday."

Peri shook her head. Just when she thought she could predict what her little friend would do, he surprised her. "Color me amazed. Possibly agog. What did the doctor say?"

Skip pulled her down for another kiss. "Doctor says we can both go. We're being released Friday."

"Oh, Skip, I'm so happy." She turned to Daria. "Did you guys plan to stay longer to take care of him, or...?"

"Amanda and I talked about it. We should stay through the weekend, make sure Dad's gonna be okay. If he runs into any problems, at least one of us will take a little extra time off."

"That's great. Now, if you don't mind, I'm going to the station and give the detectives this new information."

"What kind of visit was this? Kinda short." Skip pursed his lips in a pout.

"I got what I came for." Peri leaned in and kissed him again. "You're back to your feisty self. Besides, the faster I get this done, the more time I'll have to spend with you."

He smiled. "Go get 'em."

It took less than ten minutes to get to the police station. Logan and Spencer hadn't returned yet, but the chief was in his office.

"Donny Jackson punched me in the park."

"Want to give me some context?"

"Oh, sure." She sat down and filled him in. "It was his fingerprints, along with Jessica's, in Willem and Jared's home, and I'm 99% sure that baseball cap he was wearing when he punched me used to belong to the guy I found dead in the park this afternoon."

"Logan and Spencer are probably still at the scene. Let me give them a call. I'll call Fullerton and see where they are with this guy. Any idea where he might be?"

Peri checked her watch. "They're probably still stuck in traffic on the way to Walnut Ridge."

"We'll get him, Peri. Don't worry."

She returned to her car and headed home. *Bet Moonie got a warm, sudsy bath and a big steak. Both of those sound good, plus a little wine.* She needed to swing by the store.

It was all going to be fine. Skip would be home in a couple of days. Of course, that meant he'd want to decide about the whole marriage thing. Her plea to God ran across her mind, repeating, "save him and I'll marry him," in a staccato rhythm.

I'll think about that tomorrow.

CHAPTER 58

By 10 a.m. Saturday, Benny had called Peri three times, once to make certain she knew what time the banquet started, once to confirm that everyone knew what a "no host bar" meant, and once to make sure she knew how to dress for the evening, telling her, "I'm wearing my tux."

At the third call, she snapped. "Trust me, I clean up good."

When the phone rang for the fourth time, she nearly tossed it in a drawer, then looked at the ID. It was Jared.

"I'm calling to ask about my bill."

"Sure, what do you need to know?"

"When I'm going to receive it."

She laughed. "Sorry, I'm waiting to make certain everything's tied up. Don't worry, I'm not billing for the wait time."

"Well, whoever was harassing me has stopped, and I heard Rick's wife is in rehab, so I thought Willem and I were out of the woods."

"I'd like to say you are. But there are two things I need before I can relax. One is Donny Jackson. He's still MIA. I need to know where he is, and that he's not a threat. The other is Rick Mayfield. He's making a big announcement on Monday, and I don't know what he's going to say. Either pulling out of the race, or admitting his past indiscretions would mean you have nothing to worry about."

"What else could it be?"

"That's the thing about politicians. It could be anything else. In the meantime, Fullerton PD is still keeping an eye on your house, and I trust you two are utilizing your home security system, plus taking my other suggestions seriously."

"Yes, Ma'am. We never go anywhere without our phones, our Mace, and our emergency alarms. We always let each other know where we're going, and give each other a safe text when we get there and when we're leaving. And Willem and I have a code word for when we're in trouble." He sounded proud. "Marmalade."

Peri grimaced. "Sure you can fit that into a casual sentence?"

"Of course. 'Can you pick up some marmalade?' 'That marmalade cat's been in our backyard again.' 'I found a recipe for marmalade sauce.' See?"

"I guess it works better than I thought. At any rate, keep up the safety measures, and I'll see what Donny's status is with the police. Hopefully, Monday will bring us good news on all counts."

"We'll see you tonight, then."

"Are you coming to the banquet? That's sweet of you guys."

"We may live in Fullerton, but we've been working so much in Placentia, we feel like we've adopted it as our town. Plus, we definitely want to support the police."

"They'll appreciate that." She ended the call.

Time for some mani-pedi pampering.

CHAPTER 59

It seemed everyone in north Orange County was at the Alta Vista Country Club. The crowd was so large, the club opened up the bar as well as the banquet room to accommodate all the guests.

Peri had chosen a pair of black palazzo pants and a royal blue tunic, tastefully decorated with a few rhinestones. Her afternoon pamper session had included hairstyling, and her blonde locks were in a graceful updo.

Benny met her at the door. "Miss Peri, you look very nice. You're early. I'm glad. I'm not sure what to do now. Phil and Nancy aren't here. They played golf today and had to go home and get clean." This last statement was made with Benny's scowl of disapproval.

"It's okay, they'll be here soon. You look nice, too. I love your tux. Makes you look a little like Dino."

"Nah." He lowered his head. "I'm not anything like Dean Martin."

"Benny, look at me." She waited until his eyes darted in her direction. "I don't think you know how much like Dean Martin you are. Maybe you are very particular about things. Most people are, but you're brave enough to say it out loud. And you've done a lot of brave things that Dino only did in the movies. Benny, you've saved my life at least twice."

She pointed to the growing crowd. "And look at what you've done, for Skip and Kenneth and the rest of the department. Maybe Dean Martin would have had a fundraiser like this because he liked the people, or maybe he would have had it because it was good for his image. But you put it together because you have a good heart. That's important."

Benny stood a little taller.

"Now, I'm going to get a drink and wait for Skip."

She had planned to pick up Skip on the way, but Amanda insisted they would drive him over. It was difficult to hear on the phone whether this was the old, stiff Amanda wanting to push Peri out, or the new Amanda trying to be practical.

Still, Peri's heart was light. Skip had requested Peri's presence when he came home yesterday from the hospital. She liked helping—getting him into the family room, finding his favorite pillow, setting him up with the remote, a sandwich, and black coffee, all the way he liked it. Amanda and Daria fussed over him as well. They'd handled everything like a good team. Drew was absent from most of the festivities. Amanda had sent him to the grocery store with a list.

Now, Peri turned around in the foyer of the club to see a tall, handsome man in a tuxedo entering, his long stride shortened due to the cane he was using. Beside him were two young women in soft, flowing cocktail dresses. There was no sign of Drew.

"Skipper." Peri greeted him with a kiss. "You look pretty dashing with that cane. Like you might pull a sword from it and vanquish someone."

He smiled, that mischievous grin she loved so much. "And you take my breath."

She could have stayed in that moment longer, but tonight she had to share his company. "Girls." She opened her arms to include them both. "You look gorgeous."

As she hugged them, she asked, "Where's Drew?"

"We sent him to park the car," Daria told her. "We thought Dad would make a better entrance with a woman on each arm."

Peri laughed. "Well, gorgeous women, how about if I buy you both a drink?"

"Oh, no." Amanda stepped forward and took Peri's arm. "You bought these tickets for us. We get to buy the drinks. Dirty martini, yes?"

"Good memory."

They all strolled to the bar, keeping pace with Skip's limp. Peri saw a familiar face mixing drinks.

"Alvin, good to see you."

The older black man had been the bartender at Alta Vista for so many years, it seemed as if he must live there. He paused in his task to take Peri's hand in his two rough dark ones, wrinkled and calloused from a lifetime of hard work. "Good to see you, too."

He shook hands with Skip. "God bless you, Detective. We're all glad you're still here."

"I keep thinking you should be retiring," Skip said.

"What do I want to retire for? My wife's been gone for a long time, kids moved out, it's either work here or sit at the diner and listen to old men complain about their blood pressure. This place has better gossip, and it pays."

Drinks were ordered, including one for Drew, and they moved off to mingle with the crowd. Everyone swarmed around Skip, and Kenneth, who had arrived in a wheelchair. Peri did her best to say hello, but soon was pushed aside.

The city council members were there, members of the various clubs and organizations around the city, as well as representatives from the police departments in other towns. Peri found Jared and Willem in a group that was discussing green housing and conservation.

"Miss Peri, come give us a squish." Willem's arms invited her for a squeeze.

"Wow, you guys look great. I hope you didn't have to leave Moonie home alone."

"Oh, no," Willem said. "She's staying next door with her second favorite auntie."

"Second favorite?"

Jared beamed. "You're now her official favorite. Her other auntie plays with her and gives her cookies, but you saved her life."

"I can't tell you how happy I was to see her. Come and meet Skip's family, if I can make a dent in the crowd around him."

Turning to go, Peri saw a face she didn't expect. Excusing herself, she made a beeline for the man, who was standing alone, nursing something amber on the rocks.

"Sean, I'm surprised to see you here."

"I'm looking for Rick. He said he was coming tonight. Had me buy the tickets and everything, but he hasn't shown up."

Peri peeked at her watch. "Well, the banquet's not supposed to start for fifteen minutes. He could be running late."

Sean dismissed her with a shrug, so she pressed on.

"I heard about Leona. Sounds like it's the best thing for her. Most people can relate to having a family member with substance abuse problems. I hope Rick doesn't drop out of the race because of—"

His finger whipped around to her face so fast and so close she stepped back.

"You listen to me. Rick is not dropping out of this race. I said I would get him elected, and that's what I plan to do." Sean's face burned and the veins in his neck bulged.

His intensity frightened her for a moment, but only one. She gathered her nerve. "You're a driven man, Sean. Just the kind of manager Rick needs."

The big man relaxed, his face cooling to its normal ruddiness. "Rick's a good man, a good fit to run our community. I wouldn't be his manager if I didn't believe it."

"It must be nice to have Rick's campaign to concentrate on at the moment. I imagine you're pretty worried about Donny."

"What's there to be worried about?"

"You do know the police want to find him, right? He skipped out on his bail. They've got his fingerprints at a few places he shouldn't have been, plus his DNA, plus—

well, witnesses." She didn't mention she was one of them. "It'd be better for everyone if he turned himself in."

The veins resumed their popping on his neck. "I told you, my boy works for the Feds. He can't be wanted—he's got immunity."

"Mr. Jackson, even if your son was working for a federal agency, it doesn't give him a free pass to ignore local law enforcement. If anything, he would use his position to keep them informed."

Sean gave her a venomous glare, and moved away without comment.

That went well. She strolled toward Skip's daughters, who were shaking hands with the multitudes of grateful strangers. A server with a tray came by to clean the area and stopped for her empty glass. He was a young man, tall and thin, with slicked-back hair, and a slight limp.

As he reached for the tray, something caught Peri's eye. His forearm stretched from under his white sleeve, revealing a dragon tattoo. In mere seconds, she focused on the tail, and the word "Drachen" underneath.

He was a faker.

CHAPTER 60

Peri looked around for Chief Fletcher. It was impossible to pick out one face in the sea of colors and sounds, especially when they were all turning and entering the banquet hall. She followed along, searching for the young man with the tattoo. He had also disappeared.

"Damn," she breathed, then turned back. Fighting the current of people, she found Alvin, restocking his bar. She leaned over and spoke low. "Alvin, I need some info."

He stopped and came close, his elbows on the bar. She turned to his ear and spoke in a low voice. "There's a young man working tonight, oily hair, skinny mustache, some tattoos."

The bartender nodded. "I know the boy you're talking about, but I don't know who he is. Showed up here today, said a temp agency sent him. I been watching him. Lazy-assed smart-mouth. Has to be told what to do every single step."

"Who would know who he is?"

"Mario, the head waiter. Wears the white coat with the black piping."

"Thanks." She rejoined the throng squeezing through the double doors, still scanning the room for Tattoo Guy.

A flash of white rushed by her. She turned to see a white coat with black piping, so she strode after him.

"Mario?"

He stopped and smiled, so she asked about the temporary helper.

"I'm sorry, has he done something?" Mario looked concerned.

"No, no, I just thought I recognized him. Do you remember his name?"

"Yes, it's Ernie Valdez."

Her blood chilled. She needed to find the chief.

"Ma'am, do you need help finding your table?" A young girl pointed toward the front of the room.

She saw Skip and his daughters, and maneuvered her way to them. Skip and Kenneth had each been given a front-row table, along with Chief Fletcher. The seats facing the lectern were taken. *Good.* She could take a seat facing away and have an excuse to watch the back of the room.

Scrutinizing the crowd, she found Detective Logan sitting at a table with Blanche and her husband Paul. There were a few other people she recognized. She waved to the table and started toward them to tell Logan about Tattoo Guy. Blanche saw her and waved back, then pointed at Skip and gave her two thumbs up. Peri was almost to their table, when Benny called to her. He was standing at the lectern, in between Phil and Nancy.

"Miss Peri, sit down." Obviously Benny was feeling more confident. "We need to start eating."

His last sentence fed into the microphone, causing a wave of laughter. Benny jumped back, blushing.

Peri stopped and turned toward her table. She needed to tell Chief Fletcher, or Logan, about the Tattoo Guy. There had to be a reason for him to be here. She watched him wander around with a pitcher of iced tea.

"Miss Peri." Benny's voice became an order.

She took her seat. *I can watch Tattoo Guy from here, and get up after the announcements. Or maybe I can text the Chief. I should have asked for Logan's number.*

Phil stepped up to the microphone. "If we can have everyone seated, I want to thank you all for the generous donation of your time and money to the Help Our Police Golf Tournament and Dinner. We want to especially welcome the members of our police force who fought bravely in the recent shooting, and were injured as a result. I won't ask them to stand, but I'd like a big round of applause for Officer Kenneth Chou, and Detective Skip Carlton."

The sound in the room was deafening. Peri had set her chair sideways to see the front of the room, and could tell how uncomfortable Benny was with the din. Phil stepped forward again, holding his hands up to quiet the crowd.

"Losing Detective Craig Daniels and Officer Thomas Gomez has devastated our hearts, but not our spirits. We are holding this fundraiser to ensure that our injured officers get the help they deserve, and our departed officers get a lasting recognition of their sacrifice."

More applause drowned Phil out. He waited for it to die down.

"They will be serving the salad in a moment, and Nancy and I will be announcing the results of the golf tournament today. Also, the raffle baskets will be awarded. Before we do anything else, I want to introduce Mr. Benny Needles. Benny does not belong to any organizations, he's not a member of any councils or boards, he's just a citizen. But this is what makes Placentia great. Just a citizen came up with this idea, to raise money for the police. Just a citizen met with the planning crew of Alta Vista. Just a citizen made a huge impact."

Everyone in the room stood, cheering. Even Kenneth Chou rose from his wheelchair and balanced himself so he could applaud. At first Benny winced and stepped back, then his spine straightened as he edged forward, his mouth turning upward. Peri recognized the signs: Dino was helping him get through it.

She wiped a tear from her face. Maybe it was all the years she knew Benny and his mother that made her feel sentimental. Maybe it was acknowledging how much he was able to do with so little. Or maybe it was being in a room full of people who were just as happy as she was that Skip and Kenneth were alive, and just as sad Craig and Tom were not.

Eventually, everyone calmed down and sat, and the waiters brought out carts of food. They were efficient, covering an entire table of ten before returning for more plates. Peri eased her cell phone from her purse as a salad was placed in front of her. She scanned the room for Tattoo Guy as she composed a text to the chief.

Skip sat next to her, nudging her from time to time and giving her the raised eyebrow. There was no fooling a detective, no matter how long he'd been on layup. She shrugged at him. If she told him, he'd want to help. Detectives didn't stop because they were injured.

She looked around. Tattoo Guy was filling waters. *Good. I'll keep an eye on him.*

"Miss Peri, that's rude." Benny had been seated next to her and was watching her.

She leaned next to him and tried to whisper, "It's for work."

Neither leaning in nor whispering were in Benny's comfort zone. As soon as she leaned, he backed away. "I can't hear you when you talk like that."

The rest of the table stared. Amanda and Daria looked curious. Drew pulled off a rather highbrow irritation. Skip shook his head. Peri was glad Phil and Nancy were still giving awards.

"Sorry, but we've got a possible situation and I need to warn a few people." She turned to Benny. "I know it's rude. I won't make a habit of it."

He frowned again, but she put her head down and completed her text to Chief Fletcher.

SERVER HERE W/FAKER TATTOO. TALL GUY W/UGLY LITTLE MUSTACHE.

She pressed Send and felt better, until she got a vibration in return. The message had failed. Checking the bars, it seemed the country club was a great place to get away from it all, including cell phone service. She looked up and saw Tattoo Guy slip from the room.

Scrutinizing the tables, she found Jared and Willem's spot, except Jared wasn't there. Willem was looking right at her, an odd expression on his face. A numbness ran through her body. She turned to Skip.

"I need to talk to Willem." With as little fanfare as possible, she slid from her seat and maneuvered her way to Willem's table. "Where's Jared?"

He gazed up at her, eyes wide. "He said he had to ask the chef for some marmalade."

"Go tell Chief Fletcher. I'm on it." Rushing down the corridor to her left, she saw Jared leaving through the lobby door, Tattoo Guy behind him.

"Jared," she called out.

He stopped, but didn't turn. She kept striding toward him, trying to stop their forward movement. "I was wondering, maybe after the dinner, we could..."

Her words died away when she saw the gun being pressed against his back.

"Why don't you join us, Miss Meownohpita?" Tattoo Guy might not be a good waiter, but he was great at guns and mangling names.

She didn't argue. Locking her hand around her client's arm, they stepped into the night.

CHAPTER 61

Benny's hands curled and uncurled, from angry fists to splayed fingers. Miss Peri could be impatient and even a little mean, but she was never rude. He was having a good time, too, more or less. It was noisier than he liked, and there were too many people and he'd rather be back at his house.

Still, he felt proud he was able to do this thing for Mr. Skip and the police. It was the most grown-up he'd ever felt.

Now Miss Peri had jumped up and hurried away. That wasn't like her, to not stay and eat. His hand went into his jacket pocket, looking for his ashtray to rub, but it wasn't there. He'd left it at home because it didn't fit.

"Please enjoy your dinners." Phil interrupted his thoughts. "After, there will be dancing for anyone who's still got the energy."

"I'm starving." Nancy sat down at their table and started on her salad.

"Where's Peri?" Phil asked as he took his seat next to his wife.

"She ran away," Benny told them.

"She didn't run away. But she was in a hurry to catch someone." Skip turned to Amanda. "Could you do me a favor? See that gentleman over there, two tables over, black guy with gray hair? Could you go ask him to come to our table?"

Amanda left and returned with Chief Fletcher. *This was not good. Everyone should be sitting and eating.* Skip whispered something to Chief Fletcher, who walked over to Willem.

"Isn't anyone going to eat?" Benny pleaded.

"Yes, Mr. Needles," Daria said. "This food is delicious, by the way. I love Italian."

He smiled. "Thank you."

Benny heard soft dinner music. A DJ sat in the corner, playing one Forties and Fifties selection after another, from Sinatra to Rosemary Clooney, and of course, Dean Martin. It had been hard to find a DJ who played the right songs.

The music calmed him. In his head, he checked off another to-do from his list of what would make this a perfect evening. He pouted a little when he realized he should have added "no one leaves until they've eaten."

Peri was the first one to go, then Jared was gone, and now Chief Fletcher left the banquet.

"Benny, you're not eating," Nancy said. "Are you okay?"

"What? Me? Yes, I'm okay. Miss Peri left, though, and so did Jared. And now Chief Fletcher is gone. Where did they go?"

"I don't know, but I'm sure they had a good reason. Why don't you eat? Look, there's the chief." Nancy pointed. "See? He came back."

Fletcher went to Willem's table and said a few words. Willem got up and walked out of the room with him. He looked unhappy.

"See?" Benny gestured. "Now Willem's going."

"Benny." Skip's low voice brought him to attention. "I think I know what's happening. You know those men who were trying to hurt Jared and Willem?"

"The ones I saw kidnap Willem and Moonie?"

"Yes. We thought they weren't going to harass our friends any more, but one of the men snuck in here tonight and pretended to be a waiter. I think that man took Jared somewhere, and either Peri is following him, or he took her, too."

Daria gasped. "Oh, no, Dad, what do we do?"

"Hard as it is, we're doing it. See those men leaving?" He nodded toward the detectives who were walking out. "Those are co-workers of mine. If I had to guess, I'm thinking Willem can track Jared's phone, and everyone's counting on the man who took him to be stupid. Logan and Spencer are going to bring our friends back."

Chief Fletcher reappeared and came to their table. "Here's what's happened." The events he described matched Skip's guess.

"What an awful man to interrupt our nice dinner." Benny crossed his arms on his chest. "After we worked so hard and Miss Peri paid for her meal and she doesn't get to eat it."

"Maybe we can get their meals to go," Nancy suggested.

Benny relaxed a little. "That's good. That's a good idea."

"In the meantime, everyone needs to keep having a good time," Skip said, looking unhappy. "There's no reason to interrupt the banquet."

"Yes, Mr. Skip." Benny went back to his pasta, bobbing his head along to a happy song.

He watched Skip push his ravioli around on his plate. Skip's daughter leaned in and whispered something to her dad, and he ate a forkful of pasta. *Maybe he doesn't feel good.* He remembered the times Miss Peri was in danger and he kept her from getting shot, or falling.

What if Miss Peri needs me?

"You should eat," Phil told him. "Everyone's got their job to do. The police are going to help Peri. You need to help run this fundraiser. We're all where we need to be."

That made sense. He was where he needed to be.

CHAPTER 62

Tattoo Guy continued to poke Jared in the ribs until they'd reached Jared's older model Mercedes in the parking lot. He jerked the gun toward the car. "Get in the front seat."

Peri looked at Jared. "Who's driving?"

"I don't care," Tattoo Guy snarled. "Get. In. The. Car."

She slid behind the steering wheel and started the engine. "Where am I going?"

"Left outta the club, right on Alta Vista." Tattoo Guy was succinct. "And no funny turns or stops, or I'll splatter this guy's brains on the dash."

She glanced over to see the barrel of the pistol against Jared's skull. Praying the trigger was solid and needed to be pulled hard, she drove out of the lot and eased the car down the street.

"Drive faster."

"I don't want my friend to get shot by accident."

"That's a nice idea, but don't worry. I only shoot what I choose to shoot."

Peri tried to focus on driving the car. She recognized the kidnapper's voice from the day her office was broken into and she was held prisoner. "I thought knives were your thing."

Tattoo Guy didn't answer at first, long enough for her to worry if he was going to pull the trigger anyway. "I use what gets the job done."

"I noticed you're limping. Get bit lately?"

In a flash, she felt the hard barrel of the gun against her own head. Her foot stuttered on the accelerator, tapping it in short bursts.

"Stop that, bitch." The barrel moved away. From her peripheral vision, she saw it was back on Jared. Tattoo Guy's temper could be controlled. Good to know. "I shoulda shot that dog. And sliced your throat. Now, shut up and keep driving."

In ten minutes, he was directing her to pull up to the warehouse, where everything had started. It was crazy. What the hell did a warehouse shooting in Placentia and a man running for office in Walnut Ridge have to do with her gay client in Fullerton?

As they walked into the building, Peri evaluated the surroundings, and their chances of getting out alive. The lights, such as they were, had been turned on. Fluorescent tubes, two stories above them, flickered with that buzzing noise. The trailers were all still there, glowing a dim green. The visual made her queasy.

Tattoo Guy prodded them forward, past a small trailer with dents and bullet holes, to a large empty space. Several other young men were looking over their handguns, loading magazines, staring down scopes. Peri counted five of them. Leaning against a white Fleetwood, a tan, muscled man with a dark soul patch and a Dodgers cap relaxed, waiting for them.

"Nice to meet you at last, Donny," Peri said. "You've been pretty good at evading the police, so far."

He sneered. "I plan to keep evading them."

"You don't think they'd have this place staked out?"

"Nah." He shook his head as he stood. "They did for a while, but it wasn't getting any action. Police can't waste their resources, especially when they're two men down."

Peri suppressed an urge to beat the smile from his face. She needed to buy time. "Who's Tattoo Guy here? He doesn't look familiar to me."

"One of my lieutenants. Name's Ernesto."

Tattoo Guy lowered his gun. "I tole you not to call me that. TG, that's my name now. TG. Total Gangsta."

While they argued, Peri studied the space. There were trailers parked all around them. About six feet from them to the right was a little trailer with the door open. To the left, a small pop-up. Behind them was another trailer, and one of the gang members. The trailer to the right had four wheels and a low profile. It seemed like it would offer the most coverage.

If I can shift myself and Jared closer to that trailer, we can make a dive underneath it when the action starts.

There would be action. She was certain. And not just the police, who would be here shortly. She was betting John Smith was listening to his police scanner.

"How do you do, TG," she told Tattoo Guy. The initials could stand for the name she gave him as well. She turned to Donny. "So, how many members are in your club?"

"We lost a few recently, so not as many as I'd like."

"Brandon decided it's not what he wanted?"

A young woman appeared from the open trailer, letting the door bang. Small, brunette, and curvy. This had to be Jessica. "Brandon got the wrong idea. Just because a girl's nice to him."

"Ah, you recruited him for Donny, and he thought it was more than that."

Jessica smirked. "Pretty much."

"Donny, why would you need Jessica? Your dads worked together. It's not like you were strangers." She rocked on her heels a little, trying to act nervous and scooting to the right. No one stopped her.

"Nah, we didn't really know each other. Brandon's from money. He hangs with that crowd."

Peri was getting more certain with every word out of his mouth. "You were hoping to put some of that money into your group, maybe?"

Donny slammed his hand against one of the trailers. "He couldn't see the big picture. We're serious, man. I'm building an army. One that'll fight for our rights."

"Your right to do what, exactly?"

"Our right to have the best. First pick of jobs, homes, schools. Our rights to look down the street, look next door, and see white faces." He glared at Jared. "White *straight* faces."

"What did we ever do to—" Jared began, but Peri stopped him.

"So without Brandon's money, you had to come up with Plan B." She pointed to the trailers, taking another small step right. "You could do business in heroin, hide it in the trailers, ship it wherever, but you needed seed money. Why did you label yourselves after a notorious gang?"

"Why not? If I push them out of the way, I got their territory, and their street cred."

She could have pointed out he was an idiot, but not while TG had a gun pointed toward her. "You steal their heroin, kill one of their guys, and think you can topple them?"

"Like the cap?" He took it off and admired it, then put it back on. "Yeah, I think I can topple them. I got something they don't have."

Peri frowned. "What?"

"I got a city councilman willing to put together a task force to drive John Smith from the area."

"Rick Mayfield?"

Donny laughed. "No, not him. His opponent, Pete Marshall. He used to be a council member in Diamond Rio. There were two warring gangs when he was elected. Within six months, one gang was gone, and the other gang served him."

"So all this time, you've been trying to discredit Rick." Peri rubbed her temples. "But why kill Holly?"

"Bitch betrayed me. She's hookin' up with Marshall, I figure she can get the dirt on Rick, but she chickened out." He shook his finger at her. "Worked out okay, though. Got rid of her, smeared Rick, and laid it at your feet."

"Aw, Donny, you should have trusted her. She had the goods, but when you shot her, she dropped the flash drive."

He shrugged. "Still got what I wanted."

"Donny, why?" Sean Jackson's voice echoed around the walls.

"Dad? What the hell?"

Footsteps were heard on the concrete and Sean stepped into view, a gang member at his back, encouraging his entrance with a gun. "Donny, I don't understand."

"How did you even get here?" Donny wore a look of incredulous anger.

"I was waiting for Rick at the club, and saw this guy take Jared and Peri. I followed them."

Peri heard a groan from inside the open trailer. She looked over at it and caught a glimpse of movement behind Donny that made her want to throw up. Shadows of people, people she recognized. The shooting was going to begin soon. She clenched her rattling teeth and put her hand on Jared's arm.

"Yeah, Rick sends his regrets," Donny said. "He's kind of tied up right now. And gagged."

"Donny, I've invested all my time and money in this campaign. You know that. I've mortgaged the house, Son. I thought you were working with the Feds. You'll break me."

Donny shook his head. "Sorry, Dad, you backed the wrong horse. I tried to tell you who to manage into office."

"Let me guess," Peri said. "The plan tonight was to kill Jared and let Rick take the rap."

"Basically. Course, now that you're here, my evening just got better."

"What are you going to do with Daddy?" she asked.

Donny pulled a Glock from the back of his pants.

Sean's eyes went wide at his son. "You wouldn't."

"You might not want to shoot your dad just yet," Peri said, overriding her nausea, attempting to buy a few more seconds.

Donny pointed his gun toward her. "Why not?"

"Because you never know when any of us will come in handy." She shuffled a few inches right, taking Jared along. Again, Donny didn't stop her. "See, your lieutenant isn't the brightest bulb in the pack. He didn't frisk either of us."

Donny laughed. "You gonna tell me Fairy-Boy has a gun?"

"No. But we have phones. Phones with GPS tracking on them." She moved again, a little closer to the trailer, while she motioned toward the entrance. "Once you go out that door, the police will give you a nice twenty-one-gun salute, right in the vital organs. Especially since they know it was your gang that shot their own. And they know you're not the real Drachens."

Donny regarded her through the gun's sight. "Well, then, I might as well follow through with the plan."

"One more thing, Donny." Her words shot out, rapid-fire, as her heart galloped.

"What's that?"

"I was supposed to give you a message." She looked past him, toward the shadows she had seen earlier. "John Smith is looking for you."

As soon as she said those words, the warehouse lit up in explosions and screaming. She pushed Jared to the ground and slid under the trailer, behind the tires, dragging him with her.

TG was the first to fall. His body caught a round that sent him sailing across the floor, landing in front of her and Jared. Peri stifled her urge to get out and run, but she did manage to reach out in the midst of the battle and grab TG's gun as it slid past, pulling it close.

"Police!" someone yelled. She wasn't sure if it was one of the thugs, or if the police were really there.

The pops and bangs kept coming, bullets ricocheting and spewing chips from the floor. Shielding her face with her arms, Peri felt the sting of what she hoped was concrete striking her. She pushed her way further back under the trailer, making certain Jared was still beside her.

After an eternity, noises settled down to the shuffle of feet and scrambling of bodies, with occasional groans. Just when the silence said it was over, another cannon would blast away. Jared stayed by her side. She could hear him whispering a prayer. Turning toward him, she put her fingers on his lips. The only way she could see them escaping was by maintaining silence and hoping the police would find them.

They lay still for what seemed like hours. Peri's shoulders were cramping and her legs longed to stretch. The gun in her hand was heavy. Skip had tried to teach her to shoot, years ago, before she was an investigator. The gun was heavy then, too. She had a hard time holding it, even with two hands. The pattern on the grip was starting to irritate her palm, but if she tried to adjust it, the noise might alert whoever was left.

Who was left?

TG was still two feet from her. He hadn't moved from that spot, so she assumed he was dead. She hadn't heard Jessica since that initial round of screaming. Sean? Who knew where he was. John Smith had brought at least two men with him that she had seen, taking their positions behind Donny. She had recognized Smith on top of one of the trailers, before the crazy started.

Jared rubbed Peri's arm, getting her attention. She looked over to see shoes approaching their trailer, stopping at the tire on his side. She held her breath and carefully rolled her body in front of his, holding the gun out, trying not to tremble. If she had to shoot from this position, she wasn't even sure if she could avoid injuring them both.

She heard a familiar voice call her name. The shoes were replaced by knees, and a face lowered into their view. Peri nearly wept.

It was Logan.

CHAPTER 63

The detective helped Jared slide out first, then Peri.

"You okay?"

She looked at her ruined clothes. "I think so. Jared?"

"I'm alive. That's okay enough for me."

Peri shook her head. "We dove for it with the first shots. What happened?"

"John Smith brought along a couple of his guys. Took out three of Donny's crew, injured the rest."

"Who was wounded?" Peri asked.

"Jessica. Took a round in the shoulder, one in the hip. Serious, but she'll live."

"Our officers—they're okay?"

"Yes, we're all fine."

Peri sighed. "Wait, Sean Jackson was here, too. And where's Donny?"

"We were outside, ready to come in, when the shooting started. Sean came running out like he was jet-propelled, holding his arm. Bullet nicked him. We came in quiet, followed the sounds, got a couple of rounds off." He gestured toward the catwalk. "Smith and his crew took off. We're still sweeping the inside, but you two need to be gotten out of harm's way. Looks like Donny might have taken off, too."

They moved around the trailer, back toward the empty space and the door beyond. Peri could barely move her legs, after trying to hold them still while the adrenaline pumped through her body. Her trembling arms hung at her sides. Jared was shaking. She put her arm around him, to steady them both.

They inched their way toward the exit. She could hear the scrapings and low mutterings of others in the building. Police, CSUs, doing their job, looking for evidence. The air smelled awful, like something burnt and rotten, and the smoke from the gunfire hung around the trailers, heavy and still.

The trailers reminded her of Jessica, banging the screen door, and she remembered Rick Mayfield.

"Logan, I forgot, Rick is in that trailer." She gestured to the trailer door. The screen opened, and out walked Donny Jackson, aiming a gun at her.

"Logan!" she yelped. She still hadn't dropped TG's gun. It was at the end of her pointing hand. One more flood of adrenaline and she pulled the trigger. Two explosions, and her hand flew back, then a third blast, and she dropped the weapon to the ground, sinking to her knees after it.

Her ears rang, but she looked up at the detective, who was staring down at her. Jared knelt by her side. She could feel his hands on her shoulders and arms. He lifted her face and enunciated so she could watch his lips. "Are. You. Okay?"

She looked down. Her silk tunic was filthy, the sleeves were bloodstained, and her black pants were reduced to tattered shreds. She pushed up her sleeves to see the scratches and marks from the concrete and bullet fragments that had struck her. Her forearm was bleeding. She managed a weak smile. "It's just a flesh wound. What happened?"

The two men helped her to her feet.

"Donny tried to shoot you," Logan told her. "You got a round off. Got him in the gut, but he raised his weapon again, so I finished him."

They led her to the door, but she turned back. "Rick—"

"Is fine." Logan guided her out. "A little roughed up, but he'll be okay."

They continued past the buzzing hive of activity outside. From police to news crews, it was lights, camera, action. Logan escorted her to the paramedics.

"Check her out, Macy. She's one of us." He gave her a pat on the back, then took Jared to an officer. "Let's get your statement while it's fresh."

Macy, the ever patient and pleasant young woman in uniform, helped Peri onto the cot inside the truck, and took her vital statistics. She cleaned her wounds and gave her a blue jumpsuit to change into, since her shredded evening clothes were considered evidence. Peri tried to be a good patient, but Macy had to ask her everything two or three times until she heard it.

Got him in the gut. That's all she could hear, no matter what anyone else said.

After a thorough exam, the EMT indicated that she was fine.

I don't feel fine. She felt like someone who'd been shot at, who'd shot back, who'd hit their target, and all because one stupid boy wanted to be king of the world.

There was nothing left to do but cry.

"Oh, Peri." It was Willem's voice, soothing her, wrapping around her, along with his arms. "Thank you, thank you, for saving my Jared."

"I didn't," she stammered. "I just, I mean, I…"

"You saved my ass, and don't ever think you didn't." Jared gave her a squeeze and a kiss on the cheek. "If you ever need anything. Food, shelter, a lung. Whatever I've got, it's yours."

Macy touched her sleeve. "Peri, you're physically fine, but someone else should drive you home. Is there someone who can do that?"

"I can." Logan had reappeared. "You ready?"

Peri nodded and gave one more hug to Jared and Willem before getting into the detective's SUV. She gave him directions from the warehouse to her neighborhood.

"I'm sorry I gave you a hard time before," he told her. "Sometimes it boils down to old dogs and new tricks."

"It's okay, Detective. I'm no prize when it comes to being stubborn." She looked down at her watch.

As they neared her street, she told him to turn left instead of right, winding out of the neighborhood until they were on Alta Vista.

"Are you steering us back to the party?" he asked. "I'm no fashion plate, Peri, but you're a little…messed up."

She looked down at her navy coveralls and rhinestone-studded heels, then opened the mirror on the visor. Her hair was officially bedhead crazy. She pulled the pins out and fluffed it around her shoulders.

"There. I'm fine."

"Peri, don't you think—"

"Logan, I want to see Skip. If I don't see him, I may implode. Willem got to pick Jared up from the warehouse."

Logan grinned. "Okay. Man, you were right about being stubborn."

"Only when it counts."

The party was nearly over when she walked in. A few couples were still on the dance floor, including Phil and Nancy, and Amanda with Drew. Peri saw Skip at the bar, having a cup of something. She ran to his open arms.

"What the hell, Doll? Are you okay? What happened?"

"You're a mess, Miss Peri." Benny was at the bar, too, with a glass of milk. "Why did you change clothes? I don't like that suit."

"I am a mess, Benny. I tried to keep Jared out of trouble and got into trouble myself. But we're all okay." She exhaled. "All okay."

"Peri, you worry me." Skip held her in a strong, firm embrace. "Don't worry me anymore, okay?"

She laid her head against him, and closed her eyes. The words she wanted to say were stuck, clogged deep inside somewhere. After several ticks of the second hand, she forced them out.

"I…shot…some…one."

"What?"

"Donny pointed his gun at me. I had a gun. I pulled the trigger."

He held her closer. "Sounds like it was self-defense."

"Got him in the gut. Logan said I got him in the gut." She burrowed her face against his neck. "Oh, Skip, I've never…I've never…"

"I know, Doll. It'll be okay. I can help you."

Peri gazed into his eyes. Then she heard herself say, "I give up."

"What?"

"I give up. I quit. I'm done with being a P.I. I want to marry you and spend as much time together as doesn't drive us crazy. I love you, Skip Carlton."

Daria's squeal pierced the room. "Oh-my-god, that's so cool!" She ran over and embraced them both, until they opened their arms to let her in. Amanda joined the circle.

"Well, finally." Drew's voice sounded a lot less joyful, more like a parent who'd convinced their teenager to clean their room.

Peri looked over from the pile of people hugging her. "Ah, another country heard from. Thank you for your well wishes, Drew."

"I am happy for you." He turned to Amanda. "Should we plan a double wedding?"

"No, one wedding at a time is enough." Amanda smiled at Peri, then turned to face her fiancé. "As a matter of fact, I'm only seeing one wedding in the near future. I'm sorry, Drew. I thought I wanted to be married to you. But I need to wait for the person I'm so in love with, I'm willing to walk away from everything to be with them. That's not you."

Drew's face flushed. "Well, I...well, I..." was all he could manage.

Amanda took his arm. "Come on. I'll help you pack and find a flight."

"Want to come home with me?" Skip asked Peri.

"I said I wanted to be with you. Might as well start now." She turned to Daria. "Need a ride home?"

The trio strolled toward the exit.

"Miss Peri, Miss Peri."

Peri turned to see Benny running behind her. "Miss Peri you gotta tell me what to do."

"What's wrong?"

"The chef. Sam Hollis. Isn't it cool her name is Sam Hollis, like Dean Martin in the movie—"

"Can we skip that part, Ben?"

"Anyway, she wants me to have coffee with her."

"What's the problem?"

Benny frowned. "You know I don't drink coffee."

"So buy her a coffee and drink something else."

"But she wants me to have coffee."

Peri grinned. Sometimes her friend was too literal. "Ask her if it's okay for you to have something else. I bet she says yes."

He ran back to the banquet room, yelling, "Sam Hollis, Sam Hollis."

Skip grinned. "Ooh, a date for Benny."

Daria giggled. "Maybe it will be a double wedding, after all."

"Miss Peri." Benny was calling from the doorway. "Tomorrow can you see when Jared and Willem are going to finish my house?"

Peri smiled up at Skip. Same old Benny.

THE END

ACKNOWLEDGMENTS

I know it seems like writers are solitary critters who eschew human contact, but it's not true. It takes a village to tell a story.

My beta readers make me a better storyteller. Thank you Tameri Etherton, Claudia Whitsitt, Debbie Haas, and Gretchen Yorke.

My resident experts always help me get the details correct. All I asked was to learn how to shoot a gun. Thank you, Matt Weinstein, for giving me four hours out of your day to teach me everything about handguns, past and present.

My editor makes me a better writer. Thank you Jennifer Silva Redmond.

I must always thank Joe Felipe for his wonderful cover art.

Finally, thank you Dale for putting up with my fits of rambling while I work out plot points.

ABOUT THE AUTHOR

Gayle Carline is a typical Californian, meaning that she was born somewhere else. She moved to Orange County from Illinois in 1978, and landed in Placentia a few years later.

Her husband, Dale, bought her a laptop for Christmas in 1999 because she wanted to write. A year after that, he gave her horseback riding lessons. When she bought her first horse, she finally started writing.

These days, she divides her days between writing humor columns for her local newspaper and writing mysteries for a larger audience.

In her spare time, Gayle likes to sit down with friends and laugh over a glass of wine. And maybe plan a little murder and mayhem.

For more merriment, visit her at:
http://gaylecarline.com.

Made in the USA
Las Vegas, NV
02 April 2022

46766423R00184